Baby Does a Runner

Also by Anita Rani:

The Right Sort of Girl

Bradford born and bred, award-winning presenter Anita Rani is one of the most recognisable faces on British TV. She is a lead presenter on *Countryfile*, hosts *Woman's Hour* on Radio 4 every week and regularly presents on Radio 2. Anita is well known for her work on Channel 4, Channel 5, the BBC and most recently with Netflix. She is also a Goodwill Ambassador for the UNHCR.

You can find her on Twitter and Instagram @itsanitarani.

Anita Rani

Baby Does a Runner

ZAFFRE

First published in the UK in 2023 by
ZAFFRE

An imprint of Bonnier Books UK
4th Floor, Victoria House, Bloomsbury Square, London, England, WC1B 4DA
Owned by Bonnier Books
Sveavägen 56, Stockholm, Sweden

This is a work of fiction. Names, places, events and
incidents are either the products of the author's
imagination or used fictitiously. Any resemblance to
actual persons, living or dead, or actual
events is purely coincidental.

A CIP catalogue record for this book is
available from the British Library.

ISBN: 978-1-83877-940-5

Also available as an ebook and an audiobook

1 3 5 7 9 10 8 6 4 2

Typeset by IDSUK (Data Connection) Ltd
Printed and bound in Great Britain by Clays Ltd, Elcograf S.p.A.

Zaffre is an imprint of Bonnier Books UK
www.bonnierbooks.co.uk

It is the end of the world, and you are not here with me.

*I am so scared. I must choose to do what is best for all of us.
I will do what a mother must do and protect her children.*

*May God protect us all. And if, my love, this does not end
well, know that I have loved you with all my heart.
I know we will be together again in our next life.*

Chapter One

I'm completely lost.

'You know what I mean?'

I am nodding at Freddie, but I have no idea what he is talking about. I lost interest ages ago, letting myself be distracted by the noise of the pub, the buzz of the alcohol in my veins. His mouth is moving, words are coming out, and my eyes are staring intently at his face. Externally, I'm giving off all the correct signals to Freddie – that I am listening to and engaged with his monologue, which is mostly about our colleague Paul getting the promotion Freddie thinks *he* should have got.

We've had this conversation before.

Freddie is physically attractive: tall, with a classic swimmer's physique, and dark blond hair, always worn a little scruffy in that slightly posh way. He loves running his fingers through it when he talks, sometimes just holding it back off his face; his beautiful, clean, pretty-boy face. And he always smells expensive. Sadly, none of this compensates for the fact that Freddie can be supremely boring. Him being boring hasn't stopped me from snogging him a few times, especially if the cheap house red has kicked in, because he's nice-looking and, well, he's right there. The set-up suits me fine because it is on my terms and very, very casual. I know you're not supposed to mix work with your personal life, but when you spend so long at the office and socialise in the hours afterwards with the same people, it *becomes* your personal life.

But now I need to back myself out of this situation. So, no more of that house red, which gives me killer headaches anyway. I look around for a glass of water, silently congratulating myself

1

on remembering to hydrate, for once being sensible. But all I can see are empty bottles of wine and half-finished pints.

'Are you listening?'

'Totally, Freddie, just thirsty.'

'Here, have a sip of this.'

He hands me his pint and I drink it. So much for sensible.

We always come to the same pub – a total dive – after work. The lighting is too low, the floor is sticky, and the toilets should come with a toxic-waste hazard sign, but the music is great and I'm much happier here than at the anodyne chain bars in town. Give me a place where you can skulk into a corner and slowly head nod over your whisky or dance until 2 a.m. on a Wednesday. Always nice to have options.

It's not a group of people that could have come together in any situation other than a work-related one, united by our passion for marketing. The entire team is here today to celebrate Paul's promotion. Freddie is right: he should never have got it. Paul is outstandingly average at his job but has this amazing ability to walk into every room as if he owns it, and he has that knack for stating his opinions so confidently that you're convinced he's right – until you realise days later, he really wasn't. I'm still trying to figure out how he does this. Has he always walked through life believing he was right and no one has done him the favour of telling him otherwise?

He's with his usual gang of lackeys from accounts. They help to shore up his fragile ego by laughing like seals when required.

'Rebecca, are you heading to the bar?' Paul shouts across the table to Rebecca, then nudges one of the seals and sniggers. Rebecca is a marketing executive who knows more than Paul will ever know about 'creative synergy problem solving for start-ups' and most other things, but she's a junior and he loves the 'wind-up'; he also loves the 'bants' and the targets of his misplaced joshing are always the youngest in the office.

Rebecca looks like she's very much in the middle of a conversation and not heading anywhere close to the bar anytime soon.

'Be a sweetheart, Becks – I'd love another pint and you can grab yourself one too. Oh, come on, don't give me that look! Be a good lass, go on, get your boss a drink; we *are* celebrating *me* today and I thought we were living in the age of equality?'

I'm watching and listening to Paul's pathetic routine and still nodding at Freddie, willing Rebecca to give him the finger. *Don't get up, don't get up, don't get up!*

She got up.

As she's walking away to the bar, Paul nudges his mates with a stupid, satisfied look on his face and right on cue the lackeys from accounts do their job and begin laughing like seals.

I feel like a zoologist observing a very basic animal species.

I take another swig of Freddie's pint.

Freddie is still sharing his pain with me at not getting the promotion, expecting me to do what I aways do: comfort him, make him feel better, tell him how great he is and what an injustice it is that he didn't get the promotion.

No. The promotion should have been *mine*; every promotion in the last four years should have been. But why should Freddie be expected to know this or care? I've been at this sodding advertising agency, sitting on the same floor, working all the hours across different accounts, managing the massively overinflated client expectations with what my team can actually deliver on the miniscule budget they've set for far too long. I am everyone's big sister who needs one, which means I always end up giving a listening ear whether I'm interested or not.

In my head I'm shouting in Freddie's face, his beautiful snoggable face, 'I DON'T GIVE A SHIT!'

But no, I'm nodding and making comforting, attentive sound effects. Desperate to have a conversation with my actual workmates, Supriya and Jojo, who are cracking up over something, but I can't extract myself from Freddie. I have the curse of never wanting to be seen as rude, even if my own brain is melting inside me.

This job was meant to be temporary and yet, ten years later, I'm still doing it. I'm good at what I do, but I used to be great.

Our managing director, Siobhan (who now wants us all to call her Shiv since watching *Succession*) has perfect hearing yet fails at the basic repetition of sounds. Anyone with a vaguely non-Anglo-Saxon name gets a wonderful new one, created through the audio tuner of Siobhan's brain. She's never once managed 'Supriya' in the two years she's been with the company.

Sopra.

Supree.

Soup.

Sophie.

Sssuuuuuuu—

Oh, let's keep it simple, I'll call you Sue.

I look over at Siobhan. She's cornered the new starter, talking at him, invading his personal space. I can almost see him trying to duck the saliva molecules being spat in his direction, squinting his eyes and retracting his neck. The new ones always get trapped. I can see his eyes glancing across the room pleadingly and it crosses my mind to stage an intervention and save the poor guy, but this would mean having to speak to Siobhan and I'd rather hang with my gang, try to switch my work brain off.

For the first few years, I really bought into my career. I slowly worked my way up the greasy pole to get to management level and gave the best of my liver to it. I've worked hard. I watch the signs, read what's required of me and use initiative, but never in a way that feels like overstepping. I bring a light-hearted attitude to the office, make small talk, go for drinks – OK, perhaps too many drinks. I'm organised, I have good people skills (more than most in my office) and I am empathetic. I'm great at thinking up hooks, even for other people's campaigns. Clients specifically request that I'm lead on their projects. And nobody writes better copy than me. The writing is what I really love; I don't have to collaborate with anyone, it's just me and my words, telling a story.

Sometimes, though, when I'm in a certain kind of mood, I wonder: am I good at my job or do *people like me* just have a really good work ethic? I was brought up to excel – or at least to work as hard as possible and harder than the person next to me. Dad gave me the 'twice as hard' speech when I went off to uni – 'we have to work twice as hard to get half as far' – but I dismissed it.

'Not anymore, Dad, the world is changing.' At a snail's pace, it transpires.

The promotions I worked so hard for were never mine. First, Andrew got one, and then Sarah. My hard-working, *just happy to be here* attitude morphed slowly, my facial muscles started to feel so much heavier, my energy levels dropping alongside my ability to raise a smile.

After I didn't get the promotion the second time, I should have told them where to stick their stupid job. Or at the very least, started considering my options. I tried to ask why I wasn't considered and was told I *just wasn't quite ready yet*. That I'm so good at what I do in my current role, it would be hard to replace me. And now I've been overlooked for a promotion a third time, despite working even bloody harder to prove how good I am. I thought I was going to run the world by now, but I'm just exhausted and, yes, a bit bitter.

I wonder if Freddie could understand any of my work troubles. He thinks he's got it bad?

'If only I'd bought some when the cost was low – it's now worth . . .'

Freddie seems to have moved on from the topic of Paul and has chosen crypto currency as his next subject, lord help me. My ears have turned to the song on the speakers, which I love but can't remember the name of.

'Who is this?'

He's surprised that I've cut him off midflow and looks a bit put out.

'I have no idea. Never heard it.'

I turn to Supriya and Jojo, and oh, the sweet relief. These two are my work saviours. We've been thick as thieves ever since an away day four years back when we all discovered that we do not enjoy any activity described on an itinerary as an 'icebreaker'.

Jojo's a couple of years younger than me and Supriya's only just twenty-seven. She's Indian but fifth generation South African; she came to study business at Manchester Uni and never went back. We all share a love of drinking after work, drowning our food in chilli sauce and, of course, a mutual hatred for Siobhan.

'Who is this? I love it but can't think who it's by?' I can feel Freddie's eyes looking at the back of my head, probably a little crestfallen. But I really can't support his one-man conversation about the crypto markets. I just want to have a laugh with my mates. 'Oh, it's on the tip of my tongue . . .'

'I've never even heard it before,' says Supriya.

'You've never heard of anything, Ms Gen Z,' Jojo says back. And then the chorus kicks in and I sing along.

'Na na naaaa nanananan naa.'

Sups has already shazam'd it. 'Jermaine Jackson!' she shouts.

I make a mental note to add it to my party playlist on Spotify.

Sups reaches out to me, pulling me to my feet and dancing exaggeratedly.

'Come on, it's your birthday tomorrow, let's party!' she yells over the music, and I can feel myself laughing at Freddie's bemused expression as I abandon him and throw my arms up in the air to sing along with my friends and begin our excellent game of pulling ridiculous dance moves to make each other laugh. The booze has worked its magic: I'm feeling light and free and living exactly the sort of modern-girl life my mum is constantly warning me against . . .

Later on, there's no escaping it – it's time to brave the toilets. This type of bar requires the full thigh-engaging hover action but at least there's loo roll. The watermarked mirrors fail to disguise my drunk face or that my eyeliner is starting to slip and, oh, nice: I still have my lanyard on. I need to go home, and as I step out of the loo, I am already making a plan: *grab coat, say goodbye, bus, pyjamas, toast, maybe even some wings from the chicken shop, bed.*

I step out of the loo and all I hear is, 'Hey, Simran . . . tequila?' Simran is also not my real name. But there is no way on earth anyone I work with, no matter how much of a pal they've become, is getting to know the name on my birth certificate.

The mischief in Sup's eyes is infectious, though, so to hell with it. Pass the salt.

The lights are bright on the night bus home. But I've got my headphones plugged in with my head unwisely resting on the window, too drunk to care about whose grease my hair might be mingling with. I've sunk into the comfort of my most wistful playlist, as tempting as it is to play my brrap big jungle tunes of the nineties, but I'm winding myself down. Melancholy is a comfort to me and there's no better time to sink into the cosy swaddle of it than when inebriated on the night bus.

The bus is quicker and cheaper than a taxi and I like to sit downstairs near the driver. Bus drivers feel safe. They are council workers, official in their uniforms, hardworking, often people of colour. Safer than a taxi driver, safer than calling the police if anything goes wrong.

The night bus is in between worlds, where things are usually calmer and quieter, but everyone on it is anything but normal. At 4 a.m., if you look closely, you'll see the people who make this all possible, the sleepy-eyed workers from everywhere but the UK, heading into clean offices, clean the streets, clean up the mess from the night before. They're also the first to see the newspaper headlines about migrants invading. Sometimes it's enough to sober you up.

I'm hypnotised by the flawless voice of Joan As Police Woman singing 'The Ride' when *PING!* Snapped out of my lonely reverie, I squint down at my phone and see MUM flashing up.

Are you home?

On the night bus, I type back. Dammit, I should have lied. I'm too drunk to think quick enough to avoid this obvious trap.

Bus? Be careful. Full of drunks and druggies at this time! Inexplicably this is followed by the ambulance emoji and a croissant.

There is definitely at least one drunk on this bus.

I'm fine. Be home soon.
Were you on a date?
No!
Did you meet Aunty Vimla's nephew?

Who?

Mum, I'm tired.

Just want you to be happy. *Dancing lady emoji*
Is it worse or better to hear that via WhatsApp? I can't handle this right now.

Yes. OK, Mum.
Coming home for your birthday?

Oh. I pause, but I see Mum is writing more:

We have not seen you in over a month. Dadima misses you.

Strike 1: the mild-guilt gut punch. I love my granny and I know how happy it makes her to see me. This card is often used to get me home because it's so effective.

Dadima is my dad's mum. We've always lived with my grandparents in the traditional Indian generational family set-up. A couple gets married and the daughter-in-law moves in with the entire family because sons don't move out. Not so easy for my mum, but pretty great for a doted-on grandchild. Grandad Ranjit died when I was young, but Dadima is my heart. My phone vibrates again.

You're turning 36 and you're alone. *Unicorn sticker* That one has to be a mistake surely?

Ouch, strike 2. I'm thirty-six and not married, yes. Plenty of friends, a (fairly) successful career and my own home don't

8

count for much, apparently. My Indian mum doesn't do subtle. She doesn't worry about anything as Western or namby-pamby as protecting my feelings. For Smita Saul, my being alone in the world is just a statement of fact, one that I'm very aware of, though that might turn out to be a surprise to my mother. It's my life I'm living.

Your dad would have wanted to celebrate it with you.

And there it is, the final killer jab to finish me off, KO'd by the mention of Dad. It cripples me every time. Who'd have thought I'd be in my thirties, work stalling, with a non-existent love life and then, bam! Dad dies. It all happened so suddenly; one day he felt more tired than he'd ever felt, the next, it was terminal and before any of us had a chance to understand what was going on, we were standing around a hospital bed, weeping and saying goodbye. It happened two years ago, the worst day of my life, and life hasn't yet made sense again in quite the same way. I'm floored, and Mum knows it.

No party, Mum. I'd love just a quiet night with you both.

I'll cook a feast. *Aubergine emoji* Wow. I can't quite figure out how I would ever explain to her that it doesn't mean brinjal pickle.

That sounds great, but I meant it, no party.
So, you coming home weekend? I will tell Dadima.
I'll be there. Don't overcook. And no party.

Another unicorn sticker. Who knows what that means to her.

I get off at my stop, zipping up my jacket, phone on one hand and my keys in the other, just in case I'm jumped on my short walk home, headphones off to make sure I'm on high alert. Can't relax until I'm in the lift in my block.

There used to be a time I was so sure of myself, my mission, my purpose. I used to talk to my dad about everything – who I

9

wanted to be, how I would get there, ambition actively encouraged. Indian aunts and uncles at family gatherings will often ask five-year-olds what they want to be when they are older. The correct answer is always 'Doctor!' This encourages all the right noises, the head wobble and, 'Very good, beta, very good. Study hard and look after us all when we are old.'

My choices were always a little more baffling. First, I wanted to become a celebrity chef, because I liked the idea of eating lots of leftover food and ordering people around. And swearing, which is what most celebrity chefs seemed to do on TV. Then I wanted to become a radio DJ but had no idea where to start and my mum just pulled a funny face when I mentioned it. Deep down, I really wanted to be a writer, to make up stories, disappear into other worlds, create characters I fall in love with . . . but no one like me becomes a writer, so I buried that dream. In the end, to everyone's delight, I went off to study law at Manchester; easy for all of them to be happy about it – they weren't the ones having to study it. I made the bold move of changing my degree to English in the second year and eventually told my parents in the third year before graduation. Dad got it although he wanted to know where I'd end up with a degree in English. Well, turns out you don't need anything specific for marketing, a job I fell into the first summer after finishing my degree. But the pay was good and I enjoyed it so Dad was pleased.

I missed chatting to Dad over a glass of whisky about life. He'd encourage me to go out and live it to my 'full potential', while Mum would shout from the kitchen, 'And remember to always make your parents proud. Don't do anything to bring shame.'

I arrive at my front door, steadying myself by leaning against the frame and let myself in. One really good thing in my life still is where I now live. I adore my flat in Manchester, in an old industrial warehouse overlooking the river, converted for young professionals to make us feel suitably swish, with high ceilings and huge windows and modern finishes. Most people my age have slowly moved out to buy their starter homes with partners, nice terrace houses with gardens and side extensions, and Farrow & Ball accented walls. Not many people in their thirties are left kicking about in this block, apart from the gorgeous couple next door, Johnny and Henry, friends who have saved me on more than a few occasions by turning my maudlin drinking-sessions-for-one into impromptu kitchen dance parties.

Once in my place, I kick my shoes off in the hall, neck a glass of water, and press play on my navel-gazing playlist, filling the living room with the exquisite Nadine Shah and 'Ville Morose'. Her voice fills me up and now I'm in my space, I do what brings me the most joy and allow my body to move to the music. I move as wildly and as drunkenly as I want, and I think about my dad, and how much I miss him, and how he loved this place. My place. My sanctuary. I've made the flat completely my own, so no neutral walls to increase resale value here. It is decadent, with lush velvet curtains, vibrant walls, and bright tiles in the bathroom; I even bought myself a gold sink, because why not? And the place is overflowing with stuff, mainly books and music and posters. I own the place, so I can do what I like. I bought it five years ago and it gave my mum something to be proud of . . . for five minutes.

The first time my parents came to visit Mum brought a coconut, which she cracked in front of the flat for good luck and poured mustard oil on the doorstep – the stain has never gone. She hung chilli and lemon above the door, lit a joss stick in the kitchen, then went into each room flicking water into every single corner to bless the house. Didn't mean she liked it, though. She couldn't understand why I had bought a flat with exposed bricks.

'Is this flat even finished? Are they going to charge you for not plastering the walls?'

'It's meant to be like that, Mum, it's the style.'

'This is what people think is style these days? Poor people live like this in Indian villages, raw walls.'

'I like it. It's fantastic.' Dad got it. 'A place to call your own. You can paint the walls in any colour you like, and no one will

11

say a thing. Well done, beta, we are proud of your achievement. Let's have a cup of tea this time and a whisky next time,' he said with his brilliantly cheeky smile.

'Bas, you just keep encouraging her to drink and drink a man's drink at that. It will ruin her beauty.'

Jagtar Singh Saul, you were the best, and I miss you every day, Dad.

Chapter Two

I wake up fully clothed on my bed, with my face in a small pool of my own drool. My mouth tastes spicy, acidic, sour all at once, and as I turn to grab my phone, I spot the half-eaten plate of chicken wings. I don't remember getting Deliveroo. Huh. Just as I am reaching hungrily for the box in the full knowledge that this is what absolutely constitutes 'a bad life choice', my phone pings.

It's from my mum.

I'm cooking. Looking forward seeing you. House emoji and for some reason, three peaches.

PING

Happy Birthday. *Chick in an egg*
My head hurts.

Before heading home for dinner with Mum and Dadima, my lovely neighbours Johnny and Henry have invited me round to their place for a birthday brunch. It's just what I need after last night and with the prospect of some serious family time ahead of me.

I get myself sorted, shower, and throw on my jeans and favourite tie-dye hoodie. I'm more likely to dress up for Johnny and Henry than I am for Mum and Gran, but today I just want to be cosy. I throw a couple of painkillers down me, two paracetamols, and then grab a bottle of Prosecco from the fridge and head next door.

'Here she is, the birthday legend!' I laugh as Johnny opens the door and Henry immediately pulls a party popper.

'Guys, I am way too hungover for this level of excitement, please have mercy.'

'Baby girl, when are you *not* hungover?' Henry says as he welcomes me into their open-plan living room-kitchen-diner.

Attractive, stylish and over the top – I could be describing Johnny and Henry, or I could be describing their home. All is well whenever I am in their flat, like a second home. They have this wonderful capacity to make the outside world disappear when I'm with them. Our first meeting came just after I moved in when Johnny knocked round with a loaf of banana bread – I knew he was a kindred spirit because it was fragrant with cardamom as well as cinnamon.

Successful in their respective fields (Johnny works in TV, Henry's in marketing and often gives me tips), they are generous, kind neighbours and will always invite me round when they have friends over. Usually though I don't even need an invite, I'll just stumble into their house parties after being kicked out of the pub. I feel safe and free in their company, and they encourage me to be as wild as I want, which everyone knows is exactly what a lot of girls raised in strict households need. They have a dressing-up box full of wigs that will always come out after a certain point – I once woke up on my bed in a Dolly Parton wig, wrapped in a feather boa with fake eyelashes stuck to my cheeks and the memory of a 3 a.m. rendition of 'Here You Come Again' lingering like the taste of white wine. Their friends are funny and fabulous and there's a sense of urgency with them, that we can't waste time not being anything other than who we are. I admire their capacity to know who they are – I often wish I knew a little bit more about who *I* am.

Johnny and Henry are slightly older than me, in their mid-forties. The apartment isn't their only home, they also have a country house in the Dales and a canal boat that they rent out, plus a little dog, a Chihuahua, named Elvis. Somehow, I don't think I'll have my shit together to this extent at any point, let alone in my rapidly approaching forties, but it's nice to have friends with a dog and a place to go for the weekends, isn't it?

I've barely sat down before Johnny has popped the cork on a bottle of fizz and we all have a Prosecco in hand.

'Cheers!'

I take a sip and almost gag. God, I feel rough. Johnny sits down next to me and slings his arm around me while Henry slices his home-made sourdough at the kitchen island.

'To our hungover birthday girl,' says Johnny, clinking my glass. I take another sip. This one goes down much easier. 'We'll have you feeling better in no time, won't we, Henry?'

'When have my eggs and avo toast not worked their magic?' Henry looks over at me and frowns. 'Though we'd need a miracle to make that jumper work, darling, even on you.'

'Henry!' I shout, and he laughs. 'I thought tie-dye was my colour.'

Elvis, their excitable Chihuahua, comes bouncing in. He is wearing a glittery party hat – Elvis has a dressing-up box of his own, of course – and I bend down to pick him up and smother him with kisses.

'Well, at least someone made an effort for your birthday,' Johnny says, winking at me. Then his tone turns serious. 'So, are you going to tell us how it went last night?'

I sigh and take a big gulp of my drink. While Henry plates up, I tell them about the night before, work, the promotion, Freddie. They know all about Freddie, and they are always here to listen to me complain even when I'm bored of talking about him myself.

'I want to break up with him, not that we are together, it doesn't feel right anymore. Should never have got involved with someone at work.' It's easy to tell them what I'm really think-ing, they're astute enough to always cut through my bullshit, so I just tell them the truth, it's liberating.

'So do it. Why are you worrying?' asks Henry.

'Well . . . I don't want to hurt his feelings,' I say pathetically.

I get an eyeroll from Henry and he adds, 'So you'll carry on with something that's not right because you don't want to hurt HIS feelings? How are we going to beat the demon people pleaser out of you? We need to conduct an exorcism.'

15

I laugh. He's not wrong. I often find myself worrying about how my decisions will impact everyone else. It's crippling.

'You're right.' And then add, 'I suppose it's not really him I'm worried about, it's me. Life just feels so stagnant. What am I doing?'

'You're enjoying your life, surely? Darling, you're thirty-six, which by the way, is still no age at all.' Johnny is always so positive.

'Not when you're a woman! My eggs are drying up and no one will want me.'

'Is that seriously how you value yourself? Medical science is amazing now. If you choose to have kids at some point then you'll find a way to do it, and your life is all kinds of fabulous if you don't decide to do that: your own place in a great city, financially independent, free to snog, marry and avoid at your pleasure and leisure, FABULOUS friends. Simran, you have a life most would love – do you realise that?'

I guess I do realise it superficially, but the message I've had my entire life is that my value IS down to first my marital status and secondly whether I've had children. I don't even know if I want to get married or have offspring but that doesn't seem to be a conversation women are allowed to entertain. Certainly not young Punjabi women with a pack of matchmakers circling her, in the form of a mother and every aunty in the Yorkshire/Lancashire district. They have access to every eligible man in the Pennines. And for some reason they are all fixated on getting me hitched. Because a single woman, making choices for herself, is wild and free and that's not the done thing. It's always explained away by Mum with a 'I just want YOU to be happy'. Because of course a single women could never be gloriously happy. What Mum really means to say is 'I just want you to make ME happy and less ashamed'. It's not her fault either, she's been conditioned by the patriarchal culture but jeez, sometimes I wish she'd just allow me to be me, understand me.

Henry clocks the solemn look on my face.

'Girl, you are hungover and having an existential crisis on your birthday, this is normal. The bubbles will help, but please, let us celebrate you this morning. Look at you! You're fab and you've broken the mould for good little Indian girl.'

I look up and smile at him.

'And it's not that simple a mould to break, it's, like, the Alcatraz of moulds.'

The doorbell goes. They've invited other friends, people I've met before but don't know very well. I ditch my maudlin attitude and try to ignore the thumping headache; the painkillers will kick in soon. I'm not sure the booze is going to help but I drink it anyway and then I drink a couple more just to take the edge off the train journey back to the suburbs. Knowing that a cosy night on the sofa eating Mum's delicious food is awaiting me, I try not to worry too much about my hangover as it is going to be nursed in its favourite spot. At some point I should maybe quit drinking, or at least drink less.

'A top up, Simran?'

I jump up, snapping out of my downer mood and slapping on my goodtime smile. It's just the hangover blues. It's my birthday, let's get on it.

Chapter Three

It's probably quicker to get home via barge along the canal than take the train, given how little the powers that be have invested in northern infrastructure, but it's a great old train line, cutting through the Pennines, passing old villages and mills, and the odd, gorgeous home cut into the side of a hill. It's February; cold, rainy, and miserable. But the landscape suits the weather.

I always use this journey to daydream. I imagine a different life, another world. I look up at the Yorkshire stone cottages scattered on the hillside and think about the people who live in them and their perfect lives. I think about the mother I always seem to spot, looking out from her kitchen window, taking in the stunning views while making breakfast for a family after taking the dog for a walk on the moor, perhaps. I imagine the house smelling of baking, I imagine homework being done at the dining table with Mum and Dad helping. I imagine a piano and bookshelves and conversation about the state of the world. The perfect happy family, with so much certainty about their place and who they are, never having to answer any questions about identity and fitting in. I've had the same daydream since I was a kid. Putting myself in another life. Wishing away my Indianness, wanting to just be accepted and understanding, from a very young age, this would mean daydreaming being white and middle class.

Now, as an adult, the daydream gives me the ick, makes me feel like a traitor and I feel regret at the amount of shame I carried as a child about who I am. But my posh white friends, with their bookshelves and riding lessons and their happy, wine-quaffing parents, who went skiing in the Alps every year and looked just like Barbie and Ken, but with names like Barbara and Kenneth, seemed to have such lovely lives to little me. Their worlds were so different to mine, less complicated. That's what I believed was the ultimate in aspiration for my little child mind trying to figure out who I was.

My life was happy but there was always struggle, a bit claustrophobic, a permanent undercurrent of stress and sadness to all the adults around me, Mum, Dad, Dadima and Grandad Ranjit, and I couldn't understand why. The sadness I wished I could fix and I guess I always knew I wanted more for my life than what I saw around me, than what was expected of me. Something different.

As much as I moan about this slow-running old train, I absolutely love travelling on it, and it might be why I haven't yet bothered to buy a car, much to the bemusement of every Asian person I know. Where do you possibly put the person who chooses not to have a car on the social status order? This line would have been fantastic when it first opened, connecting the industrial North, the engine of Britain, to the coast. I think of all those mill workers and their families heading out to the seaside for the very first time, allowed a week for nothing but pleasure. And now holidays feel like a right, not a privilege, in Britain. Unless, of course, you grew up in a family like mine. Then holidays are still very much a privilege and for some, something to be denied.

'Leh, I haven't got time for holiday-shmoliday. Some of us have to take life seriously. We don't have money to waste.' This was always Mum's standard response.

But then she would also walk into any clothes shop, take one look at the price and say, 'Leh, I could make this better and cheaper at home.' Or in the supermarket, she'd see me drooling over cake or fondant fancies.

'Leh, what is this waste of money, on cake? I'll make you delicious home-made kheer, if you want something sweet.'

Or on the odd occasion when I'd want to eat junk food, like KFC.

'Leh, let's not burn our money. I'll make it better and tastier at home, with masala.'

Pleasure for the sake of pleasure just doesn't exist in my household, is seen as a frivolous waste of money. Money is precious and hard-earned and to be used seriously, not wasted on things that may bring you temporary joy.

This landscape is so familiar to me, I feel physically connected to it. I imagine how magnificent and grand these northern powerhouse towns and cities were back then – Ponti, Doni, Waki, Bratfud, Halifax – built on the back of the colonised world, I now realise. These cities are still handsome if you can see beyond the faded grandeur, the buildings covered in pigeon shit.

To me, they are beautiful. This is Yorkshire, the only land I've known.

I take a huge breath and sigh, looking at the rain pelting the window as we approach Bradford Interchange.

God, I love being Northern, but it would be so good to taste something different, to just be somewhere else.

Eventually, we slowly veer left onto the lonely line into the unlovely dead-end that is the Bradford Interchange. The trains chug in and then chug back out the same way.

I get off the train and head to the taxi rank. The guy I get makes me smile. He jumps out the car and opens the door for me, which is a first.

'Alreet, sister?' he says.

He's dressed in jeans, a long kameez, a denim jacket and some very, very new trainers.

'Sick kicks,' I say, in genuine appreciation.

'Yeah, mi Loobs. Louboutin, innit? Gotta look smart on the job, yeah.'

He is, I would guess, in his early twenties and really good-looking. I suppose I should be grateful he didn't call me auntie.

I get his life story on the journey, in a broad Yorkshire accent with that distinct South-Asian twang. He wants to take over the family taxi company, wants to take his future wife to the

Lake District, loves Liverpool Football Club, has a love-hate relationship with Bradford.

'Crap, innit, but it's our crap, yeah,' he says and laughs.

I tell him I live in Manchester, though I'm from round here.

'Manchester! What doya go an' do that fur?'

Yep, he's definitely from Bradford.

I get out the taxi and walk up the wide road to my mum's, lined with sixties semi-detached homes with well-kept gardens and sensible cars like Fords and Kias parked on the driveways, the odd flash German number outside an Asian house. You can spot a desi household a mile away: the house might be worth £150,000 but they've got the same value at least in the three cars parked outside. The Sandhu family at 42 have their Mercedes, a sporty BMW and a BMW 1 series for their daughter. The Khans at 76 have a Mercedes, a Range Rover and a Subaru for their twenty-seven-year-old, single-and-still-living-at-home son. To be fair, he did buy it himself with his wage from PC World, but then again, he pays no rent and has no bills to pay. He spent a small fortune having it wrapped bright Kermit green and spends every Sunday polishing it. The Khans also bought the house next door to theirs, number 74, for their eldest son, his wife and two kids. The two semis are now one big, detached home, with paved-over lawns to make space for all the cars. It's practical, I guess.

But before the Khans and the Sandhus, there was us, the Sauls, at number 33. We were the first Asian family to move into the area. And what a welcome we received. A few cautious hellos, a few tentative smiles, a lot of curtain twitching. Then, on our second night, someone felt the urge to post dog shit in an envelope through our letter box. Someone was filthy enough to pick up a dog poo and squish it into an envelope, therefore subjecting themselves to a far worse trauma than me finding it, feeling totally confused, showing Mum, who then promptly shoved it in the bin.

I can see our neighbour Roger at number 29 is in his front garden, weeding – his garden is his pride and joy.

'All right, lass?' Roger gives me a wave. I wave back and remember when we first moved in.

One day soon after, Mum was cooking with the kitchen door wide open – Indian cooking is potent stuff, with the fumes needing to go somewhere. We could hear Roger two doors away, in his back garden, shouting at his wife: 'What is that godawful pong? Is our street going to smell like Pakistan now?'

Mum met Roger's lovely wife, Eileen, and gave her an old yogurt pot full of the 'godawful pong' one day, her black chickpea and potato curry. From then on 'the smell of Pakistan' often coaxed Eileen and later, Roger, to drift towards our open kitchen door for a chat and a casual, 'Oh, if you're sure there's enough, yes, we'd love some curry.' Mum always has an empty yogurt pot or ice-cream tub to hand to distribute her cooking to the world. Food is always something to be shared.

Mum finds it impossible to cook anything less than a giant vat of whatever it is she's making. The worst sin would be to not make enough. She never concerns herself with food waste, because there never is any – leftovers will always get eaten or distributed to ever-willing takers. The neighbours, the postie, the milkman, the window cleaner, the builders (not even builders doing work on our house, any builders in the vicinity) will often be treated to a lavish lunch of rice, dhal, pakora, or whatever Mum can knock up in no time. It's her pleasure. Food, she says, is to be shared. She couldn't believe it when I started to attend birthday parties at primary school and realised that English food customs aren't quite so generous.

'A sandwich? That's all you had? Jelly and ice cream too? That's not going to fill you up.' She'd make sure I'd eat before every party, never realising how much I loved the little crustless sandwiches, especially cheese and cucumber on sliced white bread. My friends always had different cheese to our Kraft Cheese slices, and proper blocks of the stuff, which was placed on the table on a platter along with other varieties. Just cheese, on a plate, with a knife. Mind-boggling to little me, and now I can't get enough of the stuff. I once brought home a Stilton at Christmas, thinking we too could have a cheeseboard after the tandoori chicken Mum had made. Dadima, Mum and Dad were horrified.

'What is this smell, smelly feet, hai hai, is this what people eat?' Dadima said, shaking her head and scrunching her nose.

'It's addictive. Try it, Mum. It's earthy, like mushrooms.' We all laughed so much at the faces Mum and Dadima pulled. But after a couple more glasses of red wine, Mum was cutting slithers and eating more. 'Told you, addictive.'

Slowly, more Asian families moved into the area over the years, as they made enough money to leave their inner-city terraced houses, terrifying a few of the white folk into upping sticks . . . to move further into the sticks. Not Eileen and Roger, though. They had no plans to go anywhere and I'm glad they didn't. They would often look after me if no one was at home. Eileen would bake and bring cake over for Dadima, who has an insatiable sweet tooth. And the two of them have been an incredible support for Mum since Dad died.

As I walk up to my family home, I notice there are a lot more cars parked around our cul-de-sac than usual. *Someone must be having a party.*

I hear it before I see it. Punjabis are a rowdy lot, and there's already guffawing laughter with a bhangra soundtrack underpinning it. At least five small children are running between the cars, screaming and laughing on the drive. It's not even 6 p.m.

Mrs Sandhu's curtains are twitching; she knows I'm home before anyone at home does.

I turn around and give her window a wave.

This, I know, is Mum's idea of *no party, please.*

'Aahh, Baby, tu aagai. Baby's here, everyone!' someone shouts from the drive.

And there it is, my real name: *Baby* Saul. Not Simran, but Baby. Mum, in her infinite wisdom, didn't want to give me a name no one would use (or couldn't pronounce) so the pet name they were all calling me at the time, because, well, I *was* a sodding baby, stuck. Punjabis love a pet name. People have beautiful names with stunning meanings, sure, but they are also given some kind of cutesy nickname when they're tiny. This is the name that lingers beyond childhood, it's girlishness following you into adulthood to make sure no one is ever quite able to take you seriously. Mum plumped for something that would only really have benefitted me if I'd had a career in Bollywood. My birth certificate reads Baby Saul, and believe me, there was no running away from it at school.

Smelly baby
Jelly baby
Cry baby
Googoogaagaa baby
Baby needs a dummy
Poopoo nappy baby

It got to the point where even simply being called Baby felt like an insult. I'd cry at home over the name I hated and desperately wanted another. I would practise writing other names over and over, imagining all the different selves I could be alongside them. I wished I was more like my friend Bahadur; kids at school would try and have a go at him, mainly because they couldn't pronounce it, but rather than feel the intense shame that defined me in the playground, he would proudly declare, 'My name is Bahadur and it means brave warrior, I am from a long line of warriors and I have courage in my heart. What does *your* name mean?'

Little Jack and Sally wouldn't know what to say. When the PE teacher suggested he maybe call him Billy instead, Bahadur didn't need to repeat his line, as Jack did it for him. And we all listened to Jack because he was the only person in the year with a PlayStation and a completed Panini album, so he was basically King of the Eight-Year-Olds. Bahadur lived up to his name and no one ever changed it to something else.

I wanted an ancient Indian name, with a meaning so powerful I could stand my ground and always have a comeback line to defeat my bullies. So, one evening when I was eight, my dadima and I sat down to think of a beautiful traditional name for me. Dadima's favourite pastime was meditating, though we never called it meditation back then, it was simply called praying, or doing paath. When I was even smaller, I had loved to sit alongside her with my legs crossed, eyes semi-closed, while she recited verses of the Guru Granth Sahib. I didn't understand a single word of it, but I loved the sound of Dadima's soothing voice, somewhere between speaking and singing, chanting the Gurmukhi. I'd then join her for Simran, repeating whatever she said, experiencing my own sense of calm, of peace, so different to the whirling set of emotions I usually experienced in day-to-day life.

Dadima explained to me that we are all part of the universe, the Earth and everything on it. Doing Simran connected me to something bigger, even at that small age, that would always look after me. If I was ever stressed or worried, I would always have Simran. If we have Simran, we will always feel brave. Simran was going to be my new name. No one argued with it at home. I think Dad was mostly happy I'd picked an Indian name, unlike Uncle Kalsi's son, who had changed his name from Kuljit to Kevin. Changing my name didn't stop my family from calling me Baby, however. I'd be a Baby for life at home.

I smell home before I step through the front door. The delicious aroma of onions, garlic, spices and deep-fat frying are all wafting in my direction.

Mum is standing by the stove dressed in a beautiful mint-green saree, her makeup simple, her hair up in a bun. She's gorgeous, more elegant now in her sixties than ever before.

'Come, come, Baby, just in time, the samosas are being fried, garam garam. Do you want to wash your face, maybe put some makeup on? Everyone is here. Say hello to Shashi aunty.' Shashi aunty is helping Mum in the kitchen.

'Hi, Shashi aunty.'

'Hello, Baby, you look lovely to me,' she says back with a kind smile and continues to decant pickles into Mum's pickle tray.

'Thanks, Shashi aunty, at least someone's on my side,' I say with a smile while grabbing a home-roasted almond, covered in salt and chaat masala and popping it in my mouth. The flavour resuscitates my tastebuds.

I slide up close to Mum, who says, 'I'm always on your side.' While she is deep-frying batches of home-made samosas in a massive karahi filled with sunflower oil.

'What happened to "no party"?' I whisper in her ear, widening my eyes and showing her a big fake smile.

She pulls the same face back and whispers, 'Your dadima insisted.'

A likely story, but there is no point in arguing with either of them – especially as the party is already very much in motion. I kiss the top of Mum's head as I'm at least four inches taller than her, and grab a samosa – hot, crisp, spicy – just what my hangover needs.

'Careful, careful, you don't want to get splashed by hot oil. Spoil that beautiful face. Everyone is here for you! You are a lucky girl. Surrounded by people who want to celebrate you . . . You look tired, though, go and put some makeup on.'

I slip into the downstairs toilet under the stairs to look at my newly thirty-six-year-old face. I'm not sure who I look like, probably more like Dad. I'm getting his smile lines around my eyes, and I've definitely got his nose, which I used to hate but don't notice it as much now that I've grown into it, and it's nice to see a bit of him still with me. I'm paler than usual today, which will go down well with the aunties. I look tired because I *am* tired – and hungover with a chaser of being slightly drunk from brunch. At a family party where I am meant to be the centre of attention . . . Great. I've still got the remnants of last night's makeup around my eyes and the lipstick I put on first thing this morning has worn away. I didn't come home prepared for a party; I'm home for a night on the sofa stuffing my face, but it's time to say goodbye to that fantasy. I take a deep breath, whack on some more lippy and prepare to enter my big fat Punjabi birthday party.

I walk into the heaving dining room which connects with the living room. It had been knocked through when we'd moved in to make space for occasions just like this, so family members could have plenty of places to sit and eat, and chat and eat, and stand and eat.

Everyone turns to look at me as one.

'BABY!'

Time to run the gauntlet of friends and relatives. I will be expected to talk to everyone. I've been brought up with 'akal', good manners, which involves saying a polite 'Hello!' and 'So great to see you, how's the family?' to every single person I meet. I grab a drink and another samosa, and dive into the fray.

Sitting in the corner are the twins, Lucky and Jolly, Bubbly auntie's daughters. They are shooting their terrifying blank stares in my direction. *Do not make eye contact.* I nod in their general direction; it's much easier to skip saying hello to cousins than to aunties and they don't want to talk to me any more than I want to talk to them. The twins are seventeen and still have long plaits down their back with clothes almost certainly chosen by their mother. No wonder they look so miserable; someone needs to liberate them. Not me, obviously. To them I am as ancient as Dadima, the younger family members seeing no real difference between someone who is thirty-six and someone who is sixty-six. We're just the boring oldsters to them, another Saturday spent at an obligatory event, counting the seconds until it's time to go home. I remember it well. Too old to really want to be here, too young to have any choice in the matter.

I can feel tugging on my jeans. It's Rekha, Pinky's middle child, meaning Pinky must be here too.

Pinky, or Pinks, is my oldest mate, and her children are genuinely adorable. She's managed to have three gorgeous kids: eight-year-old Maya, six-year-old Rekha and now a baby boy called Jai. We've been friends since always. Our parents have been friends for years, and her grandparents know my grandparents as they are part of the same Punjabi community in Bradford. We were never that close when we were little but then, aged eleven, everything changed over one episode of *Top of the Pops*. We bonded over our love of All Saints.

We thought we were so grown-up, liking them; they seemed like the thinking eleven-year-old's choice of pop group. We weren't just fans, we were connoisseurs. We'd practise 'Never Ever' over and over and tried to wear our jeans as baggy and low-slung as possible without getting into trouble. And she knew me as Baby – but then, she was called Pinky, so she understood. With Pinks, my name just made sense. I didn't need to explain myself to her, ever.

'Baby Masi, can you play with me?' Pinky insists her kids call me Masi rather than generic aunty. Aunty doesn't feel right, it's too formal and could be anybody, but Masi cements our bond as sisters.

I pick her up and give her a nose kiss.

'Sure, and let's go over towards the drinks on our way . . .' But she doesn't like the sound of this and wriggles free, so I put her down. Sensible child.

I meet cousin Sammy (who is actually my second cousin) by the drinks, who is studying some kind of finance but he really wants to be a DJ. An ambition he has to keep to himself because my aunt and uncle think it's ridiculous.

'You want to be jumping up and down, playing music at weddings? What kind of profession is this?'

'Fatboy Slim and Naughty Boy make a fortune, I could produce tunes too,' he's tried to explain.

'What are these names, fat boy? Naught boy? Who will you be? Silly boy?'

'Hey, Sammy! How's life? Any big gigs yet?' I say, cheerfully bumping him with my hip.

'Pritpal's daughter's fifth birthday party,' he responds, with the least amount of enthusiasm I have ever seen on someone's face. 'But we've all got to start somewhere, even if it means a set consisting of Disney classics, some old-school bhangra for the parents, and hyped-up toddlers on sugar. Someone brought the cheap fake Haribo, with extra E-numbers or something. It was carnage.'

'Sammy, that sounds like a mega skill to me, not many DJs can play that eclectic combination. Plus, there was projectile vomiting and an overexcited audience? That is basically what you'll get in any club night, so it's good practice! You'll be playing Glastonbury before you know it!' I manage to pour myself a drink as I continue this incredibly spirited pep talk. 'Move over, Chemical Brothers, DJ Sammy Singh is headlining Saturday night!' I pump my arm up in the air and he laughs before looking at me conspiratorially.

'Hey, Baby, have you got a cigarette by any chance?' he asks, slightly cautiously but with a knowing wink.

The cheek of it! I'd never have had the guts to ask an older cousin for a cigarette at a party. No one would know I'd ever even tried one.

'No, I quit, I've never really smoked properly – and anyway, have you lost the plot? You can't smoke at a family party. It's not worth the risk, there are eyes everywhere. I though you Gen Z lot were all clean-living vegans, anyway?'

'Only every other day,' he says, with absolutely no hint of sarcasm on his face. 'Funny how we can drink ourselves legless, but smoking is a no-no.'

He's not wrong. Punjabis do love a drink, but smoking is a cardinal sin. It's bad enough if a boy is caught smoking but a girl? The shock and judgement would follow her for life. She'd be tarred with the smoker's brush. *Chi chi chi*, a wrong sort for sure. But drinking? Fill your boots.

Fresh drink in hand, I turn around and make a play for the exit, wanting to head upstairs to dump my bag and freshen up properly but they appear, en masse – my biggest fear in these situations, my arch nemesis as a single Indian woman. No, not the drunk pervy uncle, and no, not the white patriarchal structure of society, not even the terrible chalky foundations that turn my skin tone a sallow grey. It's . . . The Illuminaunty. Imagine a clap of thunder and a crack of lightning and then, out of nowhere, there they are, right up in your face, invading any and all of your personal space. If they don't already know your business, they want to know. And their directive is to find out.

This crew would be definite contenders for *The Real Housewives of Bradford*. Pindi, Jas, Shallo and Jags, the four aunties of the Apocalypse, never knowingly underdressed for any occasion. Every event, no matter how big or small, is an opportunity to glam up. By the looks of their sarees, my birthday party is a major event. They come over, a shimmering mass, their beady eyes rimmed with kohl, boring into my soul. They will sap every ounce of my energy. I must stay strong.

'Hello, aunties. You all look lovely.' First point goes to me – flattery is a strong power play with this lot. I look across them all and jump in alarm at Aunty Shallo's latest beauty experiment. Has she had her lips done? I find myself staring a little too long. All I can see is pout.

'Didn't you know it was your party, Baby? Always so casual.' Shallo's looking me up and down and I'm watching to see if her overinflated lips are going to ricochet off each other. Aunty Shallo loves to look beautiful. She was indeed a natural beauty and has known it her entire life, but since her own daughter started getting more compliments than she did, she's gone into beauty overdrive. Her face is paler than it's ever been, smoother than it's ever been, and she is in a permanent state of alarm with not a wrinkle or expression on her face. It was hard enough to trust her before she zapped away any form of natural movement, now I'm really not sure how to react, because it's hard to know what she means. Her face is the equivalent of a text message, no nuance, no reading between the lines, no emotion.

'Babeee! Looking tired, Baby, skinny as well. You not looking after yourself?' Aunty Jags jumps in.

There is no filter present whatsoever. Especially when it comes to someone they have seen grow up, because you are always a child in their eyes and that is how they'll talk to you, forever.

'Happy birthday to you, beta. How old now? So old – you probably don't even remember yourself,' Aunty Pindi adds with a high-pitched laugh.

'No, I do, I'm thirty-six. Not quite at the hot flushes stage of my life.'

'Oh, so cheeky this one!'

'Speaking as a doctor, Baby, you need to get your skates on and get married if you want a chance to have babies.' Aunty Jas coming in strong, not even a warm-up from her, she went straight for the jugular. But before I can say anything aunty Shallo remembers her own ailment.

'Oh, ha, Jas . . .' Shallo aunty momentarily takes her eyes off me. 'I need to speak to you about my itching down below. Could you recommend a cream?'

Too much information about aunty Shallo's genitalia.

After an awkward pause that felt like at least an hour, I say, 'Thank you for the warning, aunty Jas. I'm all right with not being married – I'd be terrible at it anyway.'

It's a standard response. I have a few as aunties have been trying to marry me off since I was sixteen. It's the fixation with marriage that always gets me. *Of course,* I want to meet someone. Lord knows I'm so overdue a hot, steamy romance. Freddie has been a distraction and a convenient excuse for me not having to do any actual work to try and meet someone decent because it feels like such an effort. But Indian aunties aren't bothered about romance and/or love, they are far too practical. Get married (to someone we approve of), the 'love will come later' is the mantra I've been fed.

'What are you talking about?' Pindi aunty jumps in. 'Everyone needs someone! And we want to wear our sarees, even though at your age it would most probably have to be a smaller wedding. Isn't that what you modern girls do anyway – invite only half the family, upset the other half, changing traditions, no care for old values?'

'Aah, you know there is a boy!' aunty Jags squeals and turns to look at the others. For a moment they have lost interest in me, but I'm still trapped with no way of manoeuvring away from them.

'Kaun?'

'Bavinder da munnda, Bavinder's son.'

'The one with the limp?'

'Didn't he marry that Gujarati girl from Leicester? Yes, she took him away and he never came to see his parents. She had a cast a spell on him. He was under her control. Just like Prince Harry?'

'Terrible shame, such a shock for Bavinder and her husband.'

My eyes can't roll enough.

'Maybe he just didn't want to see his parents? How is it her fault?'

I'm not quite sure what I'm listening to or whether they can actually hear themselves.

They don't care what my thoughts are.

'I saw him at a wedding recently, sitting by himself at the back, so I thought I'd see how he was doing.'

On a nosey fact-finding mission, more like.

'He looked so terrible and, my God, his bad breath, chi chi chi. He's lost the vision in one eye too, apparently – she threw something at him and he's blinded now as well as the limp, bechaara.'

'. . . But he is single.'

'Maybe he deserved the eye?' I say to no one. My comment is completely ignored as they all jabber, a chorus of voices, their faces almost blurring together.

'They have a good family business and his mother is lovely.'

I suddenly realise they are all staring at me, waiting for me to respond to their suggestion.

'I'm not really interested in marrying his mother. He sounds great so I'm sure he'll meet someone soon. Excuse me, aunties,' I try to escape, but they haven't finished yet.

'But his mother's brother married an Englishwoman a long time ago, then she left him. Remember the hoo-ha? She took the kids and they never got to know anything about their culture; their grandmother was so, so upset. Such a shame. It's always different when they marry out of culture.'

'You, Baby, have you got a gora boyfriend?'

I hastily swallow my last gulp of wine. 'What?' I haven't got a boyfriend, never mind a blond one!

'Is that why you haven't got married yet?'

Isn't this the same Shallo aunty whose daughter-in-law is Polish?

I'm stunned into silence.

'What your aunty means is nobody minds these days. You should think about getting married, time is ticking, even if he's gora, or a different caste, no one cares these days, Won't be the same but you won't be on shelf.'

Caste? Who thinks about caste these days? What are these women *on*?

'Thank you for the very useful pep talk, aunties. I just need to . . .'

I manage to extract myself from that vortex of judgement. The life was being squeezed out of me.

Good lord, my glass appears to be empty. Again. So much for slowing down.

Dinner is served. My cousin's perfect wife, Nina from India, who everyone adores, is helping Mum put out all the food on the dining table. Mum's best china service is out for the night, with steaming dishes and every spoon in the house all crammed onto the surface. She has excelled once again. Nina's favourite phrase is 'Khau na?' It translates as 'please eat'. It's all I've ever really heard her say. She always looks lovely, if a little overdressed for the occasion in a silk saree and her finest wedding gold. Or maybe she's just highlighting how underdressed I am in my jeans and hoodie. If everyone else is dressed up, maybe I need to accept I'm the odd one out.

'Hi, Baby. You must be hungry? Khau na?'

The spread is immense, Mum's gone all out. Samosas, pani puri with home-made tamarind chutney, deep-fried crispy okra coated in chaat masala and tandoori chicken tikka – and that's just the warm-up act. Then all my faves for the main event: Dhal makhana, slow-cooked black lentils with garlic finished with butter, a spicy lamb curry, stuffed karela filled with onion and spicy tamarind, and potatoes with mustard seeds, curry leaves, red chilli and tomato. My stomach rumbles at the sight of it all. I start piling my plate up. There are all the usual side dishes too – raita, pilau rice with cumin and peas, a mixed cucumber, red onion, tomato and radish salad drenched in fresh lemon, freshly fried papad, at least three different home-made pickles, plus Patak's mango chutney (of course), and finally chapatti dripping in butter. This is a birthday feast.

Mum pops her head out of the kitchen, where she is manning the chapatti production line, a dab of flour on her forehead.

'Come on, everybody, time to eat! Get it while it's garam garam.' Then she looks at me.

'Come on, Baby, make sure everybody eats, and check on your dadima.'

I look to the corner of the room and there is Dadima playing with Pinky's eldest, Maya, and chatting to Eileen from next door. I head over, plate in hand and sit on the floor in front of her, putting my head in her lap.

'Aah, my Baby is here. My piece of the moon. The best girl in the world.'

God, I love my granny.

'Yes, she is. Happy Birthday, Baby,' says Eileen. Lovely, kind-hearted Eileen. She bends over and whispers in my ear, 'I've baked you a cake.'

'Victoria sponge?' I say, hopefully. She nods. Yesssss.

'How is my Baby?' Dadima asks.

'Bit tired but happy to be home with you,' I say.

'They work you too hard; remember, life is about balance, Baby, you need to keep your energy up. Chalo, you are home with me now and I'll give you my energy,' she says, kissing my forehead. I'm feeling boosted by her power already.

'Shall I bring you some food, Dadima?'

'Thora, thora, just a little bit and no lamb – it gets stuck in my teeth and your mother makes it too spicy.'

I bring a bowl of food for Dadima and another for Eileen and then pick up my own overloaded plate and sit on the floor at Dadima's feet. It's time to feast.

The music is being cranked up. Jas aunty's Bailey's milkshake has kicked in, so she's first up on the dance floor. I need to sit down out of harm's way, so make my way to the sofas in the living room, where most of the uncles are congregated around the coffee table, drinking whisky. They won't eat dinner just yet, they'll wait until they've had a few more drinks. I collapse next to Harbans uncle, my dad's best mate.

'Ah, Baby beta, good to see you. Fancy a drink? We've opened a bottle of your father's favourite Glenmorangie.'

Having a glass of whisky with Dad was one of my favourite things in life. It was a special occasion, just the two of us, putting the world to rights or having a heart-to-heart discussion. It would drive Mum mad.

'You are spoiling this girl. Which father gives his daughter whisky, a man's drink?! It will ruin her beauty and you will give her bad habits.'

I've always loved having a drink with the uncles, which feels like admittance to a special grown-up club even now. Especially Harbans uncle with Dad. I liked getting involved in their moral and political debates, laughing at their terrible Punjabi jokes, but mainly I loved sitting with them after dinner when the whisky had mellowed their blood flow, the Jagjit Singh ghazals were playing and they talked about their lives in India. Another lifetime, another life, of freedom and school pranks, of riding motorbikes and chatting up girls, and the simplicity of life back then. I'd see their eyes well up for lost loves and lost homelands and, for a brief moment, they'd be back there, with their carefree lives, when life wasn't such a struggle, where they made sense. Or at least, I liked all this when my dad was still around.

'Yeah, why not, Unks? Just don't let Mum or Dadima catch you giving me a glass.'

'Oh yes, I don't want to be told off by Smita. She can be strict with all of us,' he says with a cheeky smile. 'Life treating you good, Baby?'

'Good enough, I suppose.' Being with Harbans uncle makes me think of Dad. I'm grateful for the whisky to take my mind off everything and just be here, surrounded by all the people who knew him.

'Your father should be here.' Harbans uncle is getting emotional, and my own eyes are starting to sting. I guess I must remind him of the best friend he's lost. There's no way I can handle a conversation about my father right now, and there's no way I can cry either. Not here. Not with these men.

I chuck back the whisky, wince, whisper an excuse about needing the loo and finally escape upstairs. In Mum's room I find Pinky breastfeeding child number three. I kiss both her and the tot on the forehead and collapse on the bed next to her.

'You almost got my boob there, Babes. How're you doing? Hungover?'

'I *was* hungover. Now I'm drunk. Again. What a birthday,' I laugh.

'Shit, I wish I was.' Pinky pulls a face. 'Do you know, in total, I'll have spent over four years of my life breastfeeding?' She scrunches her nose up as she does more sums in her head. 'Plus two years and three months of my life pregnant. That is way too much time, y'know? I would love to be drunk right now.'

'Yeah, not gonna lie, it feels bloody good and lord knows I can't handle today sober. Do babies get drunk from breastfeeding?'

'Dunno, but the last time I had a couple of glasses of wine, he slept for six hours straight.'

We giggle.

I turn to look at Pinky, and she's beautiful and somehow glamorous, even with baby Jai attached to her boob. She qualified as a lawyer, met the dream Indian son-in-law at university, Anoop, who is also a lawyer, working with his dad in the family firm. I wanted to hate Anoop when I met him, for stealing my best mate away in what was meant to be our era, our time, but he's lovely, and seems switched-on enough. He won me over by recognising that she's the smart one in their relationship. He's not one of these douchebags whose ego can't handle a successful woman and he makes her laugh, plus he cooks dinner for her frequently. I was OK to share her with him. So at twenty-five, she got married and ten years and three kids later, here we are. Our life trajectories took completely different turns and, unlike me, she's never put a foot wrong. In the eyes of her family and the Illuminaunty, she's ticked every box at the right time, plus she never has a hair out of place. Pinks would never turn up to her own birthday party in a tie-dye hoodie.

'I wasn't expecting a party.' I roll my eyes.

'Yeah, well, I wasn't expecting to have a third child either, but here we are.' That doesn't sound like the Pinky I know. There's a bitter edge to her voice; she sounds brittle and by contrast, my statement feels childish. I can tell she wants to talk, to confide something. We've got great shorthand.

I sit up and turn to her, holding her free hand in mine and ask, 'Everything OK, Pinks?'

'I'm just desperate to get back to work. I'm ready to have my life back, to have a life, to have a bit of your freedom . . . I'm sick of my only purpose in life being to feed other people and then clean up after them. I love my family, love Anoop so much, but sometimes I am so jealous of what you have, mate.' She seems agitated and upset and it takes a lot for her to get like this. Pinky is calm, considered, collected, cautious – all the things I'm not. Or at least that's how I see her.

'Where's this coming from?' I ask.

She just shrugs.

'You're welcome to have a bit of what I have. It might involve a lot fewer nappy changes, but nobody cooks for me either. No one even makes me a cup of tea. And you have sex on tap.'

Pinky tries to smile as I make a face at her, but her eyes tell a different story.

'I'm ten years married with three kids, the sex on tap days are long gone. I just want . . . I don't know what.'

'It won't be long before you can get back to work, your mother-in-law can look after them and you can join the family firm. It's set up, and you're sorted for life, happily ever after and all that?' I ask.

37

She lies the baby against her body, his head looking over her shoulder while she gently rubs his back. It's soothing to watch. *Can someone do that to me, too?*

'All so set up, isn't it? Me and my perfect life, and you who've always done what you wanted, never conformed, and got away with murder. And no one makes me tea either.'

'Hang on, I've had to battle hard to live this life of extreme isolation!' I say in mock outrage. 'And I keep the Illuminaunty occupied because my boring life is of major concern to them.'

'Your life, Baby, is anything but boring. You can do what you want when you want with who you want. You have your own flat, you are sexually available, you don't have any responsibilities, you haven't had to grow up like I have.'

Everything she's saying is true. Sounds so good in theory.

'And I got married at twenty-five because that's what was expected of me. I don't want to be ungrateful but goddam, I sometimes wish I'd fought the system like you and lived a bit, just went off and did me. There's just so much pressure put on us, isn't there? What if I hadn't felt pressure to marry Anoop, what if we'd just carried on dating? Moved in with each other? Waited to have kids?'

I keep listening with growing concern and ask, 'Surely you wouldn't change things, though?'

'Me and Anoop were going through a bit of a rough patch, you know, and then this little limpet turned up. I love my limpet, of course I do. And good God how happy Anoop's mum is that I've produced a grandson.' She rolls her eyes and exhales, then carries on.

'Nothing is wrong, really, but I dunno, it's just – just not really what I was expecting. I'm not sure there's ever equality in the house; he expects me to be on top of it all, the kids, running the place. I've had the babies but now I can't stop thinking about how much I'd love some independence. I want to properly give my career a go. I'm smart, but my life now doesn't let me use my brain, doesn't satisfy that part of me! And I do *not* want to join the family firm, I can't think of anything more suffocating. We already see his family every weekend; they're lovely people but Every. Single. Weekend. Actually, they're not that lovely. His mum never has anything nice to say to anyone apart from her own kids. "My Anoop this, and my Anoop that. My Anoop works so hard." Anyone would think no one had ever had a job before. They say opinionated women emasculated men, whatever that means. Well, in my experience Indian mothers have already done a great job at infantilising their sons. And he loves nothing more than to go to his mum's, sit on her sofa and get served like a little prince. Drives me mad! I can't remember the last time Anoop booked us something to do, spontaneously. He works, eats, drinks wine, fixes shit when the mood takes him, watches *Peaky Blinders* and sees his family. On Tuesdays he puts the bins out. And that's enough for him, apparently.' Pinky says all this in a rush.

This sounds awful. 'But not enough for you?' I gently prod.

'I'm thirty-five. I wasn't expecting life to become so predictable, so quickly, and it's not like I can leave him . . .'

Wow, wow, wow, this was not something I was ready for. 'You want to leave him?' I had no idea my best mate felt this way. Have I been a shitty, neglectful friend?

'Not really. No. I don't want to leave, but I do think about how life could have been if I'd made different choices. If I'd *had* a choice. Once my parents found out about Anoop, the only option was marriage. I love the kids, I do. But—'

At this point, the baby lets out an extraordinarily loud burp, and we crack up. Pinky dabs at him with a muslin cloth and I place my hand gently on his soft mop of baby hair. She lays him down between us.

'I am so sorry you are feeling like this. I had no idea. Have you spoken to him about it?'

'Anoop won't engage, I think he thinks it's a phase that will pass. He's more interested in drinking wine and watching Netflix. I just don't feel seen by him at all.'

Now I'm getting angry at Anoop.

'*I* see you, mate. And I feel your pain. Have you spoken to anyone else?' The baby tries to crawl away, but she pulls him back by his little chubby leg and puts him on his back between us.

'My mum, she shut me down immediately, saying it was just a phase and I picked him – and if he doesn't beat me, she doesn't understand my problem, thinks it's a modern-girl affliction, the generation that can't put up and shut up.'

'For fuck's sake! Sometimes I don't know whether I feel angry at our mothers and their generation or sorry for them and the shit they put up with. Actually, I feel both. Does he help with the kids at all?' I ask, frowning.

'Oh yeah, I'm lucky in that regard. He's a decent dad, even if the kids will only go back to sleep with me comforting them and he has work so needs the sleep. He's just being a bit of a crap husband at the moment and I'm beginning to wonder what I've done.'

'You need to talk to him, make him listen or maybe go to couples therapy? He definitely needs to stand up to his mum . . . useless twat!' I mutter the last bit and Pinky snorts.

'Fair comment, he has been recently.' She pauses. 'Maybe therapy, maybe I just need to get back to work.'

'Do it.' I say, knowing it's easier said than done and suddenly feeling pretty good about having so many options open to me still.

We sit in silence for a bit as Pinky stares thoughtfully into space. I've always loved that we can talk incessantly but just as easily sit quietly together and it never feels awkward. We really are the perfect couple.

Suddenly Pinky sits up and says, 'Babes, let's go out some time. It's been ages. Let's go raving.'

I sigh and lie back down. 'For sure! Though I'm not sure you can go raving if you're breastfeeding.'

Pinks laughs.

'What's going on with you?' she asks.

'I need something to change in my life, too. You're right, I've made my own choices so far, but it feels like I'm at a dead end. I can't get out of this bloody cul-de-sac. I feel like I've hit some kind of racist glass ceiling at work – not that I can ever prove it – and all the men I meet aren't even worth talking about. I miss my dad every day, so badly. I only seem to argue with my mum these days and my life feels almost meaningless. What's the point of any of it?'

Pink looks at me and laughs. 'Surely we're too young to be having a midlife crisis?'

'Maybe they happen younger for Indian girls?' I shrug but then carry on. Maybe it's because Pinky has shared something so intimate with me, but my feelings pour out and even take me by surprise. 'I don't even know who I am anymore. I've never felt more alone, more like an outsider. And now I'm officially over the hill at thirty-six – in any culture, not just ours! I'm heading towards complete invisibility and I haven't got anything in my life to show for it. I dedicated everything to work, but I'm stuck in a rut. They keep telling me they need me where I am, that I'm a brilliant team leader.'

'You are,' Pinky jumps in with a smile. And then I laugh.

'They've put me on the Kenyan account because they said someone BAME needs to work on it. What the hell is BAME? Are we a separate species now? I've never even set foot in Kenya!'

We both crack up laughing.

'They also want me to head up the diversity something or other. To look into what needs to change, help change the system. Told me like I was being given a big promotion. But honestly? It's just extra work for the people who have the least to gain from the training and the most to lose from the lack of it.'

Lose, lose situation.

Pinky nods sympathetically. 'My tutor at law school was fixated with me doing family law. Every time he saw me, he brought up forced marriages and honour killings.'

'And you told him you were in a forced marriage.'

'Yeah, just to see the look on his face.'

'What am I doing with my life, Pinky? It's a struggle these days to even get out of bed and that's not me, is it? I used to love life! Now it's like walking through thick custard every day.'

'I hear you, mate. Do you want me to put on Madonna, get two bottles of cheap white wine that can double up as microphones, and we can take our trousers off and jump up and down on the bed? I think I have the photos from last time, somewhere,' she says with a smile.

'Burn them!' I say.

'Or how about we sneak out and nip off down the pub for a pint and a game of pool; or rather, we can stare at the lads playing pool?' She reminds me of what we used to do.

'My God, we were brave, weren't we? How did we never get caught?'

'We're smart, innit?' She winks.

Pinky has done what she always manages to do, swerve my thoughts and get me smiling. But I'm too down for it to last long.

'To make everything worse, Pinks, it actually crossed my mind that I might need to quit drinking.'

Pinky is silent for a beat. I turn to her as she says, 'Oh, God, Babes, this sounds awful. Sounds like you need something to change fast. But please, whatever you do . . . Don't quit drinking until after our night out.' We burst out laughing at the same time.

'I know you're sad, Baby,' she continues and rubs the baby's tummy. 'You need to channel your alter ego and find your Zen space, Simran. Live up to the calming name you gave yourself, or at the very least for now, try and do some actual Simran?'

'I don't need religion, I need the universe staging some kind of life intervention. I think we both do.' I look at Pinky and give her the biggest hug. I'm feeling unusually tactile; my armour has dropped, and I say something I never usually say to anyone . . .

'I love you, Pinky.'

'And I love you. We all love you, Baby, don't forget that.'

'Oh, I remember what I wanted to ask you, Pinks . . . What in the name of Guru Nanak has Shallo aunty done to her face?'

We both crack up.

I leave Pinky in my mum's room while she finishes up with Jai and go to what was once my bedroom. I walk up the dodgy wooden steps to the attic conversion we had done years ago and enter my den, which Mum has now turned into a storeroom. Rude. Taking up most of the space is Dadima's wedding trunk. I try to imagine Dadima as a bride and my grandfather Ranjit, wonder how she might have felt on that day. My grandad died a year after I was born. I don't remember him, but I've asked questions and Dadima has told me about him. He was a quiet man, didn't give too much away, and could have a short fuse with Granny, but apparently the day I was born was the happiest anyone had ever seen him.

I brought the joy back to the house temporarily and then Grandad died. I think about Dadima losing her husband and then her son. My heart aches for her, but then my heart just aches as once again the loss of Dad pierces me. Desperate to feel closer to him, I reach for the trunk, knowing Mum has put his TV-watching blanket in there. I want to feel close to him again.

Every Indian woman of a certain generation owns a trunk, her peti, containing their trousseau for when they are married and move to their new home. Mum has one, Dadima has one, every aunty downstairs has one. I open the trunk and there is an immediate and familiar waft of mothballs. Once on its way to a new life, full of hopes and expectations alongside the wares inside, it now holds tight to memories and gathers dust.

I've never looked inside it before, never needed to; it long ago become a storage box I've always just assumed held Mum and Dadima's old sarees. But I know Dad's favourite Yorkshire wool blanket, his kambal, is in there, neatly folded right at the top. It's fraying at the edges and, touching it with only the tips of my fingers, as if preserving it like a precious artefact, I lift it out and drape it over my shoulders. I suddenly feel cold in this room, devoid of any of the traces of my childhood. I know it's the drink talking too, making me feel sad and down now I'm by myself, with only the soft touch of the blanket bringing me comfort. *It should be Dad.*

An old hand-embroidered bed sheet catches my eye, a cross-stitch done with such care and attention it stops me in my tracks. Another skill I failed at when the aunties tried to teach me.

Move on, Baby, what else is in this treasure trove?

A couple of fine silk sarees and shirts still wrapped in plastic, which must have been given as gifts at a wedding and have never been worn, are packed and ready to pass on to someone else.

An old pressure cooker – why Mum has kept it, I'll never know. It might be an antique one day, I suppose. I rummage further, listening to my internal, infernal, self-pitying dialogue. *I'll never have something as special as this peti for myself. Happy birthday, Baby.*

I move my hand further into the deep space and it meets with something unexpected – paper – and I draw out what looks like a stack of letters, tied with a red ribbon. *What are these?* I untie the ribbon and start to look through them, noting that they have been kept very carefully but are yellow with age.

I am nosy and I want to know what these could be, so I open one – the envelope has been neatly slit for me. I wonder if they're from my grandfather? I realise they have been written in Punjabi and for the first time in my life, I fully appreciate being forced to attend those classes at the gurdwara once a week with the Punjabi GCSE to follow at fourteen. I was obviously too embarrassed to ever reveal this to my friends at school.

I'm a bit rusty but I think I can just about make out enough key words to understand the gist. The handwriting is beautiful, classic, and the letter feels like a precious time capsule from the past. Imagine, Granny and Grandad exchanging love letters to each other!

I will write your name on my hand in henna. I dare not say it aloud, lest it shorten your life. But I write it here and admire it. It is a warrior king's name, as is befitting of you.

And I will say your name out loud, let it roll off my tongue, sitting here writing this letter in the dark by candlelight.

Ranjit, I will run my fingers over your name on this paper.

Oh God, I suddenly think, *please let there be no kinky stuff.* Imagine if I have discovered Grandma's sexy letters – my granny and her false teeth doing the dirty. I need to rid my mind of that thought immediately. But also, good on you, Granny, let his name roll off your tongue, you get it, girl.

My eyes jumped straight to the romance, so I scan to the bottom of the letter to see my dadima's name, Madhu. Instead, I read a name I've never heard or seen before: *Naseeb*. What a beautiful name. It means fate, I think. But who is she? And, *oh God*, why was she writing letters to my grandfather?

I rifle through the stash and find the letter dated the earliest.

January 1940
Dearest betrothed,

My first ever letter to you. I hope you like my handwriting. I hope it's not too shaky, but I am nervous.

Let us mark the date. Just after the festival of Lohri 1940, the day my father agreed to us being married.

Are we truly to be married? Am I really to be yours?

I can barely believe that I am this fortunate. Me, Naseeb Kaur, about to marry the handsome stranger who came to my village and asked for my hand. This never happens to girls like me.

Imagine if you had not been sent to work on the canals near our village? Imagine if you didn't just brazenly walk into my front yard looking for my father? Strangers usually knock on the door. Imagine if I had not been sitting there, drying my long hair in the morning sunlight, reading my book of poetry by Amrita Pritam. Imagine if you were not shocked and surprised by my ability to read, imagine if you had not been captured by my smile.

Oh, sweet destiny. How lucky I am.

And you know, when you read the newspaper to the men of the village underneath the banyan tree by the well, I would walk past, pretending I was on an errand, just to catch a glimpse of you.

And now, you are to be mine and I am to be yours.

I'm so excited I can barely contain my excitement. But contain it I must. Nirmal Masi, did you meet her when you were in my village? She's not my actual Masi, but everyone calls her Masi. She was trying to set me up to marry her distant relative, a man so much older than me. She's fuming that it hasn't happened. Says I am spoiled and indulged by my father. She says I'm shameless and I've set a terrible example for the rest of the girls in the village by picking my own husband – even though you picked me. She also says my mother-in-law will not like me as I was not chosen by her. Do you think this will be the case?

Nirmal Masi says this is what happens when you educate girls, they become too free.

Papaji made sure I was educated. It's the biggest gift, after life, that I've been given. I'm the only educated girl in the village, you know, apart from the doctor sahib's daughter, Sandeep Didi, who lives in the haveli. Sandeep Didi is incredibly modern, she has a job as a secretary and rides a bicycle. She is nineteen and still unmarried. She says she will be marrying into a family in Lahore, where she will get a job at the University of Punjab. Such big dreams. She also wears the loveliest French chiffon sarees in delicate pastel colours. Her father receives them as gifts from visiting British officers. They make my cotton shalwar kameez feel heavy when I see her wear them, and I look so plain in comparison. But these are dreams for big people, jobs and diaphanous sarees are not for me.

But I did dream, and my dream came true. I wished for you.

I have spent many hours imagining a romance for myself, a love story like the ones in the novels I read. Of lovers destined to meet, whose souls are bound through many lifetimes.

Whose love is intense and passionate, the lovers in my stories always seem to be star-crossed but I feel our fate will be better.

I must have done something good in a previous life for God to have granted my wish. You seem like a kind man. Your eyes are gentle and your voice soft.

Nirmal Masi is calling for me. I have to go and help embroider the phulkari dupatta I will be wearing on my wedding day. Our wedding day.

I only wish my mother was alive.

I will write again.

Not long now until we are together forever.

Your betrothed,

Naseeb

I try to read more to see if there has been some sort of mix-up. Maybe the letters were for another Ranjit. What was Grandad's brother called? Maybe they were to him?

My pulse quickens in fear, and I bring the pages closer to my face, to try and increase the chances of understanding. There is talk of marriage. *Who is Naseeb going to marry?* Who on earth is this woman? Why do we have all these letters? Hang on, hang on. Is she really talking about marrying Grandad? Did Grandad have a girlfriend before Granny? I gasp at this thought while trying to carefully grab the next letter, and the next, and the next. They are all love letters from Naseeb to Ranjit. And she wasn't Grandad's secret girlfriend, she was his wife. His official first wife. Grandad was married before Dadima? What is happening? My fuzzy mind is beyond confused but there's a sense of urgency to find out more.

This is a family secret that no one has ever, ever spoken about. My God, what have I stumbled across? I read on, furiously, greedily, snatching up the next letter.

February 1940

Dearest betrothed,

It is a strange feeling to be packing away my life to start a new one somewhere else. With the family I was born to be with. That's what they say, a daughter does not belong to the family in which she is born, but the family into which she will marry. They tell us this from birth. So that means I was born to be yours. Your family will be mine. Your customs and rituals, your extended family all mine. My job is to be a good daughter and for my family to never hear a complaint against me. These are the things whirring round in my head as I think about our wedding.

I am seventeen years old, and you are eighteen years old and in three weeks we will be married. The entire village is being prepared for your arrival. When you come to take me away.

I cannot believe I will be stepping into life as a wife, stepping into the unknown to become a woman, leaving behind my own family, to become part of another.

I am looking forward to my adornment as a bride. I hope you will find me beautiful.

My time has finally arrived to have the choora placed on my wrists. I hope my uncle gets the right-sized wedding bangles – at Jeeto's wedding the skin on her knuckles came clean off, even with all the ghee we put on her hands.

I will have my hands mehndi'd; they say the darker the henna, the more your mother-in-law will love you and so I'm going to keep mine on all night to make sure the colour really takes.

I will write your name on my hand in henna. I dare not say it aloud, lest it shorten your life. But I write it here and admire it. It is a warrior king's name, as is befitting of you.

And I will say your name out loud, let it roll off my tongue, sitting here writing this letter in the dark by candlelight. Ranjit . . .

I will run my fingers over your name on this paper.

I am being summoned. Nirmal Masi wants me to take her turnip and carrot pickle with me. I will be packing it into my peti. A little taste of home. It really is delicious; I hope you will all enjoy it too.

The next time we meet I will become yours in the eyes of God. To begin our long, long life together on this earthly plane. No more will I be Sheru's daughter; I will be your wife.

*They say our union was made in the stars. We have one
light in two bodies.*
Tonight, I will be looking at the stars and thinking of you.
Yours always,
Naseeb

I slump on the floor, the letters all around me, thinking of a
bride packing carrot pickle in her suitcase, is that what I read?
I'm so confused, suddenly my eyes feel so, so heavy. I'm furious
that my Punjabi is so rusty because I want to devour this secret
whole, I want to consume it all at once, in every detail.

I read on. This is a love story, there is a marriage between
Ranjit and Naseeb. I feel a sharp cold wave of shock roll through
me as I piece together the story. Dadaji, my grandfather, Ranjit,
he had a life, a life before Dadima.

*Your son saw his first gecko today. It came into the room and
scuttled up the wall. I screamed but Deepu thought it was
fascinating and wanted to touch it. Mataji came in running
with the broom. The sight of her chasing the lizard was so
funny. She was also telling it to shoo, shoo shoo and waving
the broom over her head.*

There's a son called Deep? My uncle? Half-uncle?
I pick up another letter.

*Our daughter Preet is well. She is our pride. She is so loved.
She misses her papa.*
We all do.
Come home to us soon.

And a daughter called Preet. Two children! Where are they now?
What happened to them? What would they be to me, to our
family, if they are still alive? I have uncovered an earth-shattering
story here, except it's not a story. This woman Naseeb, she
was real, these are her words, her handwriting, her letters. I'm

49

touching paper she would have touched. When? There are dates at the top, although the pencil she was writing in is beginning to fade . . . I can't believe how precious these letters are, whatever they are. What are they revealing? Right now, I'm so confused.

My eyes aren't fully able to focus, and I think of my father. I wonder if he knew his father's secret, if he kept it from the rest of us deliberately. I think about how no one ever talks in this family, and oh, God, I really shouldn't have had that last whisky. My mind is reeling, and I feel sick and panicky, overwhelmed by it all. Does everyone know apart from me? Someone knows but I have never known. No one told me.

The wooziness and the cosiness of the blanket wrapped around me as well as the dimness of the room make me feel suddenly tired, as though I could sleep for days. The weariness I feel, the hangover from last night merging with what I've drunk today, and I find myself nodding off.

'BABY nichea aa, come down.' Mum's voice is like a gravita-tional pull, and I'm yanked back to reality. The house is full of guests. It's my birthday party. And I've uncovered something major but I'm struggling to make sense of what it actually means. Love letters, in my family? The mantra has always been 'love will come later'. No one in my family has married for love, every single person has had an arranged marriage. Dadima and Grandad met on their wedding day. Mum and Dad at least met before but only once and Mum had to fly to another country, so she could hardly say she didn't want to marry him. I've never heard Dadima talk about Grandad being romantic, or loving, or affectionate. I hear about him being a bit aloof and strict. Are these letters written to the same guy? My grandfather Ranjit? These would suggest he was deeply in love with someone at least once in his life, whoever this Naseeb woman is? I grew up in a house completely devoid of romance, where no one ever talks about attraction or desire. Any time there's a snog on TV, Mum will reach for the remote. She thinks *Love Island* is inappropri-ate viewing, she calls it 'that dirty programme'.

And yet here in these letters is evidence that my grandad had a full-on love affair with someone. Naseeb. And how articulate she is in these letters to him. What a woman! She seems to be someone who also didn't do what was expected of her. Someone who didn't fit the mould.

I've already become possessive over the treasure and think about putting the letters up my jumper, but they are too precious and I realise this idea is crazy. I carefully put them back in the peti and cover them with Dad's blanket. He'll take care of them, while I go back to my party. My God, is it still my birthday?

I wobble as I walk downstairs and take a seat on the sofa and wrap my arms around myself. Pinky comes over and sits next to me. Her children clamber up her body and I hug myself tighter.

'Where did you disappear to?' she asks.

'Ugh, nothing. I'm fine, just had enough of all this,' I say, slightly more grumpily than I mean to.

'What? Are you OK?'

'Oh, yes. I'm fine,' I reply, putting on my most non-suspicious voice. I sound completely suspicious.

I look over at Dadima and my mouth goes dry. She's talking to Shallo aunty and I'm thankful she's not looking in my direction. I study her face to see if I can find any clues to how much she knows about these letters. She must know about them, they were in her trunk? Did she decide to keep them? She must have. Does Mum know about them? Did my dad know? Did he die without knowing that his father was married to someone else? And why has no one talked about any of this? I feel dizzy again. Who is keeping this secret from whom? Well, they're definitely keeping it from me, that's for sure. And if that's the case, what else are they not telling me about? Pinky keeps looking at me strangely but before she can say anything else, one of her children starts to cry and distracts her.

The rest of the party goes by in a haze. I stay glued to the sofa, turning people down whenever they attempt to drag me up to dance. All I can think about are the letters upstairs. Did

I imagine them? I'm desperate to go back and check they are still there but have to remind myself it's my birthday. I'm present physically but my mind is anywhere but in this room.

Later that night I wake up, my bedroom in total darkness now and there is no noise coming from downstairs. I look at my phone. It's 2 a.m. My head is pounding. I check the letters in the peti again, decide to put them under my pillow for safekeeping and drift back to sleep. I dream of a big party where I don't know any of the guests. I look for my family, but I can't find them. I can't find my dad. I'm panicking and feel a deep, excruciating sense of loneliness. Like I'm totally alone on Earth. I'm shouting, but no one can hear me. I'm screaming and pulling my own hair to get their attention, but no one can see. I try to run away but my legs are like cement.

The next morning, I am woken by Mum's footsteps coming up the stairs and before she opens my bedroom door, I grab the letters from under the pillow and shove them under my top, gripping the duvet to me as if my life depends on it.

'Oh, hey, Mum,' I say in an overly cheery voice.

'Good morning, sleepyhead. How are you feeling? You looked very tired yesterday. At least four people asked if you were sick. Are you OK?'

'Honestly, I'm fine. Thanks for the party, Mum, it was great. Sorry I came to bed before the last few people left.'

'It's OK, Nina helped me clear up. She's such a good girl. Come down, your dadima is making your favourite gobi paratha.'

Nina strikes again. Nina barely speaks; if she has an opinion, I've never heard it but she's a dutiful daughter-in-law who always dresses well, such a 'good girl'. I roll my eyes. Mum sees and gives me a look.

There is nothing more comforting in the world than to wake up on a weekend to the smell of home cooking. Dadima and Mum always start early and on the weekend, they go into overdrive. Waking up to paratha is sheer heaven, the distinct smoky aroma of fried butter fills the entire house, and I'm back to being a kid again.

I get up and transfer the bundle of letters to my hoodie's front pocket, then hang it on the peg on the back of my door next to the fluffy dressing gown I wear every time I'm home. I need a shower. The scalding hot water is good for my headache, and I pretend to be in a sauna rather than horribly hungover in my childhood home. I get dressed, put on my hand-knitted home socks and pad down the carpeted stairs to the breakfast of dreams.

Dadima is at the thava in her cream lucknowi embroidered shalwar kameez. I've always loved this embroidery and desperately wanted something the same, but Mum said I'm so old before my time anyway, this would just turn me into a granny. Mum has her ways of making me feel crap in a spilt second. Dadima has always looked the same my entire life: black kohl lines her eyes, gold hoops hang in her ears and a simple stud sits on her sharp, regal nose. Her face lights up when she sees me and I fall into her hug, squeezing her as though it might be the last time we meet. I always squeeze her like this. It's a hug that works like magic, I have not a worry or a fear in the world when I'm cuddling Gran. I could hug Dadima for days.

'Aaah, tandh pagaee.'

It's what she says every time we hug: 'I've gone cold' or 'You've cooled me down.' It must have something to do with sweating balls in the Indian heat. Although why anyone would want to hug in that weather, with all that sweat and body odour, is beyond me. Stick to the palms-together-and-bow, a lovely friction-free greeting, the great Indian invention.

'Chal, sit. There's dahi, achaar, butter, eat them while they are nice and garam. I've also made some chai, with fennel and cardamom and cloves, your favourite.' The aroma and the smoke in the kitchen is heady and thrilling, and I don't mind the mixture when my head is still pounding slightly from drinking so much last night.

I can't speak when I pop the first burki in my mouth, because it's piping hot and the flavour is so perfect I'm basking in the reverie. In this moment, I have not a single worry in the world. This moment right here, eating Dadima's paratha, is perfect. One thing about living alone is that you really, really appreciate it when someone else looks after you.

'Dadima?'

'Yes, Baby?'

'I have a question about Dadaji.'

'Ask, ask me anything.'

'Was Dadaji romantic?'

She smiles. 'What kind of question is this? Romantic? What am I to do with romantic? Life is not a movie. Your dadaji was not a hero from a film,' she says with a smile, somewhat embarrassed by the thought.

I laugh at her face. 'He never wooed you with any love poems?' I ask cheekily.

'Chal hat! Asking silly questions!' Dadima giggles and then her face becomes serious for a second. 'That was not for us. There was always a sadness in your dadaji and then, when we came to this country, he became quieter and quieter. All we did was struggle and work and work and work and then he found his second wife.'

'Second wife?' My eyes open wide. I'm holding my breath.

'Yes, or maybe husband – Johnnie Walker! Drinking became his first love. Oh haa! I remember once he bought me flowers for my birthday from the market. They went dry and I kept them until they crumbled.'

I exhale. I'm gutted I didn't get a different answer.

'Your father was never romantic either. That's not how real life is, Baby,' Mum pipes in.

Why does she always have to comment?

'He's only been gone a couple of years, Mum. Why do you have to talk about him like this?'

'Oh, you only remember the good bits,' she says, looking down at me as I take a sip of the hot chai in my hands.

'I only want to remember the good bits, he was my dad! I miss him every day.'

'We all miss him,' Mum responds quickly. 'I can also be angry with him. He left me so soon, and he left me with the burden of an unmarried daughter.'

I'm about to put another burki of paratha in my mouth but put it down. Here we go.

'Burden?' I blurt out. *Stay calm, stay calm.* I take a breath. 'What decade are you in, Mum? I'm hardly a burden. I have a job, I'm . . .' I can't bring myself to say what I was going to say. *Happy.* I'm not, but before I can say anything she is back at it.

'He wasn't the easiest, your dad. He was spoilt. Boys are always spoilt and then wives pick up the pieces. You only saw the good. I was the one person he could have his goes at.' She shoots a look at Dadima. Dadima who is used to Mum's outbursts, sensibly stays looking at the paratha she's about to flip.

'But you're the one who made me respect him. You constantly said, "Respect your father, don't talk to him like that," whenever I tried to argue with him.'

'That's because you must respect your father. He is your father.'

'Was. *Was* my father.' How has a lovely morning turned so quickly?

Mum's face changes; she looks distraught, shattered. And I remember that she's in so much pain, she lost her husband. My sentence feels cruel.

There's so much unsaid in this family, so much between the lines, but I'm not a psychologist who can decipher what's going on and right now my head is definitely not in the right place for this.

I'm tired. This is not the Sunday morning I was hoping for, but since we lost Dad, I find myself having a regular confrontation with my mum. Is she angry with me, or him? The boiling point between the three of us simmers and then cools. We are quick to flare up and quick to forget too, but I feel drained. So, so drained.

'Dad could be difficult with Mum, couldn't he, Dadima?' I say, wanting to make Mum feel better, that I'm not always against her, defending my dad. My dead dad, who is defenceless.

55

'I did my best with him,' Dadima says, trying her best not to show Mum has got to her. 'Do you know how hard it was to bring up Indian children in this country? We come here to do their dirty jobs and still they have no respect for us. They would spit on me in the street when your father was younger. He used to get into fights at school with the racist children. Children! I would tell him not to fight, to keep his head down, to not get into trouble, to study hard and stay quiet. Your grandfather drinking, your father so angry.' She looks shaken. 'It was a hard time, I did my best.'

'I can't imagine what you went through, Dadima,' I say, thinking about how I feel about work and how much harder it was for the generations before me. My eyes are welling up. Having a visceral reaction to what's being said. The injustice of it all.

'We thought we knew best back then. We are parents, after all. Our solution was marriage. A good bride from India and a family, this is all we knew. He resisted, said he wanted to study more, not marry, but your mother is from such a good family and then . . .' Dadima giggles, 'he saw the photograph of your mother and she is such a beauty, how could he refuse? He was lost in the beauty. Plus, he's my only son, I told him he had to get married to the girl of my choice.'

Nice one, Dadima. Mum is smiling.

'You see, marriage obsession is in our culture.'

'MUM! Leave it.' I'm about to reach boiling point again but think better of it and force myself to laugh. It works and everyone relaxes, their tense shoulders drop.

I've had Mum's marriage drip-feed narrative for so long: 'I won't be truly happy until you are settled', 'Everyone needs someone', 'Why is my daughter like this?' 'Other people's daughters . . .' 'Get married!'

And nothing will change. I get the same predictable dialogue that crushes me every time. Mum is part of the system. The system that wants women to obey. I bat it all off and yes, I get cross, a lot more than I want to. But I'm bloody exhausted by it all. By my life. I need to do something different. I need something

56

to change because evidently Mum isn't going to. I need to figure out who I am and what I really want. Everything in my life up until now seems to be a reaction to what's expected of me. How do I find out what it is I really want? I'm not sure I even know who I am, let alone what I want and how to get it. I need to do some soul-searching, switch things up somehow.

The best way I know to put out any embers of tension is by watching television together, although this too can be difficult as all three of us have different tastes. Mum adores her Indian melodramas, Granny loves the religious channels, and I can't tolerate either for more than thirty seconds. Gran and Mum would love *Sex Education*, I think, although the name alone is enough to cause a scandal. So, we stick to a crowd-pleaser, a Bollywood movie. I haven't watched an Indian film in ages, and as I flick through one of the many Indian TV channels, we realise one is showing the classic *Sholay*, one of the first Indian-style Spaghetti Western movies. It's also a film which happens to be Dad's favourite. Or, at least, it *was* his favourite.

We settle down to watch and I put my head in Dadima's lap so she can apply coconut oil to my hair, and my feet on Mum, for a foot massage at the same time. In this moment I'm in love with being an Indian daughter. Fully regressing into a small child, I allow them to pat and massage my head and feet. This is an experience I can fully endorse: the Indian mother spoiling package, best served accompanied by home-made snacks and endless cups of chai. A warm, soothing atmosphere settles in the room amongst the women, and I remember that, although we disagree on almost everything, my family are still able to make me feel safe. We laugh at the jokes in the film and all three of us sing along: 'Yeh dosti, hum naheee, tore gayeee.'

These are the moments watching a Hindi film with my family that I feel relaxed, and I suppose at my most Indian. Watching those films as a kid would transport me to another world, full of colour and magic. I'd imagine myself living the lives of the characters on screen. The village girl, the modern city girl, the princess living in an ancient palace with my own elephant to ride. The runaway bride. India was a place that was part of me, yet I knew nothing about it. Always promising myself a visit but never actually doing anything about it, my feelings towards it complicated.

At some point, I fall asleep on the sofa, only waking when Dadima strokes my hair gently and tells me to come eat something before I leave.

The train home to Manchester always feels longer, the journey has an added loneliness. I need to sort my life out, fill the void. Not necessarily because I need someone to fill the space, but because I just need to find *me* again. The me who was in control, the me who was happy and content, the me who was enjoying life. What has happened to that Baby?

As I stare out of the window into the darkening day, I remember the letters, still stashed in my hoodie. I had slept with them under my pillow, imbuing their secrets within me. It ignites something I haven't felt in a long, long time: intrigue. A deep yearning to find out more. Naseeb's words have connected with something inside me. A woman who is kind of, maybe, connected to me, who did something different, behaved in a way that wasn't expected of her.

She learned to read and write, saw the value of education, wanted more for herself. Her handwriting, her words have lodged inside me. I need to know more about her and her life. It's like a switch has been turned on – no, no, it's more physical than that, more like a gut punch.

Who was Naseeb? Why hasn't Granny ever said anything? Dadima has always said so little about her life before coming to the UK. Her generation keeps so much to themselves. They are the masters of secrets. *How many Punjabi families have skeletons in the closet, or letters in the peti?*, I wonder.

I get home and the first thing I do is try to chase away the loneliness of my slightly chilly flat by lighting some incense and putting the kettle on. Cup of Yorkshire tea in hand, I begin to organise the letters on the floor in front of me, placing them in a rough date order, starting from 1940 to 1947. Some of the dates are a bit faded as is some of the writing. They are written in pencil, none of this is helped by my adolescent Punjabi. The story begins unfolding in front of me.

There are nine letters, nine *love* letters. Letters of the heart from Naseeb to my grandfather. Letters that tell a story of another life, another lifetime. The grandfather who I never had the chance to meet or know. But this woman, this Naseeb, knew him and knew him well.

There's too much information at once.

I type a WhatsApp to Mum. *Who is Naseeb?*

I look at it and then delete it, slowly tapping away the letters while the question lingers in my mind.

Naseeb and Ranjit were in love. The kind of love that stops the world from turning and makes your heart beat to another's drum. What happened? Why had he chosen this other life, what drew him to England, drove him to drink? What happened to Naseeb to break my grandfather's heart?

These letters, her words, her innermost thoughts and feelings to my grandfather, were meant for his eyes only. He kept them because they meant something to him, who he was, who he was going to be. He must have been so far away from her for long periods of time, because had he not been, she wouldn't have had to write the letters.

The letters change tone over the years of their marriage. From the excitement and dreams for the life she will have with my grandfather as a new bride, to the difficulty of adjusting to married life. To the joy of her two children, her friendship with Anjuman, and the inevitable destiny no one at that time was able to outrun. I desperately want to go back in time and tell them all to get out, to leave, years before the violence – run and don't look back. Where was Grandad when all this was happening? Why wasn't he with them? And if he was still with Naseeb, I wouldn't exist. I have so many new emotions about my family and so many unanswered questions.

And as I'm looking at all this information, a slice of my family's history laid out in front of me, what I want to do next becomes abundantly clear. I've never been surer of anything in my life, not since I dyed my fringe electric blue. I realise in this moment that I have to *know* Naseeb. All that she was, what happened to her. The Naseeb no one speaks of. This woman whose heartfelt words I'm seeing on these fragile pages in front of me. I'm thirty-six years old and I know nothing about my family. What does that say about us? What does that say about me? I've never thought to ask my family about their time in India, I was never interested. But they also never really opened up about anything, apart from drunken nights reminiscing about their childhoods. Dadima never spoke, just batted off questions with 'Oh, that was a lifetime ago.' And 'This is our home now.' I never pushed my dad to talk about his father, my grandad, Ranjit, without whom I would never have had the opportunity to have the life I do. Suddenly I know that this feeling of emptiness I have, of disconnect, cannot be healed by wild, drunken, regretful nights in Manchester or cosy, gluttonous, frustrating nights in the Bradford suburbs. I need to go back to where it all began for my family. I need to go to India; I need to head to the motherland.

I've only ever visited India once in my life, for a family wedding when I was just a toddler. My memories are sketchy and involve playing with a stray puppy and getting sunburnt so badly I whimpered when I was put to bed. No one in my family realised that British-Indian skin might be toast when it was greeted by the blazing Indian sun, not helped by the fact that all I wanted to do was play outside with the dog. I remember the squat toilet, too, or if you were to define it by how *I* used it, the stand-over-it-with-your-legs-straight-knees-locked toilet. I was not going to squat, especially as a little person. That hole in the ground looked as if it could swallow me whole, and I didn't want to go down there.

India is a place that has almost mythical status in my mind and yet I've always been conflicted about my relationship with it.

There have been plenty of occasions when Dadima has gone back to visit and asked if I wanted to join her for the trip, and every single time I've refused. I've always disliked how I'm expected to want to go. I feel British, and I don't know what India will reveal to me about myself, about my *Indianness*. Would I feel more at home there? Or would I feel like a Westerner, disconnected from the place I came from? Maybe I'm afraid of what it might reveal. There's the poverty and the chaos and the danger and the religion. Plus, have I mentioned the toilets? Mum says she remembers me loving India, how I asked questions about everything, was happy to try all the food and sit with extended family. Apparently, my Punjabi came along effortlessly because I was so immersed in the world, in the language. But since then, she says I've become too 'gorafied' – too white – for my own good.

Maybe I was more interested in experiencing the rest of the world before I truly *knew* India. Not that I've done much of that, either; the most adventurous holiday I've had was two weeks in Mexico, and a week of that was at an all-inclusive place in Cancun. The other week really wasn't my thing: I'm not really one for backpacking, at least I don't think I am, but I imagine I could go anywhere in the world and be fine. I've just not tried it. Not really been anywhere adventurous. Even though I see myself as someone who is, I've not really done anything more adventurous than having a wee on the street behind a parked van, which then drove off mid-wee, which still makes me cringe. It was a long wee too. Spontaneous adventuring or questioning your identity were not things done in my family. I think they all massively underestimated what moving to another country might do to the generation born there. What the impact of living in two worlds would have on them. I always thought it was inevitable that I would go to India again, as an adult, but in my own time, for my own reasons. And here it was: a reason, *my* reason.

I had also experienced India through Dad's eyes. I used to love hearing his stories when I was younger – he was always so happy talking about his childhood in Amritsar, his carefree youth in Punjab.

'I had a bike back then,' he chuckled, as I sat on the floor at four years old with my long plaits snaking down my back, long enough for me to sit on. 'It was much too big for me but we didn't have a lot of choice back then. And, anyway, it got me around!' He leaned back in the armchair. 'I thought I was the absolute bee's knees.' His flip-flopped feet barely reached the pedals, but he and his friends would ride around and play practical jokes, telling ghost stories to the local kids and then ride around at night, pretending to be ghosts.

He told me of things that are borderline criminal but, somehow, in 1960s India, you could get away with, like the corporal punishment dished out to him at school. Not only were they hit with whatever implement was handy (cane, ruler, leather chappal), they were made to crouch down in a kind of yoga pose, arms looped under their legs, holding onto their ears – in the midday sun! The punishments were inventive and cruel. Dad would laugh as he told me and said for them it was normal, they didn't think of things like 'trauma' or 'child protection'. It was just discipline and they needed it.

The rest of his stories involved food or animals, or both. No vegetable or fruit ever tasted so delicious as the fruit and veg of his youth. We couldn't eat a mango without him telling us about the sweet-tasting ones he'd pick from a tree, or how he loved to chew raw sugar cane while walking in the lush fields, or about the sweet-and-sour sticky tamarind they'd buy from the shop and slowly lick while screwing up their faces at the sourness. I especially loved to hear about the monkeys and the elephants, the wild roaming cows, and the pagal kutta, or mad dogs. Every village in India seemed to have one that everyone was to avoid.

My family would tell stories of mysticism and religion and spirituality, of gurus spending weeks meditating on mountains, of shrines and temples, of palaces and kings and gods and goddesses. I would never know where the reality ended and the fiction began. To me, every story was real and believable because India was *everything*. India was magic. In India, everything was possible. It was alive, the opposite of my rather dull, clinical, cynical, grey Western world. But the conflict came the minute I'd step out of my door and the world around me told me my Indianness was something to be ashamed of. My skin dirty, my food smelly, my clothes and customs strange. My identity was something I needed to fix.

For someone who had only been to India once as a child, I felt as though I knew the place through my family. I knew the culture that my family left with, and the culture that was exported around the world through music and movies. The food I ate at home, the clothes I wore to special occasions, the music my family would listen to at home, I knew.

I didn't know the meaning of those very songs I would love to sing. I had to ask Dad to translate. He'd love to put on his vinyl LPs of ghazals and qawaāalis and explain the meaning behind the poetic lyrics, how they sound like love songs – and they are, only they are singing to the divine. Bollywood movies are the only place British-Asian kids get a sense of India, but of course it's nothing like the movies, or so Mum is always telling me. I also knew this because, growing up as an avid watcher of telly, I'd also seen every documentary involving some variety of posh-man comedian/politician/adventurer travelling around India, on a train, sharing his invaluable thoughts on the place.

But now I'm going to find out first-hand, for myself, exactly what India is like, because I'm going to go. I've never been more certain about anything in my life. I need to go to India, to my homeland of Punjab, the homeland of my father and mother and grandparents, of everyone before me, and find answers. To find out about my grandfather's life. I need to find Naseeb. But then reality kicks in. I can't just pick up and leave. I can't go to India. I have a job and a mortgage and sure, I have savings, but they're meant to be for a rainy day. Rainy days aren't 'needing to find yourself' – they're broken boilers and unexpected bills. Trips to India are for white women who do yoga and read self-help books, not brown women with family secrets to uncover. No, it was a nice fantasy while it lasted but India is just too far away. The idea of it is too far away. There is just too much to think about, too much to sort out. I have too much stuff to be getting on with at home, like sorting out my life. This is just a distraction.

I realise I've been staring out of the window for ages. Not even noticing anything. Just in my head. Feeling gloomier than ever with my existential crisis merging with a mega case of the Sunday night scaries, I stack the letters on my coffee table and head to bed.

December 1940
My heart,

How are you? I miss you, we all do.

I am so proud that you enlisted to join the British Indian Army. Who could not be proud that their husband is a soldier? You looked so handsome in your fauji's uniform the day you left. But I wish you didn't have to be so far away, or leave so soon. I know you are only away training but soon you will be at war.

I keep my days busy with all the chores around the house. Milking the cow, our beautiful buffalo who I have come to adore. I secretly call her Nirmal Masi, and it makes me chuckle. I have made a good connection with her, churning butter, making yogurt, paneer, ghee, washing clothes at the well, I'm very good at beating the stains out with the paddle (although these days I can't be too vigorous), stitching clothes, repairing clothes, cleaning the house, daily sweeping and dusting, and my favourite, cooking. Every night I imagine I'm cooking for you and not just for me and your parents.

Word has gone around the village that I can read and write, so I have agreed to write letters for some of the women. I have become the keeper of their intimate secrets, their hopes, dreams and the details of their lives. Oh, the things that women suffer in silence! I have become their confidante. And their secrets are safe with me. It is an honour to be able to use my skills to help other women in this way.

Oh! I have just felt our child move within me, they must know I am writing to their father.

64

Mataji is convinced it is a boy. She is praying for a son.

I am praying for a healthy baby. It is a shame I won't be able to do the traditional ritual of going home to be with my mother and have my first child in my father's home.

Today I really miss my mother, but Mataji and a few other women in the village will be with me here.

Yours always,
Naseeb

Chapter Four

'Pass the chilli sauce, Sups.' I'm having lunch with Supriya and Kate. We are smothering our jacket potatoes with cheese and beans in chilli sauce. It's our ritual, bonding us more strongly than our love of a mid-week tequila. It's also the cure for any consequences of our love of midweek tequila.

'I can't believe you snapped at Paul,' says Supriya.

'Yeah, well, he's always asking me to do stupid shit and I couldn't be bothered to make him a coffee if I was *making one anyway*. It's time he bloody well learned where the coffee machine was and hey, maybe he could even make me one while he's at it.' My mood is off at work.

While a lunchtime rant is fairly standard behaviour for any one of us, refusing to make Paul's coffee is very out of character for me, so the girls know that something is up.

'Everything all right, Sim?' asks Jojo cautiously.

Before I can answer, all three of us are distracted by the sight of Kunal, the ridiculously handsome account manager working on the big publishing company job.

'Jesus, why can't we ever get set up by family with a Kunal? I might be into it, if they could find someone as fit as him.' I'm temporarily snapped out of agitation.

'But the Kunals of this world don't see us,' answers Sups, eyes still following him. 'You know, the Indian man with a white girlfriend. They never look at Indian women. We're too . . . Indian. Sad, really, for him and for us.'

'He might just be in love. Anyway, you two, when was the last time *you* dated anyone Indian?' asks Jojo.

I think back to the men I've been with. I can't remember the last time I dated anyone properly, let alone an Indian man. Have I even dated an Indian man?

And then she continues: 'I always date black now, after some bad experiences. I realised I was being fetishised by white men. Do you remember that guy, Tom?'

'Oh yeah,' I say, 'the one who liked to touch your hair and comment on the texture all the time. What a douche!'

'Well exactly. Now, for me, it's important I'm with someone who understands my experience of being black, while also seeing me as more than just my skin colour. Like I can understand them and see who they truly are, you know? I also think as I've got older I've become more rooted in my Ghanaian identity, become more secure in my own identity. I want someone who can appreciate that.'

And this is why these women are my friends: we can have real, open, meaningful conversations, freely, without having to explain ourselves. Jojo is a proud, confident Ghanaian woman and I admire and envy how she feels. It makes me question what I see in the white men I usually date.

'Says the woman with a Brad Pitt screensaver!' Sups is right back at Jojo.

She laughs. 'Brad Pitt transcends. He transcends race, gender, age, the lot,' she says.

I nod but add, 'He's also the problem, right? Because that's who we have all internalised as the dream man, because that's who we've been told it is. We're conditioned to fancy the Brads of this world.'

'You're right,' Jojo continues 'Anyway, I don't want another person asking me if they can touch my hair or telling me – and this happened just the other day – that white men are the most oppressed people on Earth now.'

'Fitteh muh,' I exclaim in Punjabi. 'Shame on you!' It makes Sups laugh as it's such an old-lady phrase.

Am I the female Kunal of this world? Have I internalised self-loathing? The thought is spinning me out. I hope I'm not.

Being Indian is an important part of my identity but it's not my entire identity. I move between worlds and fancy all kinds of men, it just depends on what we have in common or, tragically, how much I've had to drink – need to change that.

'Yeah, I can bet this guy has never truly experienced oppression. My grandparents were thrown in prison during apartheid. We have it so good in comparison,' Sups chips in as Jojo and I nod, sombrely, then in her classic Sups' way lightens the mood: 'Apart from when it comes to dating. I'll date anyone, as you know, not fussy, black, brown, male, female, but dating is hell. It's not pretty out there, girls.'

We all laugh and I'm thankful to be dragged out of my internal Kunal conflict.

'And anyway, it's the system that has screwed us over. The patriarchy, colonialism and white supremacy.'

Every single one of our conversations ends with Sups drawing the same conclusion. We nod and hold our hands in prayer position and then I get serious, remembering why I've been in a strange mood all day and why I snapped at Paul.

'I mean, do any of us even know who we are? I don't think I really know who I am, not anymore. Why are we striving for this white middle-class mundanity when we have so much more about us? We have so many layers of rich history and culture which I feel that I end up hiding – and which I feel has been hidden from me. We've been denied our own history and what must that do to a person, erasing their sense of self? It's barbaric, really. I hate we have to whitewash ourselves to be accepted, I hate that we happily do it to fit in. Why should we have to fit? We are never going to.'

I grab the chilli sauce bottle to pour more heat on my bland potato.

After a long pause Jojo asks, 'You OK, Simran?'

I exhale a sense of relief at getting that out of me, poising myself to tell them more.

'How was your birthday?' Sup adds, trying to lighten the conversation once more.

'Everything is different. *I'm* different, my world is different, only I don't exactly know how yet.'

'Bloody hell, Simran, what happened in Bradford? They haven't arranged your marriage, have they?' Sups chuckles.

'No, they haven't gone that far yet . . .' I pause, deciding what to tell them. 'I found some old letters. And, well, they suggest some things in my family history have been kept from me.' I don't want to give too much away but they both lean in to really pay attention, Sups eyes widening with glee.

'Well, I need to understand more. I need to get some answers for myself, and those answers are in India. So. . .' I take a deep breath, 'I think I need to go to India.'

'Oh, wow! I wasn't expecting this turn of events. Things are getting interesting,' says Sups.

Freddie joins us at our table with his supermarket prawn salad. I really need to learn to speak quieter. He's overheard the end of our conversation.

'India? Oh, I've always wanted to go to India, but nothing would be better than going with you, Simran. To see it through your eyes, to understand it the way you understand it. To be able to explore it spiritually and really connect with the place. I bet you know all the best places to visit? Anyway, I really need to talk to you, I'm having trouble with a client and could do with some help.'

I really haven't got the patience for any of this today.

'No.'

He looks alarmed.

'No, Freddie, I'm sorry, and not just to today. No to the advice – maybe someone else can help, I'm too busy doing my own job – and no to being your Indian tour guide because I'm from sodding Bradford.' And I get up to get rid of my plate.

Sups and Jojo rise and follow me, leaving Freddie alone, in shock, at the table.

'You're heading to India?'

'To discover a family secret?'

'Who have you discussed this with?'

69

'What will you wear?'

'Imagine if you have a romance?'

'How will you go?'

'What's the weather like out there?'

I'm feeling electric. Buzzing with excitement. Now I've said it out loud, it has become real.

I can't answer any of their questions apart from:

'What about work?'

'I'll just take some time off. They won't say no . . .'

'No.'

'*What?*'

'We need you here,' says Siobhan. 'That Kenya account needs you. There's too much work to get over the line still and you are the only person who really understands what that job requires. Plus, you've agreed to head the understanding diversity scheme for the company, and that's a huge responsibility.'

I'm the last person who needs to understand the diversity scheme in the office, or the extra workload that this 'scheme' will require.

'It's not difficult for me to do a handover, it's really not that complicated. And anyway, I have plenty of holiday to take; it's not like you'd be giving me a huge amount of leave on top of that!'

I know full well that plenty of people have had six-week sabbaticals approved before – extended ski trips, driving holidays to California, weight-loss camps in Thailand.

'No, I'm afraid it's just not possible.'

'But I really need to do this. It's a personal family reason.'

'That's what happens when you have such big families, always a family reason.'

Sorry? Who needs the diversity training again?

'You can't say that, Siobhan. And I'm an only child.' I'm struggling to control my temper now, but I need to stay on top of this conversation without her getting a rise out of me. 'I'm only asking for six weeks, and I wouldn't have requested the time off if it wasn't important.'

'You might need to calm down there, Simran.'

Now I'm absolutely fuming.

How dare she speak to me like that, after all I've given to this job, to this agency. I never take time off; I've missed weddings, birthdays, funerals – I didn't even take time off to grieve my own father because I've been so foolishly dedicated to this job and to these people who don't even value me. They don't even see me. Why have I been so blindly committed to this place when they give me so little in return? They can't even give me the promotion I deserve! I should just tell her I'm going and that it's not up for discussion. I won't back down on this.

'Look, Sim . . .'

Sim?

'I'd love to be able to make it happen for you, but we can't. I wish I could.'

I take a deep breath. Don't back down.

'You know, I didn't take compassionate leave when my dad died because we had to finish the Nando's project. I just feel—'

'I've said it's not possible, Sim,' Siobhan interrupts me, any kindness in her face now gone. I stop talking and feel myself deflating. But the hype girl in my head is growing louder.

'THAT'S IT! I've had enough of being treated appallingly by this company. By you. I've worked harder than anyone else in my department and I've never been treated fairly. Always overlooked for every promotion. Well, you can stick your job where the sun don't shine, up your tight butt crack!'

I'm screaming this . . . in my head. What comes out of my mouth is, 'I think I want to quit.'

'What?' says Siobhan, eyes wide.

I'm quiet and thoughtful a moment, then I get to my feet.

'I'm not sure I've been treated very well at this place, *Shiv*. I work really hard and I believe I am undervalued and underappreciated and I just need to reassess my life. You have never really liked me or supported me, and you treat me differently to everyone else in the office – you couldn't even get my name right for the first two years of me being here. I think I've had enough. So maybe it's time for me to think about going somewhere else.'

If I wasn't shitting myself about quitting my job I'd probably laugh at the look on Siobhan's face. She sits blinking at me, before the full horror of what I've said hits her.

'OK, OK, let's talk about this. Let's stay calm and talk this through rationally. Please.' She gestures to my chair. I sit back down.

'I am sorry you feel this way, Simran, but I have supported you in many ways.'

Have you?

'We have nurtured you and given you the responsibility of leading on huge accounts. The Kenyan account, the Mr Singh pickles job, you were perfect for that—'

'Can you see a pattern?'

Everything I've had bottled up inside me about this place, making its way to the surface. I can't believe how little awareness this person has of how I've been treated, even when she's saying it out loud.

How do you even articulate microaggressions anyway?

'We have very strict policies in place to ensure we do right by our people. We value every one of you in this office and of course we need to improve but Simran . . .'

Some people are just valued more than others. She seems nervous and I'm glad. Her trying to gaslight me is pathetic.

'You are a valued member of this team and we appreciate all you do.'

There's that 'valued' word again – and I've never felt appreciated. She thinks I'm every other Asian woman in the office because we are interchangeable and all look the same to her.

'I would like to look into how we can go about improving your experience here with us.'

Improving my experience? I'm not some disgruntled customer complaining about my patchy Wi-Fi, Siobhan.

'Now, please tell me again exactly what it is you would like to do . . .'

Acknowledge what I'm saying, stop gaslighting me, diversify the management team, stop only seeing your own experience, stop being a complete bitch would be a start.

'. . . and I will speak to HR myself to make sure we can accommodate your needs.'

Is she reading this from a manual?

'We are a company that gets things right.'

What is that stupid smirk on her self-satisfied face?

'Just not with me. I'm going home.'

I walk out of that room like I'm Bridget Jones and I've just told Daniel Cleaver to shove his job, but in, you know, a brown way.

I walk into my flat and slam the front door behind me. My hands are shaking. I take a few deep breaths to calm myself down then collapse onto the sofa. A sickly feeling of panic is replacing the exhilaration I felt giving Siobhan the proverbial finger. Oh my God! What the heck have I done? Have I just quit my job? I grab my phone out of my bag and text Johnny and Henry.

> This is an emergency. Come to mine for dinner, I have tons of yogurt pots full of birthday curry.

Immediately I see Johnny is typing.

> We're both home. We can come round now?
> The sooner the better. And bring ice cream.

A couple of minutes later I hear a knock at the door. I jump up to let them in and before they can even say hello, I blurt, 'I just quit my job.'

'What?' they say together. Even Elvis, who they've brought along with the ice cream, because they know dog therapy always calms me down, looks shocked.

I bring them up to speed while we eat Mum's curry and I shovel giant spoonfuls of strawberry cheesecake ice cream down my gullet.

'I found these letters at home at the weekend. I thought they were kinky letters between my grandparents, but it turns out they're from my grandfather's first wife.'

'He had two wives?' asks Henry.

'No, something must have happened to her for Grandad to then marry my gran. Anyway, no one, ever, in my family has spoken about it. A massive family secret.'

'I can relate to that, big Irish Catholic family, riddled with secrets. My Uncle Brendan was actually my cousin. My granny brought up Aunty Mary's son as her own to stop the scandal,' says Johnny.

'So why did this lead you to quit work?' asks Henry, keeping me on track.

'Well, the discovery has changed everything for me and I have this overwhelming need to find out more about Naseeb, who she is, who I am, and to answer these questions it's obvious I need to go to India.'

'Oh yes.' Their eyes have lit up; they are thrilled with my news so far. Elvis jumps up and sits on my lap.

'All I did was ask that bloody bitch-face Siobhan for a sabbatical and she said no. Gave me some bullshit HR spiel like a marketing robot and threw in a dose of casual racism while she was at it. So I quit – or at least I think I have.'

There's a pause while they let the news sink in. Elvis readjusts himself in my lap.

'Simran, I have such a good feeling about this! This is it, your *destiny*,' says Johnny dramatically.

There's been far too many mentions of destiny in the last couple of days.

'But I could also not go. I mean, I've lost my job over this already. I've become reckless. Is that a good omen or a bad omen?'

'I thought you didn't believe in omens?' says Johnny with a raised eyebrow. 'And anyway, you can just get your mum and granny to wipe away all the bad omens and evil eyes with their magic, can't you?'

'It's not magic, it's superstition.'

'What did you say this was again? It's so delicious,' says Henry, having another mouthful of the warmed-up leftovers.

'A karela, it's a bitter gourd. Mum likes to stuff them with an onion and tamarind combination. I used to think they looked like mice when I was little, you have to pull the cotton thread off that's holding them together. It's a bit of an acquired taste so I'm really glad you like it. I'll give you some you can put in the freezer, I have enough for the entire building.'

We all sit there, Johnny and Henry eating my mum's curry while I dig into the ice cream. I take a deep breath.

'What if I have a terrible time, or I hate it, or just end up on some wild goose chase and discover nothing? This is India we're talking about.'

'It's a time-honoured white lady tradition to go to India to "find yourself", so why shouldn't you be able to do the same – and with a much better reason? Your culture is from that land, you have a legit reason to go. So go! What are you afraid of?' Johnny replies.

'Stepping into the unknown. Am I being daft, should I just stay in the comfort of what I know?'

'You are not comfortable, you are in turmoil. We know that and you know that. Could you pass me another chapatti, please?' Henry reaches over to pass Jack the chapatti.

He's not wrong.

Later, after a hot shower, I decide I should call Pinks before bed. I've been putting off talking to the one person I know will give me the right advice. I drop her a text and I get lucky because she's breastfeeding – surely one of the reasons they invented speakerphone?

'Babes, you *quit*? Just like that? Was that wise?'

Was it wise? Of course not. It was a compulsive decision made in the heat of the moment. There was nothing wise about it! But my bravado prevents me from admitting this to Pinks . . .

'I feel liberated. I feel as though I've taken the power back, but I'm also petrified that I'm making a huge mistake. I'm so unsure but I couldn't keep going as I was. I'm excited and terrified!'

'You will never be able to work there again.'

'I'm OK with that.'

'It's a small industry, especially up north, people talk.'

'I'm done with advertising and marketing.'

'What about income?'

'I've got savings, I'll figure something out.'

Silence

'You think I've made a mistake?'

I think I've made a mistake.

'No, I'm just trying to get my head around your rationale. Especially after the other night – you seemed like you were in quite a dark place. Maybe you need to speak to someone? A professional?' She sounds genuinely concerned,

I try to explain. 'I *was* in a dark place. That's precisely why I need to do this. Look, Pinks, this really feels like the universe is giving me a gift. I need to make this trip to India. What's the point in living this single and so-called "carefree" life if I'm not free? I dreamt of being the single woman with the capacity to have adventures and travel and learn and do amazing things. Well, I should do just that, rather than dream it forever, shouldn't I?'

I tell her everything. I explain about the letters and Naseeb, Grandad's wife, tell her there's so much missing that I need to know and that even though my mind keeps trying to explain to me why I shouldn't do it, there's something inside me that knows I have no choice but to go to India. To find Naseeb.

'I just don't think me finding the letters at that moment was an accident.'

'Hang on, since when are you into superstition?' asks Pinks.

'I'm not, but this really feels like a crossroads. You know, like the universe is making me an offer? I need to listen to the wisdom inside me, maybe the ancestors are speaking to me?'

'OMG, whose Instagram account did you get *that* from?'
she laughs.

My laptop pings.

'Oh God!'

'What is it?' Pinks asks.

'Siobhan has just emailed me. Oh God! Oh God!'

'Well, read it then.'

'I'm nervous, don't want to.'

'Stop being an ostrich. If you want to live life to its fullest
then start by reading this email.'

She's right. I click it.

Dear Simran,

I have spent some time considering your request for a sabbatical. You are a valued member of the company and instrumental in your team, and we would not want to lose you. After further discussion with management, we have decided to approve the sabbatical request, with HR to follow up later this week regarding dates and so forth.

If you accept the sabbatical, I hope we can put behind us the conversation that took place in my office this afternoon.

Warmest

Siobhan

'I still have my job, Pinks, and I've got my sabbatical!'

That's it, then. Nothing to stop me now.

'Bloody hell, Babes, whatever you said to her worked. I take
it back, you should feel very empowered. Am I seeing you at the
wedding next weekend? We can celebrate.'

'Oh, I nearly forgot! Rimple auntie's daughter! I can't keep
up with the number of weddings we have in one calendar
year. There is nowhere I would like to be less but I have to
take Mum and Dadima. At least you're going to be there, so
I have my wingwoman.'

I should feel happy, relieved that I can go to India and keep
my job. But there's something gnawing at me. I'm actually

disappointed. Though I was scared about leaving the agency, I also felt . . . lighter, somehow. And excited and liberated by what I had done. Gah, Baby, snap out of it! This is what you wanted. This is the best outcome you could have hoped for. Right, I'll keep telling myself that until it feels true.

'We can't do weddings without each other . . . OMG, Baby, you're off to have an adventure in India. Now you've just got to tell your mum.'

The next small job on the list.

Chapter Five

'Please don't trip, please don't trip, please don't trip.'

This is my mantra for the bride at every wedding I've ever attended. Flashback to 1992, when Sukhminder auntie's foot got caught in her fifty-kilo lehnga. Dripping in real Swarovski crystals, she hadn't quite managed to get her balance right on lifting herself from cross-legged seated position to standing position. That, plus the extra length once her Jimmy Choo stilettos had been taken off, meant that as soon as her new husband began the first of four circumnavigations of the holy book, she stacked it, hard.

Sukhminder was a particularly extravagant bride. No one had ever witnessed a lehnga quite so eye-blindingly reflective; the lights in the room were shooting lasers off those crystals as she slowly, very slowly, made her way down the aisle. Never had there been a more bling bride in Bradford.

And then she fell, in slow motion and because people were too busy protecting their eyes from the lights, no one reacted quick enough to help her. The room gasped and instantly the whispers of it being a bad omen for the marriage began, and the women began praying harder.

Poor Sukhminder aunty had to get married with a broken nose, in searing pain, with blood smeared across her cheek. If her arms hadn't been weighed down by all the kalire on her wrists, she might have saved her face.

I was a wide-eyed five-year-old who adored a wedding. I loved getting dressed up in my Indian suit, I loved wearing my bindi, just like Mum and Dadima, and I loved to sit right at the front of the gurdwara, so I could watch the ceremony up close.

I would watch the bride's face, usually with her eyes focused on the carpet in front of her, but sometimes a bride would look up and smile – or occasionally, even more shocking and free-willed – she'd look up and smile at her husband. Never the done thing back then, but times change slowly and little me soaked it all up. The drama of Sukhminder's fall was thrilling – what five-year-old doesn't want a long wedding ceremony broken up with some live unexpected action?

Here we are, thirty-one years later and I'm already in the prayer hall sitting on the floor, shoes off, head covered, awaiting the arrival of the bride. I turn around to say a quiet hello to Sukhminder aunty; she and her twenty-five-year-old daughter, Guddi, are sitting just behind me. All those whispers after The Incident that the marriage wouldn't last, that her falling was a bad omen, clearly didn't mean much.

'Nothing will ever beat your mum's wedding,' I say in Guddi's ear.

'She'll never forget it – no one will let her!' she whispers back.

Mum and Dadima are sitting at right angles to me by the wall because Dadima, along with all the other elderly women, needs to be able to rest her back.

'Why don't you take one of the seats at the back, Dadima?'

'No, I'm happy here.'

She's always intent on proving that she's not elderly or infirm and I've always enjoyed being with Dadima in this space – she's my comfort and we are gurdwara buddies.

As a kid I would always look up at her, singing along with the kirtan, knowing the words to every shabad, praying, listening to the priest tell his stories; none of it made any sense to me. Dadima would look at me as I began to fidget and reapply the scarf on my head, which was always slipping off, and tell me to sit cross-legged quietly. And if that didn't work, a humbug or a Polo mint would appear from the bottom of her handbag to keep me sweet.

During my teen years I was happier running around in the langar hall, playing with Pinky and talking about the good-looking lads who only came to the gurdwara on special occasions. They never noticed us, with our gaudy-coloured home-made shalwar kameez and teenage moustaches, the curse of the Asian girl who has yet to be introduced to threading.

I haven't been to the gurdwara or a wedding in such a long time and today it feels right to be back by Dadima's side. Plus, I know she's still packing humbugs in that bag of hers.

The guests walk down the aisle to do their matha taykna, bowing of their heads, before taking their seats on the floor. It's the perfect opportunity to oohh and aaah and look at the amazing outfits people are wearing. Weddings are *it*, the occasion everyone goes all out with their clothing and there seems to be no such thing as too much at a Punjabi wedding. Chandeliers don't have a patch on some of these outfits.

The bling factor seems only to have ramped up in the last twenty years as everyone wants to imitate the latest Bollywood wedding or designer creations. Some of the outfits weigh a ton and cost a ton.

Some of the younger lot have skipped the wedding outfits and gone straight to the 'item-girl outfit' as my mum and Dadima refer to it. They are the sexiest, with the most revealing ensembles, all body confidence, pouting lips and lash extensions so long they brush the carpet when they bow their heads.

The designs are modern, revealing, extravagant. I'm shocked that I'm shocked. I wish I had the confidence to strut my stuff like the younger generation. And if these are the outfits for the religious ceremony, I can't wait to see the numbers coming out for the reception. Weddings are the perfect opportunity to make multiple glamorous outfit changes.

Mum looks at me and shakes her head.

'You look very nice, but you could have looked so pretty if you'd worn the lengha I got you.'

'Mum, if I wasn't used to this battle, you could hurt my feelings with a comment like that.'

'I said you look nice,' she says, trying to backtrack.

Mum tries it every time, getting me some outfit I'm never going to wear, in the hope I might glam up; you'd think she might have learned by now.

'I'm going to wear my cream suit, Mum,' I'd said. 'It's beautiful.'

'It's too simple.'

'I like simple.'

'You are like Kate Middleton.'

'What's that supposed to mean?'

'She was so simple on her wedding day.'

'Mum, she was wearing a tiara, I'd hardly say she looked simple.'

'You should look dramatic, Baby, while you are still young and pretty and have your figure. Why can't you be like everyone else?'

I just look at her.

'I'll wear a pair of your Indian earrings and some bangles, accessorise tastefully.'

'This is not the place for taste, Baby, we are going to a Punjabi wedding!'

I've upped my wedding game from when I was a teenager, though. It was almost impossible for Mum to get me out of jeans and trainers.

I love my outfit, and despite her grumblings, Mum and Dadima both agree that I am the epitome of elegance. They'd stood at the bottom of the stairs this morning, cooing and fussing as I walked down to meet them.

I can scrub up for an occasion and now, as an adult, I love dressing in Indian clothes. Nothing makes me feel more feminine or graceful than when I'm draped in a saree or when I'm wearing a bindi with a dupatta delicately placed on my head. I just like to wear them in my own way.

The groom has taken his place at the front of the hall, but the bride is still to make her entrance. Pinky arrives with the three kids and, as usual, she looks incredible. She always gets it spot on. Her clothes are stylish and dramatic without being OTT. The older she's become, the better she's got at wearing Indian clothes. Effortless yet glamorous.

'You look beautiful, Baby,' she says as she sits down, then turns to hug Dadima and Mum.

'How do you do it? You look stunning and you've braved a saree in the gurdwara,' I say to Pinky.

'A lot of strategic safety pins.' Then, 'Have you told them yet? About India?' she asks.

'Ssshhh! Nope, nothing yet, so please don't say anything. I'll do it when the time is right.'

Dadima is handing out humbugs to Pinky's eldest two. She sees us both looking and passes us a handful each, smiling as we discreetly unwrap them and pop them in our mouths, just like when we were kids.

I have mixed emotions observing the wedding. I'm enjoying listening to the soothing wedding chant but I feel alien in this space, a space I used to know well. There's a feeling that I've left this part of me behind. I watch the Bride and Groom walk around the Guru Granth Sahib, the sacred circumnavigation, and wonder if I will ever do the same.

It's never been my goal, getting married. I've been force-fed the idea that the ultimate attainment for a young woman is to be married and that she'll never be fully respected or seen as respectable until she's married. The more I've been made to believe that my value is equated to being with a man, or rather being married to a man, the less I've wanted it.

Nowhere do I feel more alone with my opinions than here, in Bradford, with my Punjabi community. Most girls my age have been planning their wedding, or at least the wedding out-fits, for as long as they can remember. The day when they get to be the belle of the ball, all eyes on them for the day, or rather, the week. So why have I never once wanted this for me? All I can think of is the aftermath. It's not just a wed-ding, it's a marriage. The long haul of having to be a wife, or worse, a daughter-in-law. If those Bollywood melodramas are anything to go by, Indian mothers-in-law are the wicked witches of the East.

Which probably isn't fair as there are plenty of lovely mothers-in-law in the room I'm in, but still, I don't fancy risking it. I guess it's all the 'you truly belong to your in-laws' family' bollocks that I've absorbed over the years that really puts me off. How about I truly belong to no one but me? How about a woman is perfectly capable of looking after herself?

Life as I know it has been disrupted and maybe I'm finally now on my journey to learn how to look after myself properly because what I was doing before wasn't it. I've been sadder than I've ever been and nothing was cheering me up, listening to what I needed, nurturing me, not giving myself a hard time. Maybe these are the things I need to try: standing up to Siobhan, stepping into the unknown, booking a flight to India, finding out who I really am, spending time with me, having a new experience, discovering something about my family history. These are the things that will maybe help me grow, not getting drunk and snogging Freddie – that was fun temporarily but something had to change.

I feel bad thinking about drinking and boys in the Gurdwara.

All heads turn at once to see Shelly the bride enter the room. She shimmies her way down the aisle in a fantastic deep-red lehnga, with beautiful gold embroidery, intricate wedding henna covering her hands and going all the way up to her elbows. It must have taken the henna artist hours. She looks spectacular. A beautiful bride. I look over at Shelly's mum, Rimple aunty, and well up, thinking about how she was ostracised from the community when she divorced Shelly's dad, even though he beat her, and how she slowly gained back respect, not that she'd ever lost it. Shelly is a credit to her. The bride is smiling all the way, looking left, looking right, waving at a couple of her mates. I look around to see the eyes of all the old ladies around me widen to the size of saucepans, shocked by her brazen entrance: brides are supposed to look miserable on their wedding day.

But Shelly isn't having an arranged marriage. She's not marrying some stranger and meeting them for the first time on her wedding day, the way it used to be. She's marrying the lad she's been dating for the last seven years, so why would she feign misery? Let her smile if she wants to. I enjoy the entrance, I even give her a little wave.

'Don't encourage her!' Mum whispers and slaps my hand down.

'No more crisps,' Pinky says to Maya, who's sitting in my lap.

We've found our table in the opulently decorated reception hall. The guests – all six hundred of us – are gathered, waiting for the arrival of the newlyweds so we can begin the feast. The room we're in is vast with more foliage than the Amazon. I can barely see who is sitting across the table from me because of the giant bush centrepiece, but I know I'm with Pinky, her kids, Mum and Dadima. I take the crisps from Maya and tell her she doesn't want to fill up before the feast. There's a rumour going round it's the same caterers that did Tinku's wedding, Curry in a Hurry, who do the best deep-fried paneer fingers. Maya won't want to miss out on those. Nor the gigantic wedding cake that is currently dominating the dance floor.

We're on a table at the edge of the room, perfect for observing while not being observed. Everyone is gliding about in their finery; some of the close family have got changed into even more elaborate sarees and lehngas. I can hear pleasantries being exchanged, gossip being spread: 'I've heard he's got three nipples, is that good luck or bad?' I overhear and marital matches are being made because the Illuminaunty never takes a day off, plus this is prime hunting ground for matchmakers. Yup, I'm more than happy to sit by the wall, protected by a humongous fern away from anyone's eyeline.

Just as I'm about to bust open another packet of cheese and onion, music begins – a ridiculously loud film score – that makes us all jump. People stand up and turn towards the door, expecting the bride and groom to walk through, when Maya points up to the ceiling, 'Look! Spider-Man!'

And there, in full costume, precariously dangling from the rafters, is the groom – or rather, Spider-Man. The rope he's attached to slowly lowers him into the crowd, which is open-mouthed in a mixture of amazement and dismay, and when he's a few feet from the ground, he jumps. The room gasps as he falls with a thud, but then he jumps back up and, landing with his legs apart, begins disturbingly gyrating to the music. Goodness me, but that costume is tight! I catch Pinky's eye and we both dissolve into giggles. Meanwhile, the groom looks towards the giant cake in the centre of the dance floor, throws forward his wrist as though shooting his web, and the cake bursts open and out pops the bride. It takes a bit of manoeuvring, but Shelly gets herself and her wedding outfit out. What follows is the strangest first dance I've ever witnessed, the groom still in character and costume for the entire track.

I am absolutely losing it. This is the best thing I've ever seen. Pinky mouths to me, 'The music from *Space Jam?!*' and I worry I'm going to cry my makeup off, but it actually ends up being oddly sweet. And the kids love it, even if most of the adults look utterly horrified.

The starters take a while to arrive, and everyone runs back to their tables, although this is anything but curry in a hurry. While the bride and groom go off to change, I'm kind of sad Spider-Man's not staying. We get stuck into the starters. Plates are piled high with chicken tikka, sheek kebab, mushroom Manchurian (an Indo-Chinese dish that the Chinese have never heard of), lamb tikka, tandoori vegetables, salad, chutneys and the famous paneer fingers, which people leap on as the waiters are still bringing the bowls to the tables. These are just the starters.

We decide to leave the faux Amazon and walk around the grounds, really make the most of the very fancy setting, work off some of those starters – we've got at least an hour before the main meal. Dadima is sitting on a bench with other dadimas, talking about the perfectly designed rose garden. Mum is hanging with a bunch of aunties, all admiring the house.

'You do realise this house was probably made with colonial money? The blood of our ancestors went into building this,' a teenager points out. Her mates are on their phones in an instant, googling the history of the place.

'Ain't nothing legit about this place. Pirates and thieves, the lot of them. You're right, built by blood,' another of them pipes up.

'You younger generation, so fixated on history,' one of the aunties says. 'Admire the beauty of the building, the decoration so lovely.'

'Suits the Punjabi taste, it screams money,' I whisper to Pinky a little too loudly.

All the aunties look at me at once. Dammit, this is not what I need.

'Ah, Baby, beti, so lovely to see you after such a long time. You never come to any functions, better than all of us now, are you?'

The four aunties of the apocalypse slide towards me.

'Just busy, aunty.'

'Life will pass you by if you're not careful.'

'If you're not careful, no one will want to marry you.'

'Oh, come on. Please can we change the script, aunties? You are getting far too predictable,' I snap back but remember I need to be polite so end the sentence with a smile.

Mum, who is standing not too far away, overhears and shoots me a look that says *don't you dare say anything to shame me. Suck it up.*

'No, no, no, there are plenty of boys for Baby . . .'

Nope, what I said ricocheted right off their diamond ear-rings. Here we go. Deep breath. The kind-looking aunty smiles at me, and I almost can't believe the comment, but her sentence isn't complete yet.

'. . . everyone getting divorced these days, no one cares about respect or trying to make it work, Baby will be fine. She might not get a respectable family but plenty of rejected men needing bride number two or three.'

I'm too stunned to reply but turns out I don't need to do anything to defend myself from the aunty assault. Pinky has my back and stops me from shaming my mum, which I am very close to doing.

'Baby is the sensible one; she's far too busy making something of herself and enjoying her life – as we all know, aunties, a man is just another child to look after.'

They all look to Pinky, in unison, and smile and nod in agreement.

'Yes, yes, Pinky, your words are true. Women end up doing everything, everything.'

God, how does she do it? I'm consistently amazed at my friend; when it comes to Indian aunties, she's like a Jedi – they don't even know what she's doing but somehow, they're agreeing with her.

Just when I think we're out of the woods and begin to turn away, another aunty pipes up.

'Yes, it's true you young women are making different choices about your lives. Take my Dolly, she's in Hong Kong, very successful banker, always going on exotic holidays. She always flies me and your uncle business class to go and see her; she's so generous and I'm so proud of her. Her and Peter have a great life. How's your daughter doing, Bubbly?'

Oh no, not Bubbly aunty!

'Well, my Nikita is just perfect, I couldn't wish for a better daughter. I don't know how she does it all. Big house, beautiful children, my son-in-law so handsome and he's so fair-skinned, people think he's a Spanish. They're just coming back from the Maldives. They love the Maldives, it's their favourite holiday destination.'

I couldn't think of anywhere less interesting than the Maldives. I'm doing a massive internal eye-roll and trying desperately to extrapolate myself from this aunty ego-stroke competition when suddenly the spotlight is back on me. Again.

'How about you, Baby?'

'What about me?' I bite back, barely retaining a sheen of politeness.

'Your life? Tell us about your fabulous life? Share with your aunties, nah?'

'Oh, Baby is doing very well at work!' Mum jumps in to start my defence, looking quickly at me. She joins the group.

'I'm actually off to India,' I blurt out.

What?

'What?' says Mum.

'You are?' say the aunties. Even Dadima, who is sitting twenty feet away on the bench, hears and says, 'Huh? Where is Baby going?'

Well, it's out there now. Not quite how I planned it to happen. Not that I had a plan. I've made it public, I've announced it to the epicentre of the gossip machine, so therefore I've announced it to every Punjabi in West Yorkshire, which means if there was a part of me that believed my trip might not happen, it's out the window. There's no backing out now, I'm definitely going to India.

My adrenaline rush is making my hands shake.

'When were you going to talk to me about this?' Mum whispers in my ear; she looks shocked.

'I'll talk to you properly later,' I say.

'You've never done anything like this before!'

'Precisely why I'm doing it, Mum.'

'Where are you going, when are you going? You can stay with my sister, your masi?'

I've only just 100 per cent confirmed it's happening so I have no logistics planned, therefore I have no idea what I'll be doing or when I'm going. My excitement is turning into terror. But at least I know I'll stay with Mum's sister.

Dadima has made her way over to give me a hug.

'Such exciting news.' She loves the idea and Mum is only a little shocked but hasn't said anything negative. Their response makes me bold.

'Yes, I'm going on a trip, taking some time out from my hectic schedule and going on a journey of discovery. All these achievements in life mean nothing if we don't truly know who we are, isn't that so, aunties? First I'll find myself, and then maybe I'll find a man.'

All the aunties begin to make the right impressed noises. They can't exactly disagree.

'Well, that was one way to tell everyone,' Pinky shouts at me in the centre of the dance floor a little while later. I manoeuvre around a drunk uncle, who's trying to dance with me, or it might be the girl next to me. I can't really tell as his eyes are glazed over. The dance floor is heaving and sweaty.

Pinky and I have always loved a bhangra at weddings; we have our favourite tunes, our matching moves, we even came up with dance routines to Bollywood songs when we were younger. No matter how excruciating it is to be around aunties at a wedding, the dance floor is always a relief, the great leveller.

But today I'm just not in the mood for any of it. I push pervy drunk uncle to one side, trying not to touch his sweat patches, while simultaneously rescuing another girl out of his way at the same time. She mouths an exaggerated 'thank you'.

'Let's get a drink,' Pinky says.

'Baby, Didi can you get us a drink, please?' I hear in stereo. I've been accosted before I get to the bar by the twins, Jolly and Lucky.

'You two drink? Yeah, sure, what do you want?'

'You can't buy them a drink! They're too young and their mum will kill you.'

'They're seventeen and they need a life – I'm getting them a drink. Don't you remember we'd ask Dad to get them in for us?'

'Yeah, Uncle Ji was awesome. His presence is so missed today,' says Pinky.

I don't know how to respond. Remembering my dad unexpectedly is always a punch in the gut. From being deafened by the bhangra set the DJ is blasting out, I'm only able to hear my own breath now. I stay still for a second and swallow hard, feeling hot tears trying to escape my eyes, but I hold them down with everything I've got.

'You OK, Babes?'

'Yeah, I'm great. Whisky and sodas all round!'

The twins disappear with their drinks, or rather float away in a freaky manner.

'Remember when we were that age? You had a moustache and a long plait until you went to uni, remember?' I say to Pinky.

'Don't remind me. I tried to shave it with Dad's razor and it came back thicker. The lads at school called me handlebar,' she says.

'Cruel but funny,' I say, 'now we are older, yeah. Praise the lord for laser hair removal.'

Pinky shouts 'Amen' and I raise my glass in the air, revealing my stubbly armpit.

'We better go and sit with your mum and gran and tell them what you're up to. You can't keep avoiding them.'

'I'm not. I think they were both actually excited for me, which I wasn't expecting.'

'Why wouldn't they be? They've been trying to convince you to go to India for years. They all want us to experience the motherland. Your mum grew up there, I'm surprised she doesn't want to come with you?' Pinky knows Mum well.

'That must be avoided at all costs. I have to do this trip alone.'

'You going to tell them the reason you're going?'

'No way. Not yet. I just want to get there and try and find things out for myself. You know what Indian families are like with secrets. They want to keep them hidden. I don't want them talking me out of it or trying to convince me I shouldn't go digging. I can't take the risk. Maybe once I'm there, I'll tell them. I can keep secrets too,' I say.

We walk past all the big expensive new cars to get to Mum's little old Fiat Punto she's had forever. She needs a new one, but Dad bought her this car so now we really don't want to let it go.

'I don't need a big car, just something to get me to the shops.'

I jump in the driving seat and pray it starts first time. This car has a tendency to only work when it feels like it.

Mum is next to me, Dadima in the back.

'Here, do you need a toothpick? Chicken tikka stuck in my teeth – these things happen as you get older.' Mum's offering me a toothpick from the bottom of her bag.

'No, you're OK, Mum.'

Dadima lets out quite a large fart for such a small woman.

'Dadima! Are you playing the trombone back there?' I say while winding down all the windows.

'Well, I couldn't exactly do it in there, in the wedding. I've been holding it in.'

'We were just standing outside, though, Dadima,' I say.

'So, your trip to India –' Mum begins. 'When were you going to tell us about that?'

'Now, literally now. I'm going to India. I need a break and I think it's time to go and explore the motherland, see where we're from.'

Dadima mutters something in the back and looks out of the window but I don't quite catch what she says as Mum is suddenly very excited. Her volume has increased as though I'm already sitting in India.

'You will go on your own, kalli? You need to be careful. Maybe we should come with you. We could go and visit a few of my cousins – you know we have family in some very beautiful parts of India?'

'No!' I jump in a little too quickly. 'Sorry, Mum, but I want to experience it on my own, and I might go and stay in a yoga retreat or something, or a spa, you know, really relax, treat myself.'

Mum is nodding but I can see she's still considering her options.

'Let the girl go alone. She wants to see it her own way, not dragging us around as well.'

Nice one, Dadima.

I'm surprised by how quickly Mum agrees and now they are both getting excited.

'This is so fun! You will love it there! Oh, but so much to do, so much to organise. What about work?'

'Oh, it's OK. They've given me a sabbatical . . .' I clear my throat. 'I just need to get some info about where to stay and where to go from you and Dadima.'

'I'm so happy you are going, beta. You know, I never visited your grandfather's ancestral village.'

There's an ancestral village? I've already learned something new.

'We were married so quickly and moved straight from my home to Amritsar, where your dadaji had a job, and then, after your father arrived, we moved to the UK. Your grandfather always wanted to move here – he said this place would welcome us, it owed us. He never got over the shock of what the reality of living here was. Anyway, such is destiny! We are here – but most importantly, we have you. Our beautiful little girl about to go on a pilgrimage to her ancestral homeland . . .'

'It's not really going to be a pilgrimage, Dadima. More of an . . . extended holiday.' I try and steer her away from thinking it's anything other than a break.

'Well, keep your heart open and leave your British eyes and thoughts behind! You were brought up between worlds so that you can adapt to most. Go with the flow when you are there. And keep your wits about you, too – they can spot you Britishers a mile off. Don't behave like too much of a tourist. Impress them with your Punjabi. Show them that even though you were born abroad, you have been brought up with the right values. Respect for tradition and culture. Make us proud.'

'Erm, OK, Dadima. I'll try.' I don't know why she's acting like I'm about to board the plane right this minute.

I knew they'd be OK with me going, but I'm delighted with how into the idea they are. This is filling me with confidence about my trip.

'Now is not the time to be giving her a lesson in how to behave, we need to give her practical advice.' Mum turns to me, 'Like not staying out in the sun because you will tan. Keep spare knickers in your bag in case you get an upset tummy. Also, toilet paper, always have tissue with you. A hat, a scarf, maximum factor sunblock and hand sanitiser and a water bottle and pain-killers and . . .'

'Mum, I'll be fine! Do you think it will be OK to stay with Masiji?

'Oh God! These British children know nothing about our culture.'

She looks at Dadima and they smile at each other; at least they are bonding, even if it is at my expense.

'She's your masi. My sister. Blood relation. You can just turn up and she has to let you stay for as long as you like. This is what families do. Well, this is what Indian families do. She will be offended if you don't stay with her.'

That's my accommodation sorted then.

Mum's little sister, Honey Masi, lives in Delhi. She got married to an Indian barrister and never left India. Dadima suggests that I could always stay with her nephew in Agra and see the Taj Mahal, or her other nephew from her father's side who lives in Chandigarh, who would happily take me into the foothills of the Himalayas.

'If I have time as part of my trip, Dadima, I'd love to visit some of your family. Of course, I'd like to visit the Taj Mahal,' I say because I'd love to know more about my granny. These letters, this trip are just revealing how little I know about my family and my extended family in India.

'You're such a good girl,' Dadima says.

Mum interrupts to suggest there's always her cousins in Dehradun just waiting for us to visit, and Dehradun is beautiful.

'Very famous school there, Baby, better than these British boarding schools. We should have sent you.'

'That's a boys' school,' I say to no one in particular as they are both now arguing with each other over which of my 75,000 relatives, all of whom have been waiting their entire lives for me to visit, it would seem, I should stay with.

'How about you just let Honey Masi know I'm coming, give me her details and if, IF, I should want to stay with any other relative while I'm there, I'll call you?'

94

Mum seems placated by this. 'OK, OK. When you drop us off at home, remind me to remove the nazar from you. So many people talking about you at that wedding and now you are going to India, we need to kill the evil eye.'

The removal of the evil eye is a ritual that Mum and Dadima have been performing on me since I was born. I've learned it is better not to question it and just let it happen. Accept it as some kind of blessing. It's become such a staple of my life that it would be weird and unnerving if they didn't do it.

There's no going back now. I guess I'm heading to India.

September 1942
Hello, Deep's Father,

I hope this letter finds you safe and well.

Your son saw his first gecko today. It came into the room and scuttled up the wall. I screamed but Deepu thought it was fascinating and wanted to touch it. Mataji came in running with the broom. The sight of her chasing the lizard was so funny. She was also telling it to shoo, shoo shoo and waving the broom over her head. Mataji has energy.

Farooq Chacha's daughter-in-law, Anjuman, has become a great friend. We are united by our love of long walks (much to Mataji's annoyance!). Mataji says I shouldn't be too friendly with a Muslim woman, which is a strange thing to say as Pitaji is such good friends with all the Muslim men in the village. We all live together. Just because we choose to pray in different ways doesn't mean we don't all belong to the same family. We are all one. Do you agree? I have been helped by Anjuman and her company, and she has opened her heart to me also. The poor girl is not able to carry a child. She has already lost two, and the family are becoming impatient with her. Bechari! It is sad. So very sad. She wishes for a child every day, and I pray for her too.

I have promised her we will visit every mandir, gurdwara, masjid and church. We will leave no religion out until she has a child. I am certain our prayers will be answered.

We also have a little shadow who follows us around the village, a little girl called Billi. She will come and sit in the vehra to listen to us. She is such a funny little girl. Her green eyes are so piercing, like a god's. I sometimes wonder if she sees more than most through them. She will be a very beautiful young woman, I think. At first, she pretends to be running an errand whenever Anjuman and I sit down together. Then, she appears by the well when the two of us are washing clothes. I smiled at her that first time, and she came closer but one of the other women there slapped and shooed her away. Slapped that poor girl so hard. They treat her like an animal. Told her to go and use the well for the untouchables and not to come near this water. I will admit to you, it broke my heart. Guru Gobind Singh ji dismantled the caste system, did he not? And yet here we are with these strict rules still in place. It does not deter Billi from following us around, however. We are becoming a little gang: Anjuman, me, and Billi as our little shadow. Sometimes I let her play with Deep but please do not ever tell your mother that I let the girl touch her grandson. She would never forgive me, and she would likely wash him for days.

How is your life in Burma? I know you will be looking out for your brothers in arms, but please, my jaan, look after yourself too. You are a father now, as well as a husband.

Yours always,

Naseeb

Chapter Six

No mythical upgrade to first class for me. One day I'll treat myself to a left turn into the lounge worth thousands, welcomed with a glass of bubbles, just not today, not while I'm on a sabbatical budget. I've got a window seat, which means having to climb over two people to get to the toilet, but I have the privacy and the luxury of looking outside and daydreaming while watching the clouds. I cannot believe I am doing this, I cannot believe I am here.

I ping Mum a message just before we take off.

Extra loo roll packed so I'm off to become a proper Indian. Then, because it is the Indian daughter in me, I confirm: I'll text when I land.

She just sends a man in a turban emoji. Which is strangely appropriate. Maybe Mum is finally getting the point of emojis, I think, and then she follows up with a snowman.

My phone pings again.

How will I cope at work without you?

It's Freddie. Typical Freddie. Nothing about my trip, just all about him. Oh, the sweet relief of not having to listen to him for a few weeks.

I check my email.

Simran
    I'm delighted we were able to get you on your sabbatical.
    So important to have time away from work. We know the value of a team with a wealth of life experiences. A happy

person brings a happy attitude to work. I'm glad we were able
to sort this out and accommodate your needs.

We look forward to hearing about your trip.

Enjoy India!

And try not to think about work too much.

Warmest

Shiv

I won't be thinking about work at all.

Delete message!

It's only once we've taken off, wheels up and turned towards Delhi, when the flight attendants are up and out of their seats, that I can fully, finally, relax.

'I'll have a Bloody Mary – actually, no, a Diet Coke.' I suppose the new drink-free me starts now. 'And two bags of pretzels, please.' Let's live a little.

As I gaze out into the infinite blue and white below, I think about my mum and Dadima, fussing and nagging me to the last possible moment in the airport, worrying over my outfit and reminding me to be a good guest and to be safe and to give so-and-so the presents they've loaded my suitcase with. Before I go through the gate, I turn to them for one last hug goodbye. Mum is in her favourite trouser suit from Hobbs, wanting to look her best even when dropping me off at the airport. Dadima is wearing her baby pink shalwar kameez with powder-blue flowers embroidered along the edges, and her pale pink dupatta on her head. She loves this suit, it's one of her favourites. Pink is her favourite colour and it brings out the rosiness of her cheeks. I bend down to give her the longest hug, nuzzling into her neck. I stay there for a few seconds looking at the gold hoops weighing down her earlobes.

When I pulled away she took my face in her hands and looked deep into my eyes.

'You are a perfect soul, my child. You make us all proud. I will miss you every day.'

'Oh, Dadima, I won't be gone for long. It's only four weeks. And don't make me cry.'

Then she handed me a freezer bag with a few humbugs in it, which I put into my bag, blinking madly.

Mum kissed me on my head before pulling out a handful of chillis from her handbag that she quickly circled around my head.

'Mum, not here, not at the airport!'

'I forgot to do it earlier.'

So, with the evil eye removed, I headed off to board the plane, my heart sinking just a little.

I'm scrolling through the films available on the flight, trying to decide what to watch, but I just can't stop thinking, planning, imagining. I love that no one can contact me for the next nine hours, that I'm entirely free of my phone and distractions and all the things that were making me so unhappy: feeling stagnant and powerless at work, never seeming to be heard or acknowledged, the pressure of family constantly on my case, the drudgery of my daily routine. I'm running away from it all, hoping desperately that rupturing my life as I know it will bring change for the better, or something different at least.

I continue flicking through my movie options. I usually watch something I'd never choose normally, like a naff, schmaltzy romance, bordering on emotionally manipulative. A fully cathartic film experience. I am quick to tear up when watching a film, but I rarely cry about real things. I don't know why. I bawled my eyes out at the live action *Lady and the Tramp*. Perhaps it's a product of my upbringing. Everyone is practical and stoic, there's no room or time for emotion when you've just got to get on with life.

I can't believe I'm on my way to India for the first time in thirty-three years, to uncover a family secret everyone failed to mention to me. My grandfather had a whole other life and I'm going to be the first person to really know what he went through, the first person not to just brush it under the carpet or lock it away in a trunk. For a family that is constantly talking, we somehow manage to communicate about absolutely nothing, and I wonder why that is. We never seem to confront anything that involves actual feelings, we argue and bicker, but nothing ever changes or gets resolved. I mean, Grandad had a wife before he married Dadima! Did no one think this was worth mentioning? Did he ever talk about it? Did my father know about it? And if he did, why didn't Dad talk to me about it? I have so many questions, and I hate that it has made me feel like Dad is further away than he's ever been.

And I just know my answers, the truth, if there is such a thing, of Naseeb and Ranjit and what happened to their life isn't in Bradford. In order to understand my family history, I need to know where they came from, where they were, how they lived, so there is no option but to go to India. A visit to India was always something I was going to do, it was inevitable – I just wasn't expecting the catalyst to be so sudden. But finding the letters just made it click into place. I had to go.

So now I'm on a flight.

Indian families love to 'shield' their children, which means not tell them anything. They also love to say 'respect your elders', which means no asking questions of them, even when you are decades into adulthood yourself. But all I can feel swimming around in my mind is: *Who was Naseeb? What happened to her? Why is she not spoken about? Has she just been forgotten? Why is her memory kept hidden in the trunk?* Mum always said I asked too many questions.

The warmth of Delhi in April smacks me in the face as I step off the plane, then a heavier scent follows, musty and comforting. It's a combination of spices and incense, with an undertone of sulphur. I inhale deeply, taking in the smell of this country, the land of my ancestors. I follow the other passengers across the tarmac towards the terminal, taking in the faces around me. There's a short dark man in a high-vis vest; a woman in a blue saree; someone waiting with a wheelchair; all brown. A taller, fairer, more smartly dressed man gives me a polite and welcoming smile; a glamorous woman, also in a saree, guides people, making sure we are heading in the right direction. All Indian. A variety of shades and shapes and sizes. All Indian. Just like me.

I check my phone.

You landed safe? Poo emoji. Mum.

Indira Gandhi international airport has changed since I was last here. It's big, clean and organised. Why am I so surprised? I smile at the immigration officer but he doesn't smile back, just scrunches his thick black moustache under his nose. Do I have the odour of not really being from here? He pushes his glasses up and asks me in Hindi what the purpose of my trip is.

I can understand him perfectly, but for some reason I pretend not to. I'm just alarmed at the presumption that I can speak Hindi. I haven't spoken Punjabi in years, and Hindi even less, because when anyone expects that I can or will speak either language, it gets my back up. I speak English, for God's sake.

He repeats the question in English and I reply, 'I'm here on holiday.' Then, for some reason I feel the need to add, 'I'm here to find out about my family.'

He says nothing. Stamps my passport, looks up and hands it back to me, saying, 'Welcome home.' I feel a swooping feeling in my stomach and a sudden giddiness. Am I home?

In India, I'm classified as an NRI, a Non-Resident Indian. Which is welcoming. I have often wondered where I fit. Who am I? Am I British and brown? Just British? Am I Indian and British? Can you be both? Am I two halves? Both? Neither? No one? Is this really another place I can call home when I feel so alien, and I've never lived here? What makes somewhere home? Is it familiarity or a sense of belonging? I guess I'm about to find out.

I exit the airport and stop to take in my surroundings. It's only now that I really allow myself to feel the excitement of being here. I take it all in, a flurry of emotion rushing through me, but just as I start to feel a wave of positivity and familiarity towards my home for the next month, panic hits. All I can see is a wall of faces, strangers, all waiting for people to arrive, hundreds of people all crushed together. Families are running up towards each other, hugging, crying, cheering, and a garland is placed around someone's neck. Elsewhere a suitcase is dropped as a couple embrace. A line of drivers from various hotels groups together, and I look at a few of the Western travellers, all of whom look just as lost as me. The scene is chaos, the noise completely overwhelming, and I start to seize up, not knowing what to do with myself.

'Baby Didi! Baby Didi!'

I look around to see my cousin Ruchi, and Uncle Sunil, coming towards me, waving. I last saw my uncle when he came over with my aunt, my Masi, for Dad's funeral, but my cousin I haven't seen since she visited Bradford, back in 2009. Ruchi was fifteen then, and she's now twenty-nine and utterly stunning. She's at least five inches taller than me, her hair cut in a neat bob, dressed casually in jeans and a T-shirt. Her eyes are piercing and rimmed with kohl, and big Indian earrings brush her shoulders; she's gorgeous. I try to smooth my post-flight hair and grin. They scoop me up, welcoming me, and take me straight to their car, a very shiny, very white BMW. Their driver, Ramu, helps put my luggage in the boot and I can't help but feel extremely bougie. If this is what life in modern Delhi is like, it's making my Manchester existence look pretty shabby by comparison.

Ruchi is so excited to see me and has a million and one questions.

'Gawd, Baby didi, you look great,' Ruchi purrs in her husky voice. She has a delicious Delhi accent.

She's being generous. I look dishevelled, like I've just come off a long flight, and I'm in desperate need of a wash and some ice cubes for my eye bags.

'No, YOU look great, Ruchi. My God, you grew into a stunner. She's a stunner uncle.'

'Yes, her mother's genetics, but same size feet as me. Huge flippers for feet.' He cracks a smile at Ruchi. Who smacks him on the shoulder and says, 'Oh, Papa.'

Then she turns to me.

'Welcome to India. I'm so excited you're here, we have so much to catch up on. OMG, you must be thirsty, here . . .'

She hands me a bottle of water.

'Rule number one, no tap water, only bottle or at home we have a filter.'

I'm grateful for the water, I've got that horrible taste in my mouth you only get after being on a long-haul flight.

'Gawd, you're here for an entire month, but you know I bet it won't be long enough. Time is never enough for India.'

Her enthusiasm is infectious and relaxes me. My cousin seems to have grown into a very cool young woman.

'How's Masiji and your grandmother?' asks Ruchi.

'You should have brought them too,' my uncle adds.

'Yes, they're well.' Being here in the buzz of the motherland, I have a pang of missing my connections to the place. Maybe we *should* have come together. No, this trip had to be mine. Next time we can come together; I have already decided I want to come back.

'How is living in Manchester? It's so cool you live there. I'm a huge fan of the music. The whole Madchester scene and Tony Wilson and Factory Records.'

'Yeah?' OK, she's waaaay cooler than she even looks. 'You'll have to come and stay with me when you visit.'

She smiles and I turn to look out of the window. I'm feeling hyper and strung out and overwhelmed and tired all at once, adrenaline pumping, eyes as wide as they can be.

I try and answer their questions as best I can, but they can see I'm pretty whacked after the long flight. Thankfully, they pick up that I need some time to decompress, and they leave me in peace to take it all in.

A Bollywood soundtrack is playing on the radio. I don't know any of the songs so it must be a pretty new one, but it's

103

the perfect backdrop to the traffic chaos outside the window. There are meant to be three lanes on the road we are on, but I count at least five streams of vehicles, and wonder why on earth you'd risk having such an expensive car with so much potential for it to be pranged.

My uncle laughs as he notices my hands have gripped the seat-belt in panic more than once. 'We are used to living like this, cheek by jowl. It's a chaotic dance, but don't worry, we all know our moves.' He pauses as I spot a young driver with no helmet on a moped dangerously weaving through the cars, then chuckles. 'But yes, it's a risk, if you don't have a driver as good as Ramu.'

I can't take my eyes off the scenes outside the window and wonder how many people is it legal to have on the back of a scooter? Families of four are clinging on, women in sarees that are dangling dangerously close to wheels, with babies, toddlers and dads the only ones in helmets. It's every car, taxi, auto scooter, bus, motorbike, bicycle, pedestrian, street hawker and beggar for themselves. A child knocks on the window of our car and snaps me back into focus. She can only just see in, she's that little, with huge brown eyes and a big grin that shows off her lack of front teeth. She's selling tacky pens, brandishing them at me and chattering, but I have no money to give her. I must remember to get cash out so I don't get caught short again.

Uncle tells me not to worry, to not make eye contact and she will go away. How can I not make eye contact? How can I ignore her? I'm riding in the back of a BMW and she's standing on the street, trying to sell enough for a scrap to eat.

'How do you do it?' I ask him, looking at Ruchi, whose sympathetic eyes meet mine and Maserji says, 'All Westerners ask the same question. We have to get on with it. Yes, it's appalling, and India has a long way to go to eradicate poverty, but we all rub together in the cities and you cannot help every single child. But here, take this.'

He hands me some small change from a pot stashed in one of the car's drink holders. I open the window and hand the little girl some change and she smiles broadly, running off through the traffic, back to the relative safety of the pavement. Ruchi passes me some hand sanitiser and I take it – there's going to be a lot to get used to.

We enter the upmarket enclave where my mother told me they live, with fancy three- and four-storey houses, some split into apartments built around lush, manicured gardens. Mature trees line the streets here, and there are people, probably servants, walking healthy, fluffy dogs – not like the scrawny street ones I've seen on my way here. A big gate opens for us and we drive into the car port underneath the wide, four-storey property. My family live in an apartment on the top floor, which we travel up to in an elevator after walking through a cool, marble lobby complete with concierge. Their home is a place of stunning luxury. An airy, open hall connects the rooms, including a huge living and dining space with a balcony, covered in plants and flowers. Ruchi explains that all the double bedrooms have an en suite, including the one I am staying in. I am so happy to be here, looked after by my family.

My mum's sister is waiting for us, and she elegantly floats off the settee to give me an enormous hug, before bursting into tears. I'm emotional and exhausted but still can't cry, even at this moment, this homecoming. I'm happy, not sad. But Masiji must be thinking about her sister, my mum.

Their maid, Savita, brings me a glass of home-made lemonade, nimbu pani. I take a long sip, savouring its refreshing taste, and I allow myself a moment to process where I am and everything I am feeling. My aunt looks me over, taking in my leggings, trainers, and the long vest I'm wearing under an over-sized denim jacket. Classic British millennial attire but to her, in her bright beautiful saree, bracelets glimmering at her wrists, a full face of makeup and a professional blow-dry, I probably look like I've fallen on hard times.

I take a deep breath.

'This place is stunning, Masi, thank you so much for welcoming me into your home. I can't believe I'm actually here.'

She waves my words off as if it's nothing, as if I'm as welcome and expected here as in my home. 'Plenty of space to have you to stay, Baby. You never come to visit your masi.'

'I'm here now,' I say, partly to her, and partly to myself. Ruchi smiles at me, shaking her head slightly as Aunty tuts at my hair and lack of manicure, and I feel so glad to be here, instantly made to feel comfortable; this is my family and I relax.

My younger cousin, Rohan, walks in, tapping away on his phone and not once making eye contact with me, saying, 'It's about 1.5 million pounds sterling, London prices. Very expensive in the big Indian cities now. Some of the most expensive real estate in the world. You couldn't even afford it with your British pounds.'

What an opener. *Neither can you, mate – you're still living at home with your parents at thirty.*

'Hello, Rohan, nice to see you looking so well.'

'You could have a great life living here, rather than your dirty country. Is Bradford still cold and wet?' He still hasn't looked at me.

Ruchi smiles at me and says gently to her brother, 'You know, India isn't easy either; this country is terrifying right now. It might be a nice lifestyle for some of us, but it's not like that for everyone.'

'Let's not talk politics, Ruchi,' Masi says, fussing with some flowers on the table and shrugging. 'You girls, these days, always trying to be political. When did politics ever get a woman anything?'

'And that's how they get away with it, Mother dearest,' her daughter laughs. I like Ruchi. She's outwardly the perfect, beautiful, well-spoken Indian daughter – elegantly dressed and poised – but she clearly has more of a spark to her, and a mind of her own.

'Well, I've told my big sister to come back to India now. What is there for her and your grandmother in the UK? Nothing but mess and rain in that country. No reason to be there since your

106

dad died. Such a tragedy. But then, we never know when our time will come. It's written in our destiny, and we can't escape that,' Masi responds.

Indian people are philosophical around death. It's part of life, they'll say; when death comes it comes, they'll add, we have only got the time we are allotted and no more.

I've heard every platitude and none of them, not one, makes you feel any better about losing your dad.

'It's our home,' I say weakly, because the tiredness from the past full day of travelling is really starting to set in. I can't help but think she has a point, though, why *is* my family there? Masi isn't listening, though, she's in full flow right now. She is definitely my mother's sister.

'You look just like your father, Baby. We all miss Paaji so much. How is my sister coping?'

'She's OK. Sends her love,' I say, not really wanting to engage in a deep and meaningful conversation the minute I've arrived.

This doesn't stop Masi from going straight for the jugular.

'And what about our Baby? Still no husband or house! Come on, Baby, get cracking! Is there even a boy on the horizon? Come on, Baby, we need some joy, something to celebrate!'

I try to laugh it off and say, 'Masi, I own my own home and have a very good job, I'm doing OK!' but even as I say it, I know I don't believe it myself. I've always thought of myself as a modern career woman, free of the constraints of the domestic servitude of my mum and grandmother, but all I've ended up with is serving the likes of Shiv instead. And my apartment is not even a fifth of the size of this one . . .

Ruchi stands up suddenly and exclaims, 'Mother! Baby Didi has only just got here. She is tired from her journey, and she doesn't need you to be telling her off – she has plenty of aunties in England to do that for her, don't you, Baby?' This time I laugh for real and feel gratitude towards my cousin.

'OK, OK, chalo. Go freshen up and then let's talk about Baby's trip here and what she is going to do.' There is kindness in Masi's eyes and I know she means well – she just can't help herself. 'Your big Indian adventure, hmm, Baby?'

My big Indian adventure.

The bedroom is tastefully decorated with beautiful, hand-printed cotton sheets, elegant dark wooden furniture, the light dim and soothing thanks to the blinds, and I breathe in intoxicating fragrances of lemongrass and jasmine that pervade the whole apartment, as well as wafting from my aunt and cousin. Jasmine and lemongrass . . . I grab a few toiletries and go into the bathroom, marvelling at the marble, feeling the coolness against my toes. I clean my teeth and have a hot shower, washing away the grime of the journey and soothing the weariness from my bones. When I'm done, I lie down on the bed and set my phone's alarm for a quick nap. My mind is buzzing with everything that lies ahead, questions such as should I confide in Ruchi about the letters? I've already got such a rapport with her and I'm also thinking about what I will do while I'm here and, most importantly, what foods I will eat. The cool calm of the room soothes me and I find myself drifting off.

When I come back into the living room an hour or so later, they have done that wonderfully Indian thing of inviting more people round; a casual afternoon spiralling into a catered event with alarming efficiency. The first person I notice is a man about my age, tall, dressed entirely in black (in Delhi!) and attractive, so naturally I am caught off guard by his presence. And it *is* a presence. There's a confidence that oozes from him, and though he's not even opened his mouth yet, he just seems utterly assured of both his place in their home and the world at large. He is lounging on their sofa with his arms stretched out across the back. I glance at his shoes: flip-flops.

'Baby! Meet Sid, our neighbour. Yes, he has come in his bathroom slippers, and we are glad he feels so comfortable in our home, almost as if it is his own.' Masiji obviously clocked me staring at this man's toes.

Ruchi chips in, 'Sid has a Mumbai vibe, relaxed and like he is permanently on holiday. He is unusual for a Delhi boy.' She turns to Sid and explains, 'This is my British cousin sister, Baby. And Baby, this is Sid.'

I wince at her calling me Baby, which puts me on the back-foot. I prefer being introduced as Simran when I meet new people. New, attractive people. But the lines are blurrier here. Which version of myself am I? Can I be all of them at once? When I'm nervous like this, I tend to spout things from my mouth without thinking, so that's how I end up letting the first thing I say to this man be: 'Hello, Sid. Didn't realise there was a need to anglicise names here, too.'

He raises his eyebrows and smiles. 'It's much easier than having the English accent butcher my name.' He puts his hand out and says, 'But by all means, Siddharth, if you prefer.' Touché, Siddharth.

'Named after Buddha himself, impressive.'

'Oh, you know a bit of Indian history? Did you read a guide-book on the plane?'

The rest of the family laughs and I feel my face flush. I want to yell 'My family was born here too! I belong just like you do!' or maybe ask him if he knows any British history, before quickly realising that it would likely be a faux pas to bring up colonialism before dinner.

What is it with this guy? He seems genuinely surprised that I might know anything about India, and I detect an air of arrogance. My guard is up now, and I'm annoyed I even let myself notice he was good-looking when he is so obviously pig-headed. I am glad, at least, that I showered and changed before going into this unexpected battle. I might be a foot shorter than him but I smell good and can hold my own in an argument.

'Believe it or not, we are taught things about India in the West, you know.'

'Funny, because when I came to study at University College London, I only came across great ignorance about "the East",' he rejoins, easily and with a laugh in his voice, as if he's not taking this conversation very seriously.

'Well, *you* came all the way to London to study, so we must be doing something right over there.'

Why am I getting defensive about Britain? That is not my usual vibe. British people love nothing better than moaning about Britain – but maybe we only like it when the people who actually have to suffer through living there do it.

Ruchi quickly interjects, sensing that the conversation is about to go off-piste. 'I told Sid to swing by to meet you because I feel that you two will have plenty in common. Sid's even lived in London!'

'Well, there's a lot more to the UK than London, actually,' I find myself muttering, as if living in London isn't one of my biggest dreams. My aunt and some of the other family members begin a loud reminiscence of the family's trip to the city and how Buckingham Palace was very dirty and shabby really. I think she might be a bit of a snob.

Sid steers the conversation away from the pros and cons of London and turns to me. 'So, why the big adventure out here, then?' His simple and natural question catches me off guard. What do I say when I don't even really know what the plan is myself?

'Well, it's been a long time since I visited h—' I stop myself before saying 'home'. 'Since visiting here, I mean. So, I'm going to see India as an adult, and find out a little more about my roots.' There, nice and vague, so hopefully no more questions.

'Life-changing stuff, then? A little bit *Eat Pray Love*, a little bit *Who Do You Think You Are?*'

What is with this guy? Five minutes of conversation and already I want to punch him in what looks like a very toned abdomen. But it would not be a good start, or good guest behaviour, to offend my family's friend as soon as I arrive by being violent but how am I supposed to just let this guy needle at me? It's almost as though I took a sabbatical and impulsively booked a flight without thinking it through properly.

'And maybe I'll do some sightseeing while I'm here too.'

He can't have a problem with that, can he?

'Ah, here to do the usual tourist trail. Act like a tourist, keep your nose in the air like the other British Indians who come to visit the "homeland", thinking their ways are better.'

I stand up and pause for just a moment, in shock at his rudeness. 'Wow! Tell me what you really think, why don't you? It's almost like I didn't have to chaperone cousin Ruchi here around Madame Tussauds and the Tower of London when she visited – Indian people are clearly above such things. Oh, wait!'

Ruchi looks a little sheepish as she explains. 'Baby, Sid is just teasing you. It's because so many NRIs think they know where they are because they've watched a few Bollywood movies. They come and buy a saree or two, stay in their five-star hotels, see the Taj Mahal, hate-visit relatives they can't understand and head home. But we know you won't be like that.'

'Well, so what if I am? And why shouldn't they behave like that? They are tourists, it's not their home,' I say to Ruchi softly, my back still up a little. I feel as if I'm deflating before them. I didn't expect this kind of 'welcome' – I thought they'd understand.

'They have zero curiosity to discover it or to understand the country, and they think they are so superior, too superior to live here, but they all have an opinion on the politics,' Sid says.

I shrug. This man does not know me, does not know about my secrets, my family's history. He will never know me because, quite frankly, he is an arse. A smug, entitled, holier-than-thou arse. I bet he was just as cringe and cliché a tourist in London as these supposed NRI visitors are in Delhi. I comfort myself by picturing Sid eating in the Hard Rock Café and queuing for the London Eye.

Sid smiles. 'Do you have a plan for your travels? Someone who will help you get around, show you the ropes?'

Help? Why would I need help? 'I've travelled plenty of the world on my own and I'm sure I can tackle India just fine, thank you very much for your concern.' My smile is as fake as the interest in his voice.

'No help, I see. And you are travelling alone?'

'Why wouldn't I be travelling alone? I'm pretty good at find-ing my way. Women in the West often do things without the chaperone, or the permission, of a man.'

'OK, then.' I can see he is slightly alarmed at my reaction, but still has that annoying, friendly smile on his face. He's a ter-rible example of a modern Indian man, outwardly modern but inwardly still backwards and traditional.

Ruchi chips in. 'Didi, you've not been to India in so long, or experienced the real, modern country. It's not the India you see on your TV shows and movies. Come, Sid, let's take Didi out! We'll go tomorrow, do it properly.'

'I'm not sure she could handle it. She might be shocked. These British-Indians have led very sheltered lives, you know.' His eyes, which are staring right at me, are full of mischief, shining annoyingly bright in the afternoon sun.

'We invented drinking culture in the West,' I reply sniffily to his back. It only makes him laugh out loud, right in my face.

'You really love this West of yours.'

He's staying for dinner, of course he is.

Savita lays the table. We have a simple meal of kidney bean curry, rice, salad and keema with chapatti. Dad was right, everything does taste better here.

We all get stuck into dinner – thank God there's no great formality to eating in India. I'm self-conscious enough in front of Sid, without having to eat in front of him. Eating with your hands is a great leveller. Everyone eats Indian food in the same way. Unless you eat with your mouth open – those guys can be banished. The atmosphere is relaxed.

As we eat, I notice Ruchi and Sid's friendly ease with one another. I wonder if they're dating, though I'd be disappointed in Ruchi if so – she can do so much better than this egocentric prat.

I look away from them and turn to Honey Masi.

'So, tell me about Mum. All the things she wouldn't want you to tell me!' I laugh, and she laughs too.

She indulges me and tells me stuff I had no idea about, like how she was great at athletics, and I try and imagine Mum in a sports kit. She was a very bossy and quite strict (no surprises there!) and she was madly in love with Amitabh Bachchan's voice, she used to listen to the soundtracks to his films *Kabhi Kabhie* and *Silsila* on repeat. Well, she kept her Bollywood crush hidden from all of us.

'I must say, though, Baby, it's a nice life here . . . Funny thing is, I was desperate to go abroad. I always thought everyone who was living in Britain, or Canada, or the US must be having such a good time. Those places were so advanced, so glamorous. And now I think of my sister and the struggles you all have been through, your poor father, and how bright she is and was, and all she could have been. You know, your mother wanted to be a doctor? And instead, she is gone, to Yorkshire, and all alone without her family and the country falling apart.'

I had no idea Mum wanted to stay in India to study. It makes me sad, thinking about her having to leave behind her family, the ambitions, the life she wanted, her secret Bollywood crush, and move to another country to marry a man she'd never met. *Married at First Sight* would just be called *Marriage in India*.

There's so much about my family I have no clue about. Why haven't I asked them?

I feel Mum shows so little interest in who I am and what I really might want for my life, but then I know so little about her, what she was like as a girl.

Masi has more.

'Now I'm so glad I stayed in India. Just look at you, caught between worlds, Baby! And all that racism, in your own country! Those gore will never accept you. Neither here nor there, I think. You know nothing of your roots. Where is your belonging place? Your brown skin makes you an outsider in their land. Second-class citizen, hmm? I feel so sorry for children like you.'

'You don't need to feel sorry for me, Masi, I'm pretty grounded and Britain is my home. No identity issues here,' I say out loud. A complete lie but too complicated to get into here. Masi and

113

Sid have cornered me in some kind of pincer manoeuvre: let's put down the British-Indian, let's make her even more unsure about who she is. Not quite what I was expecting on day one. At least I have Ruchi on my side.

'So, why are you really here, Baby?'

I like Sid saying my name. What is wrong with me? I do not like this man.

'Just a break.'

'No, I don't buy it. There's a reason, a mission. Baby is on a quest,' he laughs.

The way he stares at me with that annoying twinkle in his eye when he says this, it's as if he's looking into my soul.

Why can't he just leave it?

I feel that I need to defend myself. They are making me sound like I'm a lost soul, wandering aimlessly through life, which I absolutely did feel. But I do have a mission now. And maybe it's because I'm a little wound up, my mouth opens to speak, and I give away more than I intended to.

'OK, you're right.'

Everyone goes quiet suddenly and leans in to hear what I have to say.

'I'm here to find out about my family; well, my grandfather, really. I know so little about him, about them all.'

'Now it gets interesting. Not your average tourist.'

'He was in the Army, your grandfather. He fought in Burma, I think.' Masi gives me this bit of information about my grandad.

'Precisely my point, Mas. I know snippets of information but don't have the entire story, and if I don't find out, as his only granddaughter, then his story will disappear. Dad was an only child and it's only me who is his family. I want to know what happened. I'm here to try and understand more about my relationship to India.'

'But Baby, you might not like what you find,' says Masi.

Sid is listening attentively.

'It's a dark period of history, what happened to us at that time. What happened to India in 1947. It's best to be left in

114

the past. Your generation is so fixated on history and discovery. We didn't have the time or the luxury to go on these "journeys of discovery", we just had to get on and discover through living life. The past is the past, Baby. Just see the sights on this trip – Taj Mahal, old Delhi, eat food, buy nice sarees, come to my beauty parlour, have massage, get nails done, get your bushy, bushy eyebrows threaded . . .' Masi continues, staring at my brows.

It's obvious she doesn't quite get why I'd want to know my history. Her comments make me explain my thoughts.

'Even more reason to try and understand it. Precisely because no one ever talks about it. No one discusses Partition or colonialism, not in the UK, anyway. Sure, there are documentaries when there are anniversaries, but people don't know about the murky British history; we're not taught about it in school and neither do we discuss it at home. So, I'm ignorant. When you're ignorant about what happened to you in the past or what happened to your people, your history, how will you ever truly know who you are and why you are?'

Wow, where did *that* come from? 'Know who you are and why you are?' It's as though now I'm in India, the thoughts and reasons for being here are becoming clearer. In order to know my history, I need to know what happened in India. I know so little.

Sid is nodding and smiling. He's really paying attention. I think I might have impressed him. Which makes me relax. Eugh! Why is does his approval feel so important? I shouldn't care what this bloke thinks, I need to get a grip.

'Sid loves history,' says Ruchi.

'It's a passion,' he says.

'You young ones are too fixated on the past. You need to look forwards,' says Masi but no one responds.

'So, what's your plan?' Sid asks.

'I'm going to hatch one over the next couple of days but probably get a train to Amritsar, see where my grandfather's house was, where my father was born, see the Golden Temple.'

He's still nodding and adds, 'There's a museum in Amritsar dedicated to Partition. I've not been there, have always wanted to visit, you should definitely go there too.'

Of course, he'd have a suggestion.

'Baby, you shouldn't go alone. Especially as you don't know India,' says Masi.

'I'll be fine,' I say, though the more they say I won't be, the more nervous it's making me.

'I'd come with you if I had the time off,' says Ruchi. 'Sid, didn't you need to go to Punjab anyway?'

'Yeah, I wanted to do a trip, was planning on going next week but maybe I could bring it forward.'

'Oh, what a good idea,' says Masi.

'You'd be the perfect tour guide,' says Ruchi.

Is anyone going to consult me on any of these plans? Indians love to organise other people's lives, don't they?

'No, no, no! I couldn't possibly expect that of you, Sid, and we've only just met. It's too much.'

I'd rather be trapped in a lift with the four aunties of the apocalypse for a week than go away with this guy.

Later that night when I am in my room, with the letters laid out next to me on the bed, I get a message from Mum:

Masi says you are on a history tour? You could have asked me questions.

News travels fast between these sisters.

I ping back. I might as well go to Amritsar and learn something.

OK. Golden temple is lovely. Must visit. And get eyebrows done. An orangutan emoji.

I'm mindlessly flicking through the millions of TV channels that all seem to be showing the same type of TV melodrama, all with dramatic music and intense acting. But I'm not really watching, my mind is whizzing. I'm too busy going over the last few hours, beating myself up, thinking about all the lines I should have come back to Sid with. But he caught me off guard. I'm wondering if I made a good impression and then getting annoyed with myself for wanting any kind of approval. I'm also worrying about my quest and I start considering the very generous option of having someone drive me all the way to Amritsar. I'm used to Indian generosity, so it doesn't feel strange that my cousin's mate, someone I've only just met, has offered to do this. Maybe realistically it would be good to go with someone who might know a few things, like fluency in speaking the language for starters. But on the downside, I'd have to spend time with Sid.

My phone pings: it's a message from Pinks.

How's it going? Is it everything you hoped?
Yes and no. It's weird.
It'll take time to get used to it all. It's a huge change and a huge adventure. You got this, Baby.

I sigh and reply with the fist bump emoji. I have never felt less like 'I got this'.

I feel so alone, I don't know how to explain what I need, and I'm afraid Masi might be right that I can't do this on my own. I don't know the first place to start figuring all this out and I'm going to fail Ranjit and Naseeb – and myself. Why did I think I'd be able to do this? I feel completely out of my depth. Everyone is just so confident here and they probably quite rightly have no confidence in me and my quest. I'm feeling small and far away from home. I'm feeling a little scared and unsure about what I've done. What was I thinking? India is vast and I feel like an alien here.

A tear trickles down my cheek and blotches one of the precious letters. I dab at it and there's a soft knock at the door.

It's Ruchi. In an elegant pair of floral block-print shorts pyjamas, hair piled up and her face clean and clearly covered in some kind of oil. She closes the door and comes to the bed, saying, 'I'm glad you're still up, I wanted to talk to you.'

'I actually wanted to talk to you too,' I say and I show Ruchi the letters. 'These are the real reason I'm here. I've stolen them out of Dadima's peti. And the minute I found them my life shifted gear or changed direction or spun out – everything changed.

'They are from a women called Naseeb to my grandad Ranjit. Seemingly she was his wife – his first wife. My Punjabi is rusty so it's taking me ages to read them. Don't suppose you did Punjabi in school?'

She's studying the letters.

'I only studied English and Hindi in school, but my granny made me take Punjabi as an extra subject,' Ruchi says.

'Punjabi grannies.'

We both chuckle.

She takes the letters and begins to read them. She's absorbed.

'These are incredible. What you've found is remarkable.'

'I know. And they've been kept hidden.' I shake my head in disbelief.

'That's not so unusual. They are a generation of secrets. I can't quite believe I'm reading these. She's talking about the anticipation of getting married and moving to a new village. Oh wow, she really must have caused a stir, as this wasn't an arranged marriage. Your grandfather Ranjit saw her and wanted to marry her.'

Fascinated, Ruchi helps me unravel more of Naseeb's story.

'Can you imagine? A scandal just because he fancied her and proposed. A scandal because she was obviously a hottie.

'And it's adorable that she says she loves him – they hardly know each other,' I say.

'Their standards were very different, Baby. Maybe it was a less cynical age.'

'I suppose it was a love story compared to all the other marriages at the time – more than our mothers, who had to have arranged marriages,' I say, realising just how radical and shocking it must have been.

'This Naseeb seems quite open-minded, way ahead of her time. Her best friend Anjuman was from a Muslim family. Not unusual as Punjab was a state made up of Muslims, Hindus and Sikhs, so different religions, yes, but all culturally identical.'

I'm nodding and then ask, 'And she talks about a girl called Billi, with green eyes?'

She reads on.

'Oh yes, Billi means cat. And she was from the dalit caste. The lowest caste. It's disgusting how they were treated. People thought they contaminated everything they touched. Humans can be so short-sighted and cruel. So, Naseeb was pretty radical as well as educated and obviously kind.'

'Thanks, Ruchi,' I say.

Ruchi puts down the letters.

'It's so nice to have you here, Baby Didi.'

I like my cousin's company. Being in this calm, clean, scented, perfectly lit room with my thoughtful cousin, who seems to have a genuine interest in what I'm doing, helps me relax. It's as if a weight has lifted off my shoulders, sharing the letters with someone else.

Ruchi seems a lot more put together than me, a lot less uptight. I've watched her deftly and kindly deal with her mum, who has the same ability to push buttons as mine, but Ruchi is a smooth operator, managing not to lose her temper or get into an altercation every time. How does she do it?

'Mum only has her own field of reference and I just get on with my life without needing anyone's approval,' Ruchi shares.

'I could do with a dose of that confidence,' I respond, impressed.

'You are here, aren't you? That's confidence. I have huge admiration for what you are doing.'

If it's a confidence booster, it's working.

'You know, Baby, Sid is actually a really great guy. He's one of my closest friends. He can act like an idiot too but he's pretty decent. He was probably nervous around you. He's serious about taking you to Punjab.'

He was nervous? I like this thought. Him taking me to Punjab would make things easier.

'Were you two ever a thing? Are you?' I ask.

'OMG, no!' She laughs at the thought. 'No, never. Not only have Sid and I never been a thing, but boys also aren't really my thing.' She says this in a way that feels casual but looks at me briefly then away, almost as if to test the water. How easy is it to be gay in India?, I wonder.

'Does your mum know?' I ask, also casually.

'Don't be silly! You've met her.'

We both laugh. We talk about our mothers; how different their life choices were to ours. How by the time they were our ages, they had both had children. We wonder at how much they really wanted those lives or were just going through the motions of what was expected of them. If somewhere, deep inside, they were desperate for something else.

'Apparently my mum was,' I say. 'I never knew she wanted to stay in India and study. My dad didn't want to get married either, apparently, so they both had their dreams crushed. They had to do what was expected of them, and here we are, living life as we choose – to a degree. It does make me wonder why Mum puts so much pressure on me to be so dutiful all the time. God, if I had a daughter, I'd be training her up to be a complete rebel, preparing her to burn down the system, not uphold the bloody thing.'

'Yep, it's just the constant pressure to get married – and who do these marriages serve anyway?' adds Ruchi.

'A single woman,' I begin. 'No, a single fertile single woman must not be free to roam alone because anything could happen and ultimately it comes back to what Naseeb was told: that you bring great shame on your family. The only ones who need to feel shame are the control freaks and killjoys controlling women. That lot need to get lives,' I say, frustration and determination blooming inside me.

'Because we are powerful.' She has a twinkle in her eye. 'They fear us. The sexually available, independent, free-thinking, older woman. We are a huge threat to society because of the power we hold. Why should any of us feel shame around sexuality? You know, before we were colonised, we were a sexually liberal

120

country . . . Well, we are goddesses. *You* are a goddess, Baby Didi. Embrace what you are here to do.'

Wow! I'm not sure I know what my power is, but I nod along with Ruchi. I'm in awe of her confidence. I'm not sure that following my gut is really the wisest way of living, but I'm going to take a chance. And Ruchi has an idea of where I should start, as she turns to say one last thing before leaving my room for the night.

'Baby, tomorrow we are going out, out.'

Chapter Seven

The cab drops me and Ruchi off in an area called Haus Khas, once a medieval historic enclave, now full of bars, restaurants, boutiques and young Indians out having a good time. I shouldn't be amazed, but I am. *This* India is a wonderful surprise to my naïve, and, yes, maybe even patronising, eyes. The India I visited in the eighties is nowhere to be seen. Consumerism, a huge middle class, an international outlook and a young, independent generation with money in their pockets – and hormones raging – needs, like young people all over the world, somewhere to go out and have a good time.

There are families out for dinner, couples on dates, groups of mates and an eye-watering amount of flesh on show. I realise, as we walk towards the bar, that my own upbringing has kept me sheltered and prudish. It's warm here and I didn't even think to pack a pair of shorts. I've been conditioned to constantly be aware of what I'm wearing and where I'm wearing it. Back home, if I'm in any family environment, I just know to dress modestly, so I presumed if I was coming to the epicentre of Indians, the same rule would apply. Apparently not, not here anyway. From what I can judge from walking around, the fewer clothes you wear places you higher up in the social pecking order. Only the rich can afford to get away socially with shorts in public and only the rich can get into most of these bars and restaurants.

Ruchi sparks up a cigarette as we walk, then offers me one, which I decline. The street is bustling and alive in a way I've never experienced before. People shout, sing, link arms, bump into those next to them and only laugh together. It's as though the air is drunk and trying to make everyone fall in love. This is going to be a whole new vibe. Like I'm going to not only fit in but have a good time doing it. This is one of the coolest places I've ever been and, what's more, I'm surrounded by Indians. *I'm not the only brown face in the room.* For the first time in my life, I'm not the odd one out. Something inside me feels strangely whole, something I've never felt before. I can breathe easy. I don't have to worry about being singled out, about not being found attractive – or the opposite, some exotic catch of the day for men with a 'fetish'. I delight in the utterly unfamiliar but welcome feeling of just being one of the crowd.

I share this thought with Ruchi.

'The first time in my life I'm going to blend in.'

She laughs and exhales the cigarette smoke.

'You stick out so much. You might look Indian but it's obvious you're not an Indian, Indian.'

'What do you mean?'

'It's everything about you. Your fairer skin—'

'You're fairer than me,' I say to her.

'OK, then. It's the way you dress, your mannerisms, the way you're looking around like you've never seen anything like this before, and how you keep taking pictures of everything on your phone.' I swiftly put my phone in my pocket. 'It's your look of amazement and confusion. Yep, it's obvious you're not one of us. You NRIs are a different breed.'

'I get it,' I say. 'But I still feel as though I blend in here in a way I never can or will, back home in England. I feel like I belong – no matter how much I might stick out like a sore thumb.'

'A sore thumb?' Ruchi is confused.

So much for blending in.

We walk into the bar where we are meeting Sid and a few of his friends, and head straight to get a drink. There are a lot of very attractive people in this place. Why am I surprised, again? It physically pains me to say it, but maybe Annoying Sid is right, maybe we do come with some kind of internal prejudice when we visit, because I can, hand on heart, say that I did not expect this. This vibrancy, this kind of life, this kind of *living*. Right there and then I decide I have to decolonise my own brain. I've obviously bought into some kind of narrative about India and Indians and yep, there's clearly some deep self-loathing going on here too. I don't like it, it doesn't serve me, and I want to embrace this feeling, change my perspective and liberate myself.

I shake off those feelings as best I can as we head to the rooftop, which overlooks some thirteenth-century ruins bordering a lake. It's lit up and breathtaking. Sid is with three friends, two men and a woman. They are all very good-looking and well-dressed, and I'm suddenly glad of Ruchi's makeup tips and the fact I brought some decent clothes with me. They have an ease and a confidence in themselves, with each other, in this space, which they do not apologise for taking up. The woman is currently regaling them with a story and I can see them all laughing and drinking as she is waving her hands, gesticulating wildly alongside her punchlines. I look at her and feel jealousy creep into my soul. I would like to feel like that, please. I would like to be like others when I'm in a bar back home, to not always be dreading that inevitable question: 'Where're you from, then? I mean, *really* from?'

It seems like everyone in the place has a bloody amazing-looking margarita in their hand, and I spy chicken tikka and masala chips ready to be snapped up. A great rooftop bar with a fantastic view *and* amazing food? This is perfect. I take a sip of my own margarita and get a strong hit of tequila and zingy lime and spice. Just what I need.

Ruchi spots me eyeing the chicken. 'We are a nation of foodies, so of course there is food everywhere. We even have it in nightclubs.'

She grabs my hand as I blurt out, 'You have clubs?' bringing me right into the attention of Sid.

'We even have flushing toilets,' he says dryly.

Goddammit, of course they have clubs. I need to play it cooler. Sid's friends must think I'm a moron from some backwater.

'Yes, Sid,' pipes up the girl, and I wince, but she continues, 'but don't forget that more people have access to a mobile phone

124

than a flushing toilet in this country.' She turns to smile at me, holds out her hand, and says, 'It's lovely to meet you, Baby. Sid has told us all about you. I'm Shazia, sit next to me and tell me everything.'

Dear Lord, he's told them about me? What's he said? It can't be all bad if Shazia's being so welcoming, but I glance at him accusatorily anyway and take another gulp of my drink as I sit down.

Drinks and conversation are flowing, and I stick by the side of Ruchi and Shazia all night, as we discuss what it means to be an Indian woman today. There is a lot of talk about relationships, about young people who still end up marrying partners their parents approve of. How teenagers are becoming more free, more open, but once women get married, no matter how educated, independent or high-flying, they are still expected to bow to the role of wife and mother after marriage. The class and caste divide, the wealth divide, the religious divide. There's a lot of divides, it seems.

Shazia happens to mention Sid's ex-girlfriend, and I look over. He catches my eye and holds my gaze as he says to the others, 'Baby thinks she can explore India on her own.'

'And she can,' pipes up Shazia. Beautiful Shazia, I could kiss her for standing up for me, but she continues somewhat bitterly, 'She'll have an easier time travelling round my country than I do.'

I look at her quizzically.

'Being a woman – and a Muslim – in India these days really puts you in a vulnerable category,' she says, leaning into me.

'Oh, come on, let's not start this one up again. We spent at least seven hours discussing feminism last week.'

'Is there anything more important?' Shazia asks, displaying her gorgeous smile. She turns to me and says, 'You seem like someone who can look after themselves. I mean, the reality is that there's not a country in the world where a woman can truly travel alone in and feel safe. Just stay alert and you'll be fine. You *can* speak the language, right?'

Now I feel even more terrified about the prospect of travelling alone. I can understand Punjabi, but I've never really used it. I've always felt too embarrassed to say anything in case someone heard me. Now, I'm embarrassed that I don't as I shake my head.

'It's OK, English is the unofficial national language of India, so you'll be fine. Plus, so many Indians refuse to speak Hindi themselves. So, what are you here to explore?' she asks.

The margaritas have obviously started to get to me, because before I can hold my tongue and keep my secrets to myself, I blurt out, 'I'm here on a secret quest to find the answer to a missing family secret.'

And then put my finger on my lips.

Ruchi joins in. 'You should see these amazing letters Baby has found; she's uncovered a whole other life her grandfather had before he moved to England. And the letters are so romantic!'

Well, it's out there now and so I continue.

'You are now all in my elite secret knowers club.'

Which at this rate is everyone apart from Dadima and Mum.

'I don't really know where to start,' I admit. 'I assume that something happened to my grandfather's wife – perhaps she died – but I don't know how or when or why or if her children survived. I don't know *anything*, and without her dying, he wouldn't have married my dadima and . . . well . . . I wouldn't exist,' I tail off, feeling the tequila has articulated rather more than I would have been happy to share.

Shazia looks at me and says matter-of-factly, 'Sid would be your perfect companion, you know – he's such a history nerd. If anyone would know how to track more information down, it would be him. But I hope you're prepared, Baby; this country has a brutal history, thanks in no small part to your country. I want you to discover your truth, it's so important, but remember to try and find within it a way to heal.'

I'm left feeling a sense of unease at the way she emphasised 'your country'. Britain was definitely not 'my country' when it was busy colonising the world. I'm there as a result of colonialism, but what they did to India, they did to my people. It's my history, it impacted my family.

'Trust me, you need Sid. The history buff.' She laughs.

I grimace. 'History bore, you mean.'

Ruchi and Shazia burst into laughter, and I feel exceptionally pleased with myself. I grab another drink as the group breaks up a little, expanding and drawing in others, as the music gets softer. I see Sid making a beeline for me and put my hand up. 'I don't need anyone to guide me,' I say, and put a tandoori chicken lollipop in my mouth and look around for a napkin to stop me wiping my hands on my dress. India Me is not as sloppy as Manchester Me. Not yet anyway.

Sid shakes his head, smiles, and nods. In the quiet moments that follow, as he hands me a paper napkin and in doing so, briefly glances at my legs, I decide to ask him all about *his* life. Give him a taste of his own medicine.

'So, you were in London studying then?' I say, somewhat aggressively crossing one leg over the other and feeling entirely pleased with myself for no real reason.

He looks as though I've startled him out of a reverie. 'Yeah, for a few years.'

'Let me guess: medicine? No, wait! Economics?' He seems like the kind of guy who likes numbers more than people.

'Now who's stereotyping? No, I studied Fine Art.'

I am genuinely, for the first time in my life, stumped by a man. An *Indian* man who studied Fine Art is a first for me.

'My parents, they fully expected me to move abroad, maybe stay in London or head to the States after, but I came back home, and managed to set up my own design agency.'

I decide to ignore how impressive it is that Sid owns his own business, and instead ask, 'What made you come back?'

'What can't I do here that you can do elsewhere? It's one of the most exciting and dynamic countries on Earth, frustrating as hell, yes, but nothing beats the street food in India.'

It all comes out in a rush, and he continues, a little more considered.

127

'India has everything for me. I've studied in the best global institutions, and I'm privileged to be able to live a very good life here.' He looks out at the Delhi skyline. 'And did I mention the street food?' He nods at the lollipop I've just finished decimating in my hand, and I nod in agreement.

'What made you move to Manchester?' he asks.

'The men and the money.' We both laugh. OK, now I like making him laugh.

His smile is outstanding because of the beautiful laughter lines around his eyes, and my God, his eyelashes! Thick, dark and long, I'd usually say they were wasted on a man, but I can't stop looking at them on him. I find myself studying the beautiful face of this annoying man as Ruchi makes sure my hand is never empty, keeping up a regular supply of margaritas and a chicken lollipop or crisp every now and again.

He asks me questions about my life and I try and answer them with the same casual, confident air. I want to paint my life as great, as successful and fulfilling as his, and so I start to get a bit creative with some of the details.

'Oh, yeah, my career is going really well. I work in advertising too!' Am I being too loud? Who knows? 'Yeah, yeah. Leading on a new account at the moment, project managing, you know, all that jazz. Constantly thinking about moving up, but really love being with the team, you know, on the ground. I find what I do really fulfilling. And Manchester is thriving, it's such a creative place to live and work, so much cooler than somewhere like London.'

I say all of this looking out towards the water, facing away from him, so he can't see the rather dead look in my eyes. I can't turn back to face him, and so we stand alone in silence for a few minutes until Ruchi says it's time to head home.

Fabricating the perfect life for myself has really worn me out, and I gladly bundle into the car with everyone else. Squished next to Ruchi, I lean on her as we leave the outskirts and head back towards the city.

I fall asleep in the cab and don't wake until we're back near home. My head is spinning. I shift myself closer to the open window for some fresh air, and notice we've already dropped off Sid's friends, and he's in the back with me, Ruchi giving directions in the front.

Oh God, I think I'm going to be sick! I breathe in deeply and notice a bottle of water appearing in front of my face. *Sid.* Helpful Sid, not Annoying Sid anymore.

His voice is a low, deep whisper as he says, 'Don't worry, happens to the best of us. But seems like us Easterners can drink you under the table, eh, Baby?' I get immediate chills at him saying my name, his mouth pressed close to my ear, but he needs to give the East v West thing a rest. I don't laugh, I'm tired and woozy.

'Thank you for the water,' is all I manage to say.

Sid looks a little put out, and rightly knows he's pushed just a little too far tonight. I'm tired and already hungover, and don't want to be reminded again of how I don't fit in here, either. I want to be able to call my dad. I want to *want* to call my mum.

'Baby, I . . . I'm sorry if I upset you.'

I blink away the one small tear that has surprisingly appeared on my lower lashes and turn towards him with a smile. 'You didn't, I'm just tired, and emotional. I didn't know if I would miss home, but I definitely didn't think I would bring so much of my . . .'

My what? My baggage? My mess of a life?

'My grief. For my dad.' It hits me in that moment. 'He would have loved this, he would have loved to have come with me. We lost him two years ago and I miss him. Very much. He would have been the best chaperone for little old British softy me.' I smile to show I'm teasing. 'He would have been the greatest at showing me around, at explaining our history. He would have known where we came from and helped me get where I'm going. I wasted so much time and now I can never ask him what I really want to ask: about his family, about our experiences here, in India.'

I realise I've been monologuing at him while Ruchi snores gently in the front. She's nodded off, but Sid is looking right at me, right into my eyes, and puts his hand on mine.

'I'm so sorry about your father, Baby. I am sure he would have been proud of you for coming all this way. I didn't mention it earlier, but I think you are very brave.' He notices his hand has been on mine for slightly longer than is appropriate, so lifts it off as he continues, 'And I insist on helping you off on your journey, in his spirit.'

I don't know how it happens, and I suspect tequila has had a significant part to play, but I agree to let Sid, Annoying Sid, take me to Punjab the day after next, to accompany me on the start of my trip.

'But what about work?'

'I work for myself.'

So that's that, then. He will drive me where I need to go. For once, and this definitely is the fault of the tequila, I don't put up a fight. It would be nice, I agree in my head, to have someone help me a little bit. Support me. And it's not like I need his help, or I'm asking for it. He offered! I smile as I begin to drift off. Oh yes, I have Annoying, Helpful Sid wrapped around my finger.

It's only when I wake as we arrive at the house in the early hours of the morning, head pounding, that agreeing to travel with a man I've only just met seems like yet another impulsive decision made without thought for the realities of the situation. I'm in a country I don't know, about to embark on a deeply personal journey to uncover my family's secret, with a complete stranger. *What have I done?*

Chapter Eight

The next morning I pick up my phone as soon as I wake up and start recording a voice note to Pinky, 'Yo, Pinks. Mate.' I clear my throat as it's dropped an octave.

'Sorry. Why didn't you tell me India was so cool? I'm the odd one out here. My cousin Ruchi is intimidatingly together and grew into a Megababe! I'll send you a pic, she's HOT and gay and she just knows who she is. My tiny backwards British mind is already blown. I've been on a night out and had a great time. Although now I wish I'd drunk a bit more water. Anyhoo, there's a lad, mate of Ruchi's . . . don't get excited, he's a total arrogant pain in the arse but I'm not gonna lie, mate, he is FIT AS. And he's driving me to Punjab. I know this sounds mad, but it made sense last night. Anyway, gotta go, think my masi has arranged for an astrologer to come round. I'm still terrified in my gut but I'm having a good time and I've already seen so much that's opened my eyes. I can smell something delicious being cooked in the kitchen. Might come back a little rounder than when I left. Squeeze the kids for me. Hope Anoop has sorted out his act. Bloody love you.'

Call ended, I take a quick hot shower and try the intense cold water blast trick to wake me up. I last ten seconds but it works. Feeling more human, I head out to find the food.

Masiji and Ruchi are delighted when they hear I've decided to take the offer of a lift.

'Oh, what a relief, sachi Baby! I would not have been able to sleep knowing that you were alone in Punjab, at least now I have no worries.' Masiji places a masala omelette in front of me, the sight of which my slightly shrivelled, hungover brain is very grateful for.

Having a companion is not quite what I had in mind when I set off on this trip. It's meant to be my adventure, my moment of introspection and discovery. Finding myself, alone. What have those beautiful white women who travel and discover India for themselves been doing then? They all seem to be in control, floating around, discovering their spirituality. Yet here I am, an Indian woman with relatives who are terrified if I step foot out of the front door without a chaperone. What? Am I less capable than Julia Roberts? Apparently so, as I am heading off on my secret voyage of discovery and personal growth with a random. But not before I've consulted an astrologer.

'Oh, he's here! Baby, meet Pandit Om Prakashji.'

I'm confronted by a boss-eyed man in a crisp white shirt, black trousers, an eighties leather briefcase, wearing a ring with a different stone on every finger. A couple of gold medallions around his neck are visible, as he's kept one too many buttons undone on his shirt, enough to see his hairy black and grey chest wires. *Who on earth is this character?* He nods in my general direction, and I have to check behind to make sure it's not someone else he's looking at. It transpires that Masiji has been on the phone to Mum, and they thought it best to get my Vedic astrology birth chart done before I go off to discover who I am.

My aunt finds the journey I'm about to undertake both funny and self-indulgent. She doesn't really get what I'm up to or why I'm doing it. She thinks there are more important things a woman of my age should be thinking about, like getting married and planning a family. Yes, Masiji has definitely been talking to my mother, and together they've hatched a genius plan to bypass me and anything I want to happen in my life, to ask a fortune teller what will happen instead, to give them piece of mind. They are obsessed with attaching meaning to everything and, because my choices so far in life make no sense to them, here is their solution.

'Thank you so much for thinking of me, Masiji. But sadly, I don't believe in this –' I smile in the direction of the fortune teller, who is now watching me. '– mumbo jumbo,' I whisper. Of course, I know it won't make the slightest difference, as I'm still a baby to them, who doesn't know what's best for her. It is very conflicting to be constantly reminded of how old I am, and to be treated like a child at the same time.

Masiji responds simply, 'It's a science.'

'But I don't believe in it. And no, it's not.'

'What difference does that make?' She chooses to respond to only the first part of my answer.

'It will make no difference to my life.'

'Well, in that case, you have nothing to lose by just doing it.'

'They might say something bad, which will get into my head and manipulate my mind, just before I go off!'

'It's just guidance. And I thought you said you didn't believe in it anyway?'

'I refuse to pay the guy. He's a charlatan.'

'I'll pay.'

I'm just not going to win this one. Mum and her sister are so alike. Everything is a war by attrition. You will, you *must* submit. It's going to happen whether I want it to or not and, as I've learned from living with my mother, sometimes it's just easier to go along with it.

He sits down at the dining table and is brought out a cup of tea with a couple of biscuits. He refuses at first as they are not very good for his 'sugar'. 'Sugar' is an Indian euphemism for diabetes. But the 'sugar' isn't getting in the way of the biscuits today, and he decides instead to inhale one just a moment later. A crumb lands in a bit of chest hair and I fixate on it, but he seems oblivious, opening his laptop and asking me to sit down. Not once does he look at me during this entire sequence of events.

I sit in the chair next to him and Masiji quickly puts herself on a chair next to me, shunting up close so she, too, can get in on the action. I can feel the pressure of her right arm and somehow feel Mum too, as though by being this physically close, they will bend my destiny to their will.

Looking down at his laptop, the man asks me for my date of birth, place and time of birth, which I didn't have a clue about, but Masiji jumps in.

'Time of birth was 3.10 a.m.'

I look at her.

'What?' she says. 'I asked your mother.'

Then my name is needed. When I say Baby, it is the only time he ever looks at me during this whole charade.

'Still a little Baby, huh?'

'Certainly feels that way sometimes,' I respond, getting more weirded out by the second.

'Sweet Baby or naughty Baby?'

I'm not sure how to take what he has just said. His face gives nothing away, and an awkward silence develops, but he soon presses the return key and instantly my birth chart is brought up before him. No lengthy calculations are required any more, this is an instant digital-life charting. Up pops a rectangle with the positions of the stars and the planets at the exact time I was born. And Pandit Om Prakash begins.

I'm strong-willed but also weak.
I know my mind but also listen to other people too much.
I have a passion for life but there is suffering.

I sound completely confused as a human being. I am a stream of contradictions, and yet . . . I can't argue with any of it.

'Ask questions, Baby!' Masiji encourages. I know what she wants me to ask, but I change tack.

'What will my work situation be?'

'Struggle,' he says.

Perfect. My heart sinks a bit, even though I know it's a bunch of nonsense.

'But paths will open before you, once you stop the struggle in your mind. Your struggle is internal. This is important moment in your life timing.'

I'm nodding away, fighting a losing battle with my cynicism as it is overwhelmed by my need for guidance of any kind, even the slightly vague variety.

'Life is long but final life cycle.'

Masiji gasps, but I've not understood. 'Moksha! You are on your last life, Baby, no more reincarnation for you.'

If this is good or bad, I'm not sure. I like the idea of coming back as another person, or even some sort of creature, but apparently we are all trying to attain Moksha. Do Sikhs even believe in reincarnation? I thought we just did Simran to be one with God? I guess we like to cover all bases in my family.

I'm still questioning what the point of this exercise is when Masi jumps in with the killer question, the reason she asked this bloke over in the first place.

'And what about marriage, children?'

Yep, definitely been colluding with Mum. 'Will this girl ever get married?' is something I have heard time and again. Now, at thirty-six, things are getting serious: why am I still not married, and is there something wrong with me? Why do I not show any signs of wanting to be hitched?

I've thought about this a lot, because Mum forced me to think about it a lot. Sometimes, I would answer her back flippantly, just to annoy her, because there is no one more up in your business than an Indian mum. But I have always, even with Dad still around, thought how strange it is how every woman is expected to buy into the idea of marriage. I've never seen what women get out of it. Look at my parents – my mum never said my dad's name, *ever*. It's not the done thing, so it wasn't done. The marriage system was designed by men for men, so that they could be looked after and do whatever they want, with women facilitating their needs and dreams. Women bear them heirs and make sure they are sustained with food. Now, I've just discovered my own mother had no desire to be married, which explains a lot. Call me cynical, but you can only go by what you've seen.

Mum and Dad were often arguing. I don't think I ever even witnessed what love or romance looks like, not really, and I've certainly never been encouraged to explore it. Don't get me wrong, it'd be wonderful to have a decent relationship with someone, a *proper* relationship, that involves sharing conversations and ideas and laughs. Proper belly laughs, too, and

135

adventures and, yes, amazing sex. I want to be adored, who doesn't? And I want to adore someone else. I just don't see why you need a piece of paper and a ceremony watched by hundreds of people to do just that.

Now that I have my future up on this guy's screen, though, I might as well see if it says 'passionate romance' in my stars.

I pipe up and say, 'Fine, OK, will I meet someone?'

The pandit looks at his chart and says yes. I'm relieved, of course. My aunt is over-the-top delighted: 'Oh, thank God!' she shouts, throwing her arms in the air dramatically.

'What a stress relief it will be for your poor mother, she deserves some happiness.'

Of course, it's my job to provide it. No pressure.

'Mum's fine!'

'She had a tough time with your father, and now she's having a tough time with you,' she says and now I think she's just rude.

'Mas, they bickered yes, but it wasn't all bad. You weren't even there And please don't make me feel like a shit daughter.'

I think she's alarmed at my change of tone and that I said shit. I could have said a lot worser but she's my masi.

I instantly feel like I've offended her, even though she offended me first, but I can hear Mum's voice telling me to be respectful to my masi, so I try to lighten the mood.

'Well, it's good news for all, because, according to this, I will meet someone.'

The pandit interrupts quickly, 'But she won't settle. Not for a while.'

OK, now I'm disappointed. I'm going to be single forever. The pandit looks up at me and says, 'Look, Baby beti, this is just guidance. Your destiny is in your hands. For you, what I see is that you can have whatever you want, you just have to want it, truly want it. But your journey right now is about questions and answers. Your questions will deepen your soul, and the answers will grow who you are in ways you can't imagine. You have so much to give, and you *will* find joy. Find the answers to your questions. Settle your soul.'

I'm gripped by his sage words. He's spot on, I've come here with so many questions. But what happens when I find the answers, if I find anything at all? Will my quest grow me and change me? It's hard to imagine how. You'd think by thirty-six you should know a bit about who you are but I've never been more unsure. Maybe I've been avoiding having to spend time with myself. Is that why I obsess about work, date guys who I know are a waste of time, drink too much? Am I just avoiding me?

I've heard so many people talk about going on internal journeys and truly knowing themselves. I didn't think that was what I was here to do. That stuff's for privileged new-age Southerners, along with gong baths and expensive leggings. But maybe I need to relax a bit more and trust myself. After all, I'm in the land of spirituality, I've come to the source. People talk about the life-changing effect of India; well, let's see what it can do for me. Or rather, what I let her do for me. What I allow in. As he says, my destiny is in my hands.

He looks at Masiji. 'So many parents look to their children to live their own lives and fantasies. Baby beti has a good destiny, but it hers, no one else's. Not Mumiji or Masiji. Kismet belongs to Baby beti.'

He then smiles at me, and finally wipes away those biscuit crumbs.

August 1943
Hello, Jaan

Are you smiling? I hope having this letter in your hands has made your heart smile.

A wise guru came to the next village last week. Anjuman and I went to see him. Your father was telling us not to go, he said all these men are crooks. But what if he is not? Anjuman needs all the reassurance she can get, so we went. Of course, Billi, our little green-eyed shadow, followed.

He told me many things. He says we are to have a daughter. This is news of great joy but of course I would not share this private detail with anyone other than you, my dear. People would tell me it is a curse if I revealed what he said.

The guru also told me I brought great joy to the people in my family, although I have not felt this for a while. He also told me there was to be great loss in my life. This I could not bear to hear. Naturally I had to pay the pandit to do a puja for blessings and to remove any evil eye which may be looking at us. He also suggested I wear my birthstone, which is a garnet. He says it will make me see clearly and make good decisions. I wonder what decisions I will ever have to make other than what to prepare for dinner?

The best news was that he also told Anjuman that there is a child in her destiny. We were so happy we went and prayed to give thanks at the Shiv mandir and then went to tie a red string at the Muslim peer's shrine.

It was a great day. We picked sugar cane from the field and sucked it all the way home.

I saw a newspaper and read about the Quit India campaign, and Congress and the Muslim League. I hope all these men see sense soon.

Please, please take care.

I await your letter.

You are in my prayers.

Your Jaan

Chapter Nine

Sid arrives bang on time at 5 a.m. It's a good nine-hour drive to Amritsar and he decided we should avoid the rush-hour Delhi traffic. Masi is up with Savita in the kitchen. They've made me a masala omelette, again. I'm not hungry at all but feel obliged to wolf it down – it still tastes better than any omelette I've ever had in Manchester.

After a lot of faff, we eventually head down to the car at half six.

Ruchi comes with us downstairs, bleary-eyed and still in her pyjamas. Sid's rather flash-looking 4x4 is parked outside. He offers to put my suitcase in the boot, and I instinctively jump in the back.

He gets into the driver's seat and looks over his shoulder at me.

'I'm not your cab driver, Baby.'

Ruchi laughs and says, 'I can tell this is going to be a roaring success,' as I sheepishly get out and move into the front seat, cheeks smarting. God, I didn't think he'd actually be driving! No one does that here, not when they own their own business as he does. It really is going to be just the two of us.

I say my goodbyes to Ruchi and Masi and Uncle and even Rohan, who have all come down to wave me off. Masi pulls a handful of chillies out of her pocket and circles them around my head, to remove the evil eye. Another directive from Mum, no doubt. I'm sad to be leaving them, especially Ruchi. She's been my anchor and I've felt so comfortable in her company; it'll be very different without her on this trip but I need to do this. I think back to the astrologer's words, about how my answers will grow me in ways I can't imagine. Time to find out what that means.

After not even ten minutes in the car together, during which we say precisely nothing at all, we are in the worst traffic jam I've ever experienced in my life. We have air conditioning and for that I am grateful, but it does not feel like an auspicious start.

I feel compelled to talk, to fill in the spaces, for this not to be awkward. This man, with no connection to me other than being a neighbour to my family, is navigating this journey with me. I have no idea how far he is willing to take me, but at this point, with the masala omelette repeating on me, I will take anything.

'So, thanks again for going on this drive with me. Well, for driving me. But not being my driver, ha ha, for being a great . . . neighbourhood friend! To my family. You're not my friend. I mean, it's not like we couldn't be friends, but I think you have to like someone to be friends and I . . .' I do a little burp and a tiny bit of sick comes into my mouth. Oh, God, the revenge of the masala omelette. I have to slow myself down, drink the water this annoyingly prepared man has thought to put in the passenger side-pocket of the car door. My energy is giddy and nervous, and he's so calm, grounded and together. I change tack, hoping to change the atmosphere of the car by getting him to do most of the talking.

'Looks like that early morning fog is burning off?'

A weather question always works back home but I get no reaction.

'Traffic's so bad,' I say. 'Have you driven to Punjab before?'

I sound manic.

'Lots.' Great. One-word answers.

'So, what's business like at the moment?' Why was my voice so high-pitched asking that?

'It's good, can't complain.'

Goddammit, this is not going to work unless he gives me something to work with.

I persevere, and he answers my questions very politely. He does a lot of work in the arts, with music festivals and art exhibitions, and is paid handsomely for his talents, which are obvious from hearing him speak. His voice is beautiful and deep – not Barry White deep, just nice, you know? There's something about it, maybe the way he pronounces his s's. There's a resonance which connects with my internal organs.

His real passion is Indian history, and now I have finally managed to get him talking about himself, nodding vigorously as he speaks so that he doesn't stop, I feel myself drifting off, staring out of the window at the unfamiliar landscape.

'It tells us about our past, yes, but also so much about humanity; we can see patterns over time that could maybe help us live better in the future; discovering a story is like solving a mystery.'

He glances at me and lifts his eyebrows. The sun catches them and his brown eyes shine at me, their brightness catching me off guard. There's a kindness and innocence in his eyes. He's excited, talking about his passion.

'Or you, Baby, can reveal just one person's history and then explain so much about who they are in the present.'

I'm still listening. Thinking again what my grandfather Ranjit's story might reveal about me, wondering how it can tell me anything when it still feels so abstract and far away.

'And I enjoy Indian history because I want to understand my country. But there are so many different versions to the same story. To you, Churchill was a hero but to us, he was a villain who has the blood of millions on his hands. And you celebrate your royal family, an institution that colonised the world. They were callous, cruel. But again you'd never know this.'

I'm still nodding, the sun now shining off his forehead. He has really lovely skin.

'Your grandad fought in Burma during the Second World War, your masi mentioned?'

'Yeah, but I don't know much.'

'I bet you didn't know that the regiments there were made up of what was then the British Empire's soldiers. Indians, of course, two million Indian men joined the Second World War.'

The figure shocks me

'And there were also Gurkhas from Nepal and soldiers from all over East and West Africa.'

He really is passionate and anything but boring. I don't have to feign interest. I had never considered the things he's saying.

I'm taking in the scene around me, amazed by the motorway; I was expecting the roads to be a lot worse, a potholed dirt track, really. *Keep that thought to yourself*, I hear my brain say to my mouth, aware that I don't want to keep offending Sid and making myself look like a complete idiot at the same time. But, oops, there it goes again, my mouth opens before I know it and out plops my thought.

This time he laughs. 'It's all relatively new, the infrastructure. We are getting there, slowly. Not like China, where one man clicks his fingers and roads, buildings and entire cities are built. Here, in India, we have a lot to contend with. Corruption, poverty, bureaucracy and—'

He slams on the brakes as a cow saunters past us on the freeway. He gestures as it pauses in the middle of the road, looks at us, and carries on. 'India!' he exclaims, as if what just happened makes perfect sense for this country.

I've been on sensory overload from the minute I stepped off the plane onto Indian soil. Every cliché about this place is true. There is just so much to take in and every part of me is over-stimulated or maybe just properly stimulated for the first time by colour, taste, noise, smell.

We are passing street shopkeepers opening up, there are lots of brands I recognise – Nike, Starbucks, Marks & Spencer – there are expensive-looking designer saree shops and jewellers specialising in gold. I make a mental note to take a look on my way home. I will definitely need to shop for sarees for Mum and Dadima, and me. We pass a giant shopping mall and then the built-up city starts to peter out. I begin to notice fields, and a large factory in the distance. We pass a bus stop with hundreds of people waiting. Their faces and clothes are very different to the people I saw on my night out. No flesh on show at the bus stop. Women in sarees going to work, men in office shirts, children in immaculate school uniforms, girls with ribbons in their hair. The shops have turned into street stalls selling tea, fruit and veg, a cigarette stall, a vendor simply making omelettes. My stomach gurgles.

'Those omelettes are delicious – as is that chai stand. You hungry?'

I shake my head.

I have a feeling of being alive like never before. The world is hyper real. It's vibrant and alive and I'm soaking it all in.

My body and its functions had only been performing to fifty per cent before and it's as though every part of me has ramped up. I'm functioning on a much higher plane, so alert and excited my brain seems to be fizzing.

We are soon off the motorway onto the famous GT road which, my driver and guide informs me, was once an ancient trade route, one of Asia's oldest roads. It runs from Bangladesh all the way through northern India, Pakistan and into Afghanistan. The British named it the Grand Trunk Road.

I already know all this so I chip in, wanting to show I'm not just some ignorant NRI.

'Yeah, they built roads and railways and created the judiciary and the civil service, so I was taught my entire life, but as you said, they were callous and had one motive to make their own country rich, so I guess the infrastructure was built to get soldiers in and goods out and the rule of law allowed them to control everything.'

'Precisely,' he says, vigorously nodding and smiling.

I'm happy to be engaging in a conversation about Indian history. The only other people I can have conversations like this with are Supriya and Jojo. There's a short pause before I add, 'Clever, ruthless bastards.'

He laughs. I made him laugh! This thrills me.

'I like the way you say bastard,' he says.

'Swearing sounds great in a Yorkshire accent. And very satisfying.' I smile. 'Did you ever visit Yorkshire while you were at UCL? It is actually one of the best places on Earth. I grew up not far from Brontë country and the famous moors. It's one of my favourite places on Earth. Sometimes I head on up to Ilkley Moor on my own, just for a long walk. You know, really to be in nature.'

'Alone?' he asks.

'It helps me think up there, when I need to get away from everything. It's peaceful and OMG, so, so beautiful, especially when it's carpeted in purple heather. Nature is the best therapy, I think. You'd love it.'

'Would I?'

'You'd have to be an imbecile not to fall in love with Yorkshire,' I say with a smile.

'And it's people?' he says.

Oh, cheeky!

'Best in't world,' I say in my thickest West Yorkshire accent, making him laugh again before adding, 'They are very loveable too.'

'I had a friend from Leeds at UCL,' he says, running his fingers through his hair.

I have a pang of wanting to know what his hair feels like.

He puts his hand back on the steering wheel and I notice he's wearing a couple of chunky silver rings. I like that he wears a bit of jewellery. He's got something a bit rock 'n' roll about him. I admit he's sexy to myself.

'Girlfriend?' My mouth plopping things out again.

'No, a massive rugby player called Geoffrey; he was a beer-drinking buddy.' He's grinning but I want to know more about his personal life.

'Did you have a girlfriend back then? How about now, how's the love life?' I'm trying to sound casual.

'Nothing serious back then or now. There was someone about a year ago, but it didn't work out. We wanted different things. Nice girl but we were just different. How about you?'

Me. How honest should I be? Say that I prefer things that are casual and on my terms so I never have to get into anything too deep and meaningful? Or that I've been consistently crap at relationships?

'Nothing serious. Never met anyone who gets me.'

He looks at me seriously.

'I see you.' And for a moment it feels like he really does, our eyes just looking at each other's . . . What does he see?

And then he breaks the tension with, 'There's nothing complicated about you. You're simple.' He laughs.

'I am very complicated with many hidden depths,' I say, wishing he could really see me.

The conversation has been easy and non-stop but it's petering out as the journey wears on and wears us out. The radio is playing faintly in the background, my ears picking up a classic song from the seventies, one of Dad's favourites, a song I love too. I start humming it under my breath. Sid's arm reaches across and turns the volume up.

And I sing along looking out of the window. As Sid joins in with the chorus.

'Phir ho na juda haan ye vaada raa.'

'My God! this could be a scene from a Hindi movie,' I say.

Sid grins over at me briefly then flicks his eyes back to the road, 'Yeah, it's a typical Bollywood scenario, the two thrown together, they hate each other at the beginning and then love blossoms over a song in a road-trip montage. It's classic.' Then he adds, 'OK, hate is a strong word.'

'Perhaps you've just met your match.' I smile.

We both laugh a little awkwardly. Am I now full-on flirting with this guy? I quickly change the subject.

'I love that song, it was one of my dad's favourites.'

'He had good taste. It's beautiful.'

There's a pause. A silence. I don't want him to feel bad or awkward, but I don't have the energy to fill the space, to say anything else. The lump in my throat won't let me speak. So, I don't.

Thinking of my dad has knocked me. I thought I'd come here and feel this extra connection to him, but if anything, he feels more distant than ever. My dad is invoked whenever I'm home in Yorkshire, under his TV blanket watching *Question Time*; or when I'm drinking whisky sodas in old-man pubs with sticky floors and bar stools that look ready to collapse. He's in the grey skies and moody moors and drystone walls, he's cutting the lawn in the spring, he's our semi-detached house, surrounded by our British family.

'Are you OK?' he asks, after a couple of minutes of silence.

'Yeah, I'm OK. Just tired.'

But really, it's not OK. It will never be OK. Dad has gone and my soul has a deep wound, a black hole where he should be, that has spun me out of orbit. I'm untethered and alone. Isolated. And yet there's some deep comfort in my loneliness. I put my head against the window, remembering how shit life can feel, how shit my life is. I'm lost in my own mind, in my grief, in my self-pity, my eyes aren't focused on anything around me. I'm deep in my mind contemplating why I'm here, feeling angry with everything, no way of coping with my pain, wishing I was back in Manchester so I could at least step out for a drink tonight. That dimwit Freddie even pops into my mind. That's all I'm worth, a situationship with a bore from my office. Why am I even on this journey? Why am I here?

'Welcome to Punjab.' Sid looks at me with a smile. 'We are officially in your tribal heartland.'

I'm snapped out of the wormhole of despair I'd spiralled into and focus on what's happening outside the window. Brought into the present, I'm reminded by Sid's words why I am here.

The landscape has slowly changed on the drive. We are surrounded by flat, lush plains, growing crops. There's the odd house in a field. The view opened up and I can see the horizon. I take a deep breath.

He gives me a potted history, bringing the landscape around me to life.

'The land of the five rivers. These plains used to flood but the British built a canal irrigation system; they were clever! The land became rich and fertile and it turned this state into the breadbasket of India.'

A thought flashes in my mind about the letters. Didn't Naseeb mention Ranjit worked on the canals? Is this why he was in her village? Did he then join the army later, sign up for the war effort?

Sid is still talking.

'No meal is complete here without a chapatti drenched in butter. The land of the formidable Punjabis – your lot.' He glances over at me with a grin.

Was that a compliment? I'm enjoying his potted history commentary.

My tummy rumbles.

'It was ruled by the warrior king, Maharaja Ranjit Singh, and the last state to be annexed by the British, it was from here they took the famous Koh-i-noor diamond that now forms part of the British Crown Jewels. They also took the rightful heir to the throne of Punjab to Britain as a young boy, Maharaja Duleep Singh, and never let him set foot in Punjab again.'

'How do I not know this stuff?'

This is it. I'm here. I'm in Dad's home, Dadaji's land. And Mum's. And Dadima's. In fact, every single person in my ancestry apart from me. This is the motherland. My tribal heartland. It's more beautiful than I was expecting. But as for any instant connection? There's nothing. I just feel like a tourist taking in new surrounds.

I look out across yellow fields of mustard, saag and then wheat, kanak. The food I grew up eating. Growing here in abundance.

'It's an important region, it produces huge amounts of wheat and rice, which have helped India become self-reliant on food. And most of India is still rural.'

Looking out at the landscape I feel a sense of calm and curiosity. The despair I felt only half an hour ago is being soothed by the scene outside the window. The land is flat, lush green and bright yellow as we are pass field after field of crops. The sun is shining, for the first time since the Delhi smog I see a blue sky. The day is warming up. We pass mandirs and temples and little shrines. I see one man walking along the road taking a step and then lying flat on the ground with his arms stretched above his head in prayer position; he gets up, takes another step before once again lying flat on the ground. Sid explains he will be fulfilling a pact with God, probably on his way to a temple; he will do this every step of the way, either praying for something or in gratitude for something. Then I shriek with joy when we slowly drive past an elephant. An elephant in Punjab?

'You'll see everything everywhere in India.'

It's not wild but owned, which makes me a little sad for the animal, although Sid tells me they are usually well looked-after by their owners. I'm not convinced, but I'm still thrilled at the sight of its majestic massive beauty, lumbering down the road. There are young farmers moving on herds of buffalo; buffalo provides milk here and some still work the fields. It's simultaneously modern and old-fashioned.

At one point we get stuck behind a tractor being driven by a man in a turban. Attached to the back is a trolley carrying a group of old women. The scene delights me. Ordinarily I'd be losing patience at this point in a long car journey, desperate to get to my destination (and let's face it, desperate for the loo) but I can't take my eyes off the old women. I'm looking at their beautiful faces, heads covered with their light dupattas, all wearing shalwar kameez, noses pierced, ears pierced, wearing different coloured bangles made from glass and one is wearing a thick cuff that looks so cool that I make a mental note to try

148

and find one similar for myself. I notice light tattoos on their wrists and wonder what they represent. I recognise their faces and feel something from them. A warmth. They remind me of Dadima. My dadima who was always so different to everyone else's gran. My dadima who I never wanted to come and pick me up from school, in case the other children, the white children, saw my granny dressed in her shalwar kameez and thought racist thoughts about her and me, would say racist things to my face about my granny, my family, me. I remember being crippled with shame about Dadima and who I am in the outside world. At home, Dadima was my world, but she was so out of place when she stepped out. Apart from in our world, our little Punjabi community.

The community I couldn't wait to get the hell away from, the community whose members were vital for each other. It's how they survived when they first arrived in the UK, where they faced overt racism at every turn. 'You can't rent here', 'you can't work there', 'we don't want you living next to us', 'we don't want you in our land'. What they went through, just so that I could grow up feeling stomach-churning shame. My life was – and has been – ruled by my old foe, shame, at every turn.

And here now, watching these women on the trolley, chatting away, relaxed, in their own land, my gorgeous granny is put into context. Here, Dadima makes sense. Here, *I* make sense in a way I've never felt before. I smile and wave like a tourist at the women and they smile back.

I relax. I'm comforted. This car journey is making me feel such a sense of joy. With a perfect old-school Bollywood soundtrack on the radio, it's like an entire part of me I keep under wraps most of the time, in big public spaces at least, is now out in this big public space because here, it's the norm. My tiny repressed British brain is exploding.

We are now on a single road and this one does have potholes; overtaking isn't easy. They have a unique system of letting people know that they want to overtake and that's by beeping the horn. The ornately decorated trucks we passed on the motorway actually have it written on the back, 'Horn please, OK'. To let them know you are there and need to over-take. Also, they might not be looking in their wing mirrors, or have wing mirrors at all, for that matter. Some clichés are true, and driving in India is clearly a case of taking your life into your own hands.

Chapter Ten

How many potential death traps can one quiet road in the Punjabi countryside have? This drive could be turned into a computer game: swerve the cow, dog, child, woman carrying a clay pot on her head, woman carrying a huge basket of vegetables, horse, horse and cart, cart, buffalo, buffalo and cart, herd of buffalo and the numerous godforsaken potholes that are rapidly becoming a literal pain in my arse. Bouncing around on high alert, I'm in a mild state of panic, which Sid is finding highly amusing.

This is all part of the Punjabi experience, he tells me. 'This is India!' He's about to let out a huge laugh at the scowl on my face when we dip into another pothole, except, this time, the bang that accompanies the dip changes his mood instantly.

We roll to a stop, right in the middle of the road. There's no attempting to move the car to the side, because there isn't anywhere to move it to. There are fields on both sides of us, swaying wheat doing nothing to shield us from the mid-afternoon sun. I put the hazard lights on and jump out to take a look.

'A nail, gone straight through the front left tyre,' Sid says with a frown, kneeling in front of the car.

Perfect. 'OK, so let's get the jack and the spare and change it.' Dad taught me how to change a tyre before I'd even passed my test. He said it was a basic life skill and, even though he made me sign up to the AA so I'd never actually have to change one, it was important I knew how to do it.

Knowing how to do things for yourself was important to Dad. His daughter was going to be fully equipped with the capacity to not have to rely on anyone to do anything for her. 'You can stand on your own feet!' he always told me. *It worked a bit too well, Dad.* He was so different to other Indian dads, who barely engaged with their daughters. Maybe it was because Dad was an only child and then he only had me, no sons to fix tyres with. But I think he genuinely wanted me to experience life, maybe do the things he never got to do.

Funny how I've discovered neither of my parents particularly wanted to get married but they didn't have a choice in the matter, and Dad never once pushed the marriage agenda with me, it was only ever Mum. Is that how the patriarchy works? Indoctrinate the women about their role and let them push the agenda onto the next generation? My dad was always different, I felt.

Although Mum would say, 'He wants to see you married too but he'll never say it.'

I look around the vast, empty landscape, thinking how this is possibly one of the worst places to get a flat, when I'm suddenly aware of a small crowd of people approaching us. *How, and when, did they get here?* They've seemingly come out of nowhere and it looks as if at least fifty people, who weren't anywhere to be seen five minutes ago, have gathered. Everyone is pushing to see the palaver, and a lot of eyes are staring at me. I stare back at one little lad, no more than ten, but he doesn't flinch or look away, so I frown and stick my tongue out, and he does the same with a cheeky smile.

We have caused a bit of a traffic jam in the few minutes since we've broken down, not that it seems to have bothered anyone. There is no waiting patiently here, you just go about your day. A rickshaw driver swerves past the car, taking a detour through the field next to us, followed by a motorbike and two young women on a scooter. I smile at them as they glide past and they smile back. One is dressed in a bright-pink shalwar kameez, the other in jeans. I wonder what they are up to, what their lives are like. I wonder if *they'd* go on a road trip, in a foreign country, with a stranger.

Behind the scooter is a goat farmer and his gang of at least twenty-five goats. I didn't realise goats could grow to such a beastly size, or be this menacing. I start backing up towards Sid. *What is the collective noun for goats?*, I wonder. Damn, if I had watched more *Countryfile,* I'd know. For some reason I've always remembered a barrel of monkeys and wonder when I will see one. Luckily for us, a large, modern, shiny red tractor pulls up behind us, and a tall middle-aged man in a checked turban jumps down.

He parts the crowd and approaching Sid, has a conversation in Punjabi to assess the damage and see what can be done. I understand some of it, so I chip in – in English.

'We just need to change the tyre, it's easy enough to do.'

'I don't have a spare,' Sid says to me.

'You don't have a spare?! Who goes on a road trip without a spare tyre?' I say, a little too loudly.

Both Sid and the farmer look at me. Sid informs the farmer that I'm his cousin, visiting from England. Only, there is no word for cousin in Punjabi. You have to explain the relationship like: my mother's sister's daughter, or my father's older brother's daughter, or my father's younger brother's wife's sister's daughter . . . Punjabis love a familial connection. So, I'm now Sid's Masi's daughter, because we are in rural India, and the rules are different here.

The farmer nods as if to say, 'Ahh, that makes sense – English gobshite, thinks she knows best.' They carry on their conversation in Punjabi and the farmer takes his iPhone out of his chest pocket to call the mechanic.

'This could take a while,' Sid says to me. 'Nothing happens quickly here. It *will* happen, just not fast.'

Fine. 'This is India!' I say to no one.

We are in the middle of nowhere, 30km from the nearest town and with just a few villages scattered around. We are in the sticks. The car eventually does get collected by a local mechanic from a village not too far away. Even though it's only a tyre change, he won't be able to get one until the morning.

153

'Well, looks like we'll need to find a hotel then,' I say to Sid.

'Hotel? A *hotel*, Baby? Where do you think I'm going to find one of those, exactly?' he asks, with all the tact he is famous for.

'Or Airbnb? I don't mind,' I say, suddenly noticing that my phone battery is quite a bit lower than I'm comfortable with.

He looks at me, exasperated, and explains, 'There aren't hotels out here. But maybe the farmer could help us out. Again.'

The farmer has the largest house in the next village, a farmhouse right on the outskirts, and he has generously offered to let us stay. He can accommodate the two of us in his son and brother's old rooms, on the ground floor of his two-storey home. It's not an ideal situation, but I'm so out of my depth I have to trust my instinct that this man is genuine, and trust that Sid is a good judge of character too. Hopefully we're not walking into the Punjabi version of *The Texas Chainsaw Massacre*. I've heard horror stories of the lawlessness in rural Punjab, and land disputes are common. But that's surely nothing to do with us, two unlucky city folk with no valuables?

We hitch a lift on the tractor to the farmer's house, winding down single-track lanes that haven't changed in years. We pass a few hay bales shaped like pointy domes in fields and a few solitary small two-room houses made by mud, it seems. Then I see a sandy-coloured village appear. Most of the houses are small, single-stories made from brick, with flat roofs that are also terraces. The farmer's house is the largest I can see and we pass a well just on the outskirts.

'Every village in Punjab has a well,' we are informed by the farmer. He's smiling at my obvious wonder and joy. This moment could not be more different to my actual life, the one I have left behind and not thought about, or missed, for a second. *I'm here*, I think. I'm in Punjab, I can finally feel my dad closer to me, and who doesn't love getting to ride a tractor? I am with *my* people! Here they are, salt of the earth, living on what they can grow!

The farmer's home is surrounded by a high brick wall. We enter through an elaborate, old, carved-wood double-door and find ourselves in a completely different world. The house is huge. The ground floor is the old family farmhouse, with a grain store attached and kept in the original fashion, but with a modernised kitchen. The second floor looks to have been added more recently, with en suite bedrooms, and the biggest TV I've ever seen. The farmer sees me gaping at this.

'I like to watch Tom Cruise, like I'm at the movies,' he explains.

I have discovered the farmer's name is Jyot Singh, but Sid calls him paji, and I follow his lead. Jyot switches the TV on to show us his surround sound and nearly blows our ears off with the blast of bhangra that comes through his state-of-the-art speakers.

'Drink?' he asks, pointing to his bar.

The house has a large courtyard out in front, the vehra, which is common in all village homes. This one the family seem to have kept the way it would have been fifty, or even maybe 100, years ago.

'I feel as if I've stepped back in time,' I say to Sid and the farmer overhears.

'It's both old and new. It's our ancestral home but as we made enough money, we have expanded it and changed things. The ground out here used to be made of a mixture of mud and cow dung and it would have to be newly spread every so often to keep it smooth and dust-free. We now have a brick floor. See, modern.'

'Cow dung?' I pull a face.

'Punjab wouldn't be Punjab without cow dung.' The farmer laughs and Sid laughs at my very British reaction.

'Punjab was fuelled by shit!' Jyot guffaws. He's got a hearty laugh. He then twists his moustache and looks at me. 'We were recycling and being sustainable for a long, long time; before gas, our fuel was dry cow pats and yes, even our houses were made from it. Nature gives us everything we need.'

Alongside the modern kitchen, the house still has the traditional outdoor 'choola', the farmer explains, because his mother still enjoyed cooking outdoors and couldn't get used to standing at the gas hob. They also have a borehole with a hand pump in their courtyard, which they used to access water before the tank was installed.

It's a fascinating example of the merging of old and new and shows homage to the past with the respect it deserves while being realistic of the demands of modern life. *I could live here*, I think to myself. *This feels like a home. Or at least a regular holiday destination.*

Jyot's wife, Lakhvinder, cooks us dinner and lays out the dinner table as though we are family guests. I try to insist that they don't need to go to any trouble for us, and then remember I'm at the source of my culture, where Punjabi hospitality originates, and I can't fight it with my overly polite, English ways. I don't want to either, not really. These people, these warm and friendly people, have opened their home up to us – to the core. Not only are they giving us a bed for the night after helping us with our car trouble, but they are also feeding us, welcoming us, enveloping us in the Punjab. Sid speaks up and requests that we eat our dinner outside, in the traditional way.

'Please, no need for formality! Plus, Baby is from England and you know them, they should experience the culture properly.'

So, the charpoys are placed in a semi-circle in the courtyard and dinner is served to us by the farmer's wife. I get up to offer her a hand and go straight into the kitchen without being asked. Mum would be proud, for once! My Indian-woman reflex has finally kicked in. Funny how the Indian-man reflex is to know to just sit there. And then Sid surprises me by getting up to help carry the food out from the kitchen.

Nice work, Siddharth.

The sun is setting and there's a chill in the air. It's been gloriously warm all day but gets much cooler at night. They've lit an outdoor wood fire in the middle of the semi-circle, the smell evoking my first visit to India. It comes back to me, a bitter-sweet memory of a happier, freer time, with Dad in India. Just like then, we are eating from metal thaals, with small round bowls containing delicious curries, all familiar and yet tastier than I've ever had. Traditional saag and makki di roti, roti made from corn, salad, home-made pickle, yogurt, chapatti. Nothing over the top and fancy, but simple, home-cooked food which tastes incredible. We sit around the fire, and I'm treated to home-made butter, and Jyot insists I try his wife's home-made cream mallai as well. I'm so full, I can't breathe and it's a delicious feeling. But how can I undo the top button of my jeans without them noticing?

'I grew up on this farm with my younger brother. We should both be working on it, but my brother was desperate to go abroad. The youngsters see so many people from Punjab with foreign money and big cars in clean and organised modern countries and they want that lifestyle. My brother didn't want to farm.'

I'm finding Jyot's story fascinating.

'So he left, first to the Middle East, then to Germany and eventually managed to get to Canada, to Toronto.'

'What did he do?' I ask, somewhat naively it feels based on the look everyone gives me.

'Nothing. Illegal.'

'Oh.'

Jyot continues to explain how his brother lived as an illegal immigrant until he got married and finally managed to get set-tled status. His life was so hard, doing manual labour, living under the radar, but he saved his money and now has a job as a truck driver. He explains that people in Punjab just see the money he makes, the life he now lives, and don't see the suf-fering and pain behind the cash. Jyot was in two minds himself when his only son said he wanted to join his uncle in Canada. Reluctantly, he accepted that his son could have a good life there, but only allowed him to go if he went via the correct channels. He didn't want him to end up living like a fugitive, doing terrible work the white folk don't want to do, when he had an education and a decent life in India. There was no persuading him to stay and he left for Canada on a student visa, to study for his masters, and is staying with his uncle. It's a problem in Punjab, where most families have someone or know someone who is living abroad. Most people want to leave for a better life, Sid tells me.

'Young people don't want to work hard on the land. They want easy life. They see the pounds and dollars brought back from abroad! Many of the properties built in Punjab have been made with foreign money, and so they think life is easier there. They go, and we stay behind. I don't blame them, being a farmer is hard. The suicide rates are high and ultimately I don't want my son or younger brother to struggle like our father, like me.'

I wonder how long it will be before Jyot and Lakhvinder will go to join their son in Canada. And I wonder what reasons my own grandfather had when he decided to leave.

'My grandfather, Ranjit Singh, left India from Punjab in 1965 for perhaps that reason, I suppose – a better life. I wonder what kind of person I would be, what kind of family he would have had, if he had stayed.'

I smile at Jyot and his wife and wonder about my family. Would my father still be alive if he had grown up here? Would the heaviness in my grandfather's heart still have driven him to drink, to the despair I know haunted him? Would my mother be happier, having stayed in India, had an easier life? Would I have been like Jyot's son, yearning for a life away from this place, which to my foreign eyes seems like paradise?

Sid looks at me, the embers glowing in his eyes.

'My grandfather, he was from Amritsar, which is where I'm heading to. To learn more about him.'

I stop, because I can't really go on, or answer any questions, because, to my increasing shame, I don't *know* anything else. Did Dadima ever tell me the full story? Was I too wrapped up in my own life to notice this family lore being passed down? Is that what living in England, in that cold, utterly alien land-scape, did to us? Wipe out the need to remember? I feel so sure now, as the fire crackles, that I was too busy trying to figure out my own place in the world to be bothered about anyone else's story. Why didn't I ask more questions? I know so little about anything, about Grandfather Ranjit, about Dadima, even. And about who I am.

Jyot and Lakhvinder tell us how they now have a new project that is keeping them occupied: finding their son a wife. They want him to marry a girl from a good family in India. They don't want him to settle with an Indian girl from abroad – they are too independent, have lost the culture and don't value tradition.

'She will be too independent for our son's needs.' Maybe it's their own needs they are thinking of.

Oh Lord, it's all starting to get a bit personal and I'm about to chip in with my own thoughts on the issue when they are saved from my tirade by the electricity cutting out. The house is bathed in complete darkness, apart from the glow of the fire.

'We might well be a nation growing in its wealth, but the electricity still cuts out,' Jyot laughs. The farmer has a generator which they will put on especially for us. Sid decides we don't need it, though. Apparently, being in the pitch-black is part of the authentic Punjabi experience. God knows how I'll remove my mascara now, but I don't want him to see my scowl, so I remain tight-lipped and go with it.

Jyot and Lakhvinder give us two traditional blankets to wrap around us to stave off the cold then head to bed, leaving the two of us sitting out on the charpoys. I appreciate being left alone, a gift from this couple who instinctively seem to know that a little quiet on this journey has been hard to come by. I can feel the crickets humming like a vibrating pulse through my body. In the distance, a dog barks. I feel cosy, and shut my eyes, until Sid pipes up.

'Well, what an adventure this is turning out to be.' I can feel his eyes boring into my head but can't give him the satisfaction of answering. I am too busy enjoying the peace. 'And if I wasn't with you, how on earth would you have navigated your way?' He pauses, I can only assume, to take on his final form as monstrous Annoying Sid. I open an eye to peek at him, but no, he's just looking at my legs, sprawled out to get the heat of the fire.

'If I wasn't with you, I'd have got the train and been in Amritsar by now!' I snap him out of his leggy reverie.

'And miss all this?' He gestures around us.

He's right, this is more than I could have hoped for. Sitting on the charpoy in the darkness, I imagine my father as a boy. I imagine my grandparents being in surroundings just like this one, for most of their lives, doing exactly the same thing as me in this moment: sitting around a fire after dinner, a simple meal served on the floor. This is it. This is *how* my ancestors lived, this is *where* they lived.

I look at the outdoor cooking choola and imagine my great-grandmother, and her mother, and her mother, cooking the same recipes the same way. I can almost hear their laughter as they prepare the okra or slice onions or stir black dhal that's been simmering for hours. I can smell the aroma. I'm somewhere I know, because this place is in me. I feel a sense of calm settle from my head to my feet and know that this is right. Truly, honestly, right. I feel different here, and I feel stronger. I know I haven't even started on my quest for answers yet, but I think I can get there.

'Tell me more about your grandfather Ranjit.'

Maybe it's because I'm utterly exhausted after the day travelling, or maybe it's because we are sitting under a perfect sky with more stars than I've ever seen. Maybe it's the glow of the fire lighting his perfect cheekbones, or down to the spark the Chivas Regal we've drunk has lit in me, but the truth tumbles out.

'He's the reason I'm here – or at least, his wife is.'

'Your grandmother?'

'No, not quite.'

I realise it might be easier to get answers by telling Sid what I'm doing here. Especially as he is someone who knows a little about Punjabi history. Not just because I'm starting to trust him, wanting to share something, to open up.

So, the truth comes out.

'I stumbled upon some . . . family treasure, I suppose. Letters, in a trunk, not even locked away, just tucked in with old sarees and never-used dowry items. The letters are from a woman called Naseeb, to my grandfather. I don't know much about her, but I'm here to find answers. I want to know who she was, and I want to know what happened to her.'

'Yes, Ruchi mentioned letters but I didn't want to pry. Did you ask your mum or Dadima or Masi about them?' Sid's eyes are kind as he probes.

For most people with different families, families who share feelings and can actually be attentive to each other's needs, this would have been the obvious place to start.

'I figured this secret had been kept secret for a reason, so therefore I kept my discovery a secret too. And I guess this is how families have secrets, right? Which I am now perpetuating . . . Huh.'

For a brief moment I feel a pang of guilt. I kind of lied to Mum and Dadima about why I'm here, how I'm chasing ghosts of our past – *their* past – and they have no idea. Or rather, they do know, a bit but not the full extent. They know nothing about my fixation with Naseeb.

'The only people who know about the letters are Ruchi, my friend Pinky, a couple of friends at work, my next-door neighbours and now you.'

'That sounds like a lot of people to me,' he says to himself and I carry on.

'I barely know you and I'm telling you this; it feels mad.' I look him straight in the eyes and, for a brief moment, I really do feel ridiculous, as though I've just exposed myself and my silly mission to this man who already thinks I'm an idiot. I'm

161

embarrassed by why I'm here and I'm embarrassed that I'm being so earnest with him.

He stares back and we hold each other's gaze.

'Baby, this is very cool. What an incredible reason to be in India, to discover your family's story. I can see why you kept it to yourself. Indian mothers can be intense.'

He said my name. And I really, really liked it.

'You don't think I'm ridiculous?'

'Far from it,' he says. 'I respect it. And I'd like to help you.'

And I am desperate for him to help me. I *need* him. Not just for the practical stuff of speaking the language, charming local farmers, driving me around. I actually love being in his company. I feel so present when I'm with him. Excited. I like our looks to each other that linger a bit too long. I like listening to him talking while studying his physique. The tension between us in the dark is intense. I almost can't cope with the romance of it.

I spring up and grab a lit candle, not saying anything as I make my way inside the house and run to my room. I wrapped the letters in everything and anything I could find, these precious treasures of my past. Tissue paper, a paper envelope, then a more sturdy one, then I finally tied the package neatly in the ribbon I first found them tied up with. I like to imagine my grandfather tying up that very same ribbon, preserving this part of his life as carefully as he could. It makes me feel closer to him.

I return to Sid and hand him the letters, feeling exhilarated at sharing something so intimate with him. We sit together in silence as he carefully looks through the pages, his eyes widening the more he reads.

'This is . . . astounding. These are historical documents from a hugely important time, pre-Independent India. When this country was one with Pakistan, we were all Indians. Then came the devastating time . . . and so few documents like this have survived, written by women, especially ordinary women in a time when we know many did not have any literacy skills. Naseeb is clearly not just literate – she was highly intelligent and articulate.'

162

I know this. History GCSE taught me that history is told through the eyes of men, and through those skewed lenses, never do we understand the history of women and how society functioned from their perspective. The letters are important to me, to my family, but I never thought of them as being important to everyone else, too. Yes, they *are* history, and I fear I hadn't fully grasped what these letters are about, what they contain. They aren't just the story of Naseeb, of my grandfather, but of India too.

'This is your grandfather's first wife. What we have here is her living testimony of what she went through during Partition.'

This is the word I was afraid of hearing. I think I'd always known, deep down, that this was where this was heading. That something terrible must have happened to separate Naseeb and Ranjit, to end their life together, end their love.

I'm nodding, overwhelmed by his reaction. Awed by the thought that history – or at least, what I have the luxury of thinking of as history – directly impacted my family, my existence. I feel chilled to the bone.

I take the letters and look through the pages, seeing them in a different light now. Seeing their value as a portal to another time and place that no longer exists. They were written at a crucial moment in the Destiny of India, after which nothing was ever the same again.

'Naseeb had two children, Deep and Preet. Deep must have been around five or six and the little girl, Preet, just one or two, still a baby. My grandfather had this whole other life. A wife, children – a family. A family he loved. A wife who loved him, from what I can tell. And all I knew about him was that he fought in the war. Nothing more. At the end he was just an old man who liked to drink. Oh, Sid, all that pain he must have been carrying inside, with no way of expressing it! I need to find out whatever I can about his first family. I need to honour my grandfather's story. I need to *know* his story. I've never felt surer of anything in my life.'

I pause.

I feel Sid looking at me as I stare into the night.

'It will be my honour to help you, if you'll have me?'

Who says that? I wonder. *My honour.* This annoying, beautiful man, that's who. The stars are shining, our hosts are nowhere to be seen, the night is lit by our shared secrets and not a small amount of electricity in our bodies. We are sitting next to each other on the charpoy. He's still looking at the letter. I'm leaning to look at the page. Our heads are so close I can feel my hair faintly brush his and the sensation is heightened . . . Goddam, he smells so good! Just a mild hint of his scent as my hand brushes his arm. He turns to say something and we are so close, I notice his lips glistening.

Everything is perfectly set up to kiss him, in this perfect moment. I feel unbelievably emotional, so raw and so flipping horny.

But I can't. This is my trip. Even though this man is waving the most green flags I've ever witnessed, I can't be distracted. I need to stay focused on why I'm here. Also, we can't risk the farmer seeing two supposed cousins kissing. That might raise alarm bells.

'This trip may just change your life, Baby,' Sid says, then touches my cheek before going into the house. I can't help but smile again, more broadly, clutching the letters in my hands, watching as he disappears into the night.

I can't move. I sit in silence savouring the moment. Breathing deeply. My heart is pounding.

In bed, I take my phone out to leave Pinky another voice note.

'I don't know when you'll get this, because the electricity is down in the house I'm staying in. A stranger's house. I know that sounds well dodgy but that's not important. I'm safe and having a proper, if tiring, adventure.

'I'm discovering more about Naseeb through the letters. Because she was educated, she used to write letters for the women of the village to their sons and husbands at war and families who were far away. So she became the keeper of all their secrets. She would have known the feelings and thoughts

164

of all these women, she must have been so trustworthy for them to come to her. Imagine having to carry all those stories, having all that information and not being a total blabbermouth gossip with it all, like Shallo aunty, or Jas aunty. The more I discover about her, the more I wish I knew her. But through these letters she's coming to life.

'Already I'm feeling closer to my history, Pinks, *our* history; this is our land, after all, and I'm starting to see it that way.

'I'm making connections in more ways than one, though, mate.

'Headline news about the lad, Sid: he's smart and good company and funny – and Pinks, he's INSANELY sexy. Smells good enough to lick. And I very nearly bloomin' did.

'We were under a moonlit sky, sitting on charpoys, talking about the letters, and we nearly kissed.

'But we didn't. It's not right. Not yet. If it happens at all. I need to keep this trip veggie, don't I? Do I? There's definitely chemistry and I'm going to leave it at that.

'What is going on? Aaaarrrrgh!

'I won't leave you a podcast, I need my battery juice. I'll keep you posted.'

May, 1944
Jaan,

Please tell me how you are, I am so worried.

Shakuntala chachi lost her only son fighting this war. I used to help her write letters to him. All she would ever tell him was to make sure he is eating. She was planning his marriage for his return. He was nineteen. She is inconsolable. We spent time with her today and she only smacks her chest and wails.

I am sorry, I am sure you do not want to hear bad news, not when you are fighting away.

Let me tell you that your son is getting bigger and cheekier every day. He is so spoiled by your mother. She takes him everywhere with her. She even has him sleeping with her.

At times I wonder what my role is in the home other than to do the chores. I don't mind doing them, Mataji is old but there is something missing in my life.

You are missing.

Yes, I have Anjuman and Billi and our son.

But I want you.

Come home to me soon.

You are in my prayers.

Yours always,

Naseeb

Chapter Eleven

The almost eight-hour journey to Amritsar flew by with Sid. After thanking the farmer and his wife, who dropped us off at the mechanic to pick up the car and refused to let us pay them anything, we were on our way. There was an easy rapport between us now; any self-consciousness I'd felt before had dissipated and I was perfectly happy to chat absolute nonsense with him. Last night had changed something. We were in a more comfortable place. Not literally, of course; Sid's car wasn't built for these provincial roads and my bum was suffering the consequences.

We finally make it to Amritsar, the holiest city for Sikhs, home to the Golden Temple, the most important spiritual sight for Sikh religion. People make the pilgrimage to visit the Golden Temple – or the Harmandir Sahib as it's also known – from all over the world. Dadima has a tiny golden temple lamp on her bedside table, and she has a CD of shabads she listens to on her ancient CD player. Sometimes she tunes in online to listen to the kirtan coming live from the Golden Temple. I have asked her if it makes her feel closer to God.

'That is a silly question, Baby. God lives in you, not in the Golden Temple, or any temple but the place is very spiritual and the kirtan magnificent. When you go there one day you will experience it for yourself.'

It's been a long time since I found comfort in religion. Plus, the older I've got, the less it makes sense. Although I do get a pang of annoyance every time a white person tries to introduce me to 'mindfulness'. My people literally invented it! My mum was doing 'mindfulness' while I was in her womb, only we call it meditation or prayer. But not everyone likes those words, so we'll reposition it as 'mindfulness', to give it a more palatable Western twist. Marketing really is a dark art. Like vegan chicken.

I realise while I'm having this rant in my head, how much I'm not missing my job one bit.

I also realise that Sid is asking me a question.

'Shall we head to your grandparents' house, where your father was born? Is that a good place to start?'

'Feels right to visit the Golden Temple. For my dadima.'

'Of course. I love going there. Let's get blessed.' He smiles.

Amritsar is a big, bustling city but we drive towards the centre to park the car near the site. Most of the central area is pedestrianised and done quite recently by the looks of it, for there are old narrow alleyways that shoot off the main wide walkway. We pass shops selling trinkets and artefacts, all Sikh paraphernalia, hundreds of steel karas in different sizes to be worn on the wrist are twinkling at me, reflecting the light, I look down at my own bare wrist, most Sikhs wear one to identify themselves but I took mine off. I don't practice the religion so I didn't feel the need to, but somehow today it feels bare. There are prayer books and turban shops and shops selling dry foods and spices. I must remember to pick up something religious for Dadima, the tackier the better. I wonder if there's anything that glows in the dark? We also pass a McDonald's and a Domino's Pizza.

Sid laughs at my shock as I take in all the fast-food chains here, in this holiest of holy places.

'They are vegetarian. No meat is sold here.'

Turns out Indians, a food-loving nation with one of the best cuisines on the planet, the country that gave the world the first holistic system of medicine, Ayurveda, which promotes balance in life, and acknowledged 5000 years ago – yes, that's 5000! – the connection between what we put into our bodies and our overall health, the country that understood the nutrients and properties and health benefits of spices and vegetables and a balanced diet millennia ago, that very same India can't get enough of American junk food.

168

'Gen X and Y who grew up just as the Indian economy opened up in the nineties, the MTV, Channel V, Sony TV generation, they grew up on a diet of Bollywood and *Friends*, bhangra and hip-hop, and they wanted a bite of that all-American burger.' He says burger with a really thick Indian accent and it makes me chuckle.

'Hey, are you laughing at my accent?' He nudges me playfully on the arm. And my body tingles

'Some of us are allowed to if the context is right,' I shoot back.

I hadn't really noticed Sid's accent; it's definitely Indian but has a transatlantic thing going for it too. Certain words sound American and others English. It's kind of sexy.

'And now with our wealth and sedentary lifestyles, we are getting fat and getting diabetes.'

'Jeez, it's cultural colonisation. Someone's making fat cheques off people getting fat,' I say.

'Probably an Indian.'

Again we laugh.

We take off our shoes and cover our heads before entering the Gurdwara. It is unlike any Gurdwara I have ever been to. The Leeds Road Gurdwara on a Sunday morning during wedding season is chaos, but compared to here, it is a calm, intimate gathering of people. There are thousands of people walking in and out, dropping off and collecting shoes.

First, remove your soles, then save your souls.

I'm completely disorientated. Sid grabs my shoes off me and gives them to a man who gives us a token. OK, so there is a system. We walk to one of the two entrances, passing through a shallow pool of water to cleanse our feet first. I try not to think of other people's verrucas or athlete's foot.

We climb up the steps through the archway and I'm stunned into silence.

There in front of me is the magnificent Golden Temple, an image I've seen my entire life and now I'm finally here and it doesn't disappoint.

It's shimmering golden building, surrounded by water, standing in the middle of a lake with a walkway to enter on one side. It's magnificent and I'm transfixed, taking it in. What a stunning vision someone had. A place designed and built to make people feel awe, peace and reverence. And it seems to be working – at least the awe bit, anyway.

I pause to take it in.

Though I am surrounded by thousands of people, the temple is somehow serene and quiet.

'Isn't it something?' Sid is by my side, taking it all in too.

'The photos don't really prepare you for it,' I say, still taking in the sight in front of me.

'We are a nation of religions and magnificent places of worship and temples galore. Believe me, I've visited a lot, all over the country but this place really is unique and very special.'

I'm so grateful to have Sid with me.

There's a beautiful soundtrack of shabads being played through what must be very powerful speakers, echoing around the four walls.

'That's the kirtan that's being sung inside. We should do what everyone is doing, descend these steps and circumnavigate the lake and pay our respects to the Guru Granth Sahib inside the building.' This I knew to do but I like that he's forward planning. I'm excited about seeing it from the inside.

There really are thousands of people here but there's no hustle and it's quiet and so peaceful.

I spend a bit of time watching the people from all walks of life from all over the world. Some sitting around the lake having quiet conversations, others sitting alone in contemplation, and many people blessing themselves with the water from the lake. Some blokes have stripped to their undies and are fully submerging themselves.

'Funny, isn't it, that the hair is still covered,' I observe.

'I suppose, but it's respectful to cover the hair and take a dip for blessings. I'd never thought about it before. Your Western eyes are giving me something to think about.' He smiles down at me. 'If women want to do the same and fully submerge, there's a small area covered over and protected to preserve dignity, but you can also just stand on the side and splash yourself with the water if you want to.'

For a nation that famously hates to queue, everyone is very respectful here. I like that it still feels informal with children and families all around me and I feel that I'm in a place that is familiar. The sounds, the faces, the knowing what to do – going to the Gurdwara is the same wherever you are in the world, I suppose.

I'm craving my Gurdwara buddy, though. I wish Dadima was here with me now. I think about how important the temple is in her life back in Bradford and now appreciate why. The temple is so much more than a place for spiritual solace in the UK; the temple is culture, it is community, familiarity, a piece of home in a foreign land. It's a place where Dadima could fully be herself.

I feel a pang of guilt for not going for so many years. For me, it's a place to dodge aunties. I make a mental note to take a trip as soon as I get back with Mum and Dadima. She'll love that I want to.

The queue moves slowly but eventually we shuffle our way inside, a little too close to an uncle with oversized multi-coloured turban – got to give him props for his style sense though.

I'm awestruck. It's much smaller inside than it looks. In the centre, on the ground floor, is the Holy Book, the Guru Granth Sahib, where pilgrims are bowing their heads. There's an old man with an excellent long white beard sitting behind it, fanning the book, which is revered as the last remaining Guru. To one side are the Gianis, the priests, playing the harmonium and singing the magnificent kirtan with soothing voices. I look up and see only balconies; it's just as ornate inside as out, with intricate patterns on the golden walls and arches. It's more like a palace.

My eyes are welling up without me realising.

My experience of visiting the Golden Temple is grounding, humbling and has made me homesick. Maybe I should drop them a text.

171

Once back out by the lake, I get Sid to take a picture of me in front of it and send it to Mum.

Thinking of you both and thinking of Dad and Grandad. It's more beautiful in real life.

I can see instant typing.

Who are you with? Who is this Sid? Are you OK? Nice photo. How is the weather? Make sure you stay out of the sun. *Ball of yarn emoji*. That's new for her.

So, word about who I'm with has got back to Blighty. Masi and Mum must have had a long discussion about everything. What do I say in response that they don't read anything into? If I say he's nice, they'll think I want to marry him. That is how their brains work.

Sid is fine, knows Punjabi so is handy.

You know Punjabi. Speak it. Don't be shy. And stay out of the sun. *ghost emoji*

We next visit Jallianwala Bhagh to see where General Dyer, a British officer, ordered his troops to open fire on a gathering of families on Vaisakhi in a park. It's only when I see the place that my heart stops. The green open space is surrounded by a wall and there is only one entrance. It was through this narrow alley that Dyer marched in his troops along with a tank. The families didn't stand a chance.

I clench my fists. This is so much more than I was prepared for.

Inside, it's more like a tourist park, with families sitting around and enjoying themselves. Which doesn't sit right with what happened here.

'This happened just after the First World War. India had sent a million men to join the war effort, in the hope that such help would allow them to have dominion status afterwards, but the opposite happened.'

I love that Sid has all this knowledge at his fingertips and he's able to explain it so well.

172

'They passed something called the Rowlatt Act in March 1919, giving the British the power to hold trials without juries and imprison anyone they suspected of a seditious act, so basically, the police could arrest anyone without a reason.'

'What?'

'They feared the threat of nationalist "terrorism" as they saw it.'

'It wasn't even their country – they were the terrorists!' I say, practically shouting.

Sid carries on.

'So here on 19th April people had gathered to celebrate Biasakhi, but the Brits said it was a political gathering and General Dyer decided to march in his troops and, without any warning, opened fire.'

I'm screwing my face up with the pain and shock of the story.

'They only stopped when their ammunition ran out.'

We look at each other.

'And we don't know the exact figure of how many people died. Between 300 to over a thousand.'

I look away from him.

'Fucking bastards!'

I'm seeing my connection to this land and what was done to it in a completely new light. I'd never before thought of myself in the context of India. Why would I? I'm from Bradford. But now I know you can be from two places at once; there's a place I am physically connected to and the other I am spiritually entwined with. We were never taught anything about Empire or colonialism in school – nothing – and yet British history for a good three hundred years was India. But all we hear about are the two World Wars and how great the Victorians were. No doubt they were great – the Industrial Revolution in Britain was a marvel – but how did they get there? How were all those feats of engineering funded? How was it getting so rich in the first place? With a great deal of blood on its hands. The blood of my people.

'I think I'm ready to leave now.' The past seems so immediate here. It's as if I can feel the anguish of those whose lives were taken here; the grief is overwhelming.

Sid watches me for a moment before putting his arm around me. The weight of it is a comfort.

'Come on, let's go.' He releases me and I am surprised to miss the feel of him, the pleasant scent of his cologne.

'OK, so where next then, Baby? This is your quest.'

He's attempting to lighten my mood and I'm grateful to him. I pull out a piece of paper from my bag.

'I want to go to my family home. Well, the house where my gran and grandad lived before they moved to England.'

He takes the paper from me, his fingers brushing against my palm.

'Great,' he says, looking at the address. 'This isn't too far away. Shall we grab something to eat then hit the road? I promise not to take you to any foreign fast-food joints. Indian for us Indians.' He grins.

I roll my eyes, but inwardly I feel a thrill. Finally, he sees me as one of his own. I am Indian, and I have never felt more so.

We eat on the go, picking up a couple of freshly made buttery parathas from a street stall, then a quick pitstop for a decent coffee because Sid is craving coffee and set off for the village, Sid estimating it'll only take about forty-five minutes to get there.

I feel antsy. I keep checking the car clock. I wipe my palms on my trousers, and take a deep breath, willing myself to be calm but the drive feels longer than our trip from Delhi.

I can't believe I'm going to see their home! My heart is racing. Finally, I'll have another piece of the jigsaw. An insight into my past, into my family's roots. It feels like the true start of my journey to get answers.

We reach a big roundabout. Sid misses an opportunity to pull out and horns start going behind us. I turn to him. He's frowning, playing with the sat nav. Another horn goes. Sid hits the steering wheel and pulls out, driving all the way round the roundabout before coming off on the same road we've just been on. He drives down the road a little before pulling in.

'Is everything all right?' I ask.

'Baby, I'm sorry.'

I almost don't dare ask.

'What for?' I whisper.

'The village isn't there anymore. Your family's home – it's gone.' He looks at me and takes my hand. 'Baby, I'm so sorry.'

For the first time since my dad died, I cry.

He puts his hand on my shoulder.

'Hey, Baby, you want to talk about it?' he asks softly.

'I don't know why but I foolishly somehow thought this place would be it. It would answer my questions. I'd find out about everything in their old home. But they sold it years ago because after Grandad died, Dad wasn't really very interested in keeping a property in India. Mum wanted to keep it, though, probably to feel as though she still had some connection to the place, not that any of us were going to go and stay there. They sold it and I'd never even given it one moment of thought, until now, being in India and feeling emotions I'd never expected about the place. I'm so annoyed with myself for knowing so little.'

'Don't beat yourself up. You are here finding everything out because you now want answers. Of course it's emotional, you are absorbing so much information, it's bringing up many feelings.'

I nod and wipe my tears.

I'm sad, surprisingly sad, at it not being here. But it's only deepened my resolve to find out about my family. How do I know so little?

'Hey, don't worry! There is somewhere we could go that might help.'

I look up at him with determination in my eyes.

'Let's go.'

We travel back towards where we were by the Golden Temple to The Partition Museum.

'We were right here two hours ago and could have seen it then,' I say, slightly annoyed.

175

'Ouch! I'm following *your* lead, Baby.'

'What do I know?' I'm enjoying having a go at him with a smile. 'Well, I've now run out of ideas completely. So I'm in your hands.' Wishing I was holding his hands.

The Partition Museum only opened in 2015 and it's here that my eyes are truly opened to what happened in 1947.

'This is the first-ever monument of any kind dedicated to the Partition and it's really to remember the people who were affected.'

It's not a vast museum, just a few rooms, but it sets the scene and tells the story of what happened. I'm transfixed looking at all the displays of artefacts like letters of life after Partition and people's belongings that they took with them, coins, necklaces and pocket watches.

I'm watching testimonial videos of people who lived through it, who witnessed the violence and chaos.

I'm thinking about the million people who didn't survive.

And then the map. The reason for the bloodshed. The map of the line that was drawn by a lawyer from London, Cyril Radcliffe, who'd never been to India before, who had no particular geographical or cartographical skills and who was given one of the most highly pressured jobs in history.

Sid is talking to a beautiful middle-aged woman in a stunning saree. She looks over at me before they finish their conversation and come towards me. I'm still studying the map.

'He had only six weeks to do the job,' she says. Her name is Seema and she works at the museum.

'I'll never complain about feeling pressure at work again.' I point at the map. 'He missed a bit.'

'Ah yes, Kashmir. Heaven on earth. Beautiful land, beautiful people. What a tragic mess.'

'Well, if the British left a gaping wound to keep us at each other's throats, they succeeded,' says Sid, and then adds, 'Bastards!' In a perfect Yorkshire accent.

'So Sid has told me about these letters you have? How wonderful!'

176

He did what? I shoot him a look. He looks guilty and gives me an apologetic shrug.

'Could I take a look?' Seema asks, her eyes twinkling.

I have to think twice as no one outside the inner sanctum of trust knows about them.

I take out a letter but keep it in my hand. I'm nervous at too many people seeing these delicate portals to the past, my family's past, certainly not before my family know anything about what I'm up to, so they still feel like my secret, my treasure. But if anyone should see, it's Seema – she may be the only person who can help me.

'This is remarkable. What a treasure trove you have stumbled across.' She is peering very closely at it.

'I'm trying to find out what happened to Naseeb, the woman who wrote the letters. Is there any kind of archive of the names of the people who lived through Partition? Where their houses were pre-Partition, where they moved to? I'm desperate to find anything out.'

Sid has walked away to look at one of the exhibits. Maybe he's feeling guilty about overstepping the mark. I'm glad he feels a bit bad but also don't want to hurt his feelings. Goddam, my inner people pleaser!

'I'm afraid we don't have any kind of archive here. We are still very much trying to build up the museum. And on that, if you are interested, we'd be very interested in acquiring Naseeb's letters from you, to be kept safely here?' She looks at me hopefully.

I step back and clutch the letter close to my chest. 'No way!'

She seems a little put out.

Maybe my reaction was too strong. But hell no, lady, you're not getting your hands on my treasure. I've only just found the letters myself.

'Of course, they are a sacred family heirloom, and you should keep them. But some advice if you don't mind. Please look after the paper, keep them in an airtight container if you can. And if ever you should want to pass them on to be looked after for generations to come, then please remember us.'

I feel a little embarrassed by my Gollum-like possession over my 'preciousesssss'. I'd love for these letters to be preserved for the future, and where better to bequeath them eventually?

'Thank you, I'll absolutely bear you in mind,' I say.

She nods and smiles then.

'I can't help you further, I'm afraid, but I do know that a register of births and deaths is kept in Haridwar. You should go there next; perhaps you will discover more.'

We thank her and leave, dropping some money into the donations box on the way out.

I say nothing as we walk towards the car. Giving him the silent treatment for betraying my trust. And then eventually I speak.

'When I said I was in your hands, I didn't mean for you to take over completely. You didn't have the right to tell her about the letters. *My* letters.'

'She was the perfect person to tell. I'm sorry, I didn't think it would upset you. I thought you wanted my help? Or do you just want me as a chauffeur to drive you across India?'

He's not backing down.

'Well, I'm sorry you're so put out by all of this. If you don't want to be here, just leave. Just go.'

There's a short silence and then he says in a calmer tone, 'The problem is, Baby, I don't want to leave. In fact, there's nowhere I'd rather be. Which makes me feel like a complete idiot, to be honest.'

This makes me smile.

'You were an idiot before I met you,' I say and punch his arm.

'It's just been a really full-on day. I'm feeling emotionally raw and absorbing so much information, plus the disappointment of not finding out anything concrete. I guess I just took it out on you . . . I don't want you to leave either – I need a chauffeur to get me to Haridwar, wherever that is.'

'At your service, madam.'

Haridwar is a sacred town on the banks of the Ganges. Not too far away apparently. Only another eight-hour drive!

'Hey, Pinks. How are you doing? Today has been . . . full-on. God, I can't believe I'm crying on this voice note. You know I never cry – but Pinks, it's just so much, too much to comprehend. We went to the museum, and I simply wasn't ready, nothing in my life until now had helped me prepare for this experience. How do we know so little about the horror of what happened during Partition? How has no one talked to us, how have we not spoken about it? This huge part of our history? Who we are? I didn't *know*. And I feel ashamed. How those women suffered, it's just . . . I hope you're not listening to this in front of the kids. They shouldn't hear this, not yet anyway. But those women, their bodies used to wage war. Like they were nothing. Just property, possessions, worthless commodities. Not just by those who had once been their neighbours and friends, but their own families were killing them. The men, they were transformed into animals, there's no other way to describe it.

'Do you think it's because men feel such great shame at their thoughts about women that they have to destroy us? They killed their own women, beheaded their own wives, daughters, sisters rather than have them abducted or murdered or raped by the others. *Our* women, Pinks. If we'd been born only eighty years earlier, not even a lifetime, it could have been us. This is getting deep, I know, and probably not really a voice note topic, but I just had to get my thoughts out to someone.

'I just can't believe that these communities, who had lived together side by side as friends for centuries, then turned on each other. All hell broke loose. After 300 years of taking from India, the Brits sliced the place up and made a run for it. Leaving India to suffer, to bleed, to die. First, Calcutta and then Punjab, erupted into hell. Hell.'

I breathe.

'It's a lot for me to process. I'm sorry I left this message. Please don't worry about me. I'm fine. It's just a lot.'

Another deep breath.

'Amritsar had no answers about my family. I still don't know what happened to Naseeb but we're heading to a place called Haridwar now, on the banks of the Ganges. They hold records of people's family trees there, apparently, so maybe I'll get some answers finally.

'I doubt there'll be anything about my family, I can't imagine anyone being that organised. I'm yet to be convinced there's any kind of organised ancestry registration in India at all. Sid has kindly agreed to drive me there.

'Anyway, love you and love to the kids. Next VN will hopefully be less heavy, lol!'

I sign off with a false note of cheer that I don't really feel.

Chapter Twelve

We had a playlist provided by the best DJ in the world that no one has ever heard of (me), enough snacks to fuel around fifty men (or . . . me), and a couple of comfort stops (one of which scarred me for life). Stepping in human faeces while wearing flip-flops is not an experience I would wish on anyone and the smell has possibly melted something in my nostrils. I'm glad Mum forced me to pack my own Andrex now. Apart from that hiccup, the road trip was pretty sweet, punctuated by a lot of laughter, a lot of singing, watching the changing landscape and – what more could a girl want? – beautiful, effortless silences.

Sid and I have spent a lot of time together in this car, breathing the same air. I wonder if he's tired. The driving is intense and long and it's India, so the experience is challenging and I'm only the passenger. I wonder how he's feeling.

'Thank you.'

He glances at me.

'Thank you for driving me and agreeing to go on this escapade. You really didn't need to do any of it, but you did, and I really appreciate it, so thank you.' *Oh no, I've ruined the carefree vibe.*

'Firstly, you don't have to thank me, I'm doing this because I want to. I mean, it was a risk, you might have been terrible company, or an awful person.'

He makes me smile.

'Are you sure you're OK driving?' We're on hour five out of eight at this point, and even though he has stamina, this would kill anyone.

'You wanna drive?'

Driving for me is freedom; I've loved it ever since I passed my test. It was the first time in my life I was able to have some independence. No more waiting at the bus stop, hoping the service was running on time. I could jump in the car and go wherever I wanted, which usually involved taking Dadima to Costco, but still . . . what Asian woman doesn't love buying in bulk? I had all these plans to go on adventurous road trips but the furthest I got was a trip to Leeds with the family to an all-you-can eat Asian buffet. Everyone loved it and I ate my body weight in those pointless spring rolls with the sweet chilli dip and managed to get flashed by a speed camera on the way home. Leeds to Bradford is ten miles! So much for a life on the open road.

'Yeah, I really would love to drive.'

Sid pulls over, and we switch sides.

'Ooh, this seat has been kept nice and warm by your hot butt cheeks.' OMG, did I say that out loud?

'Thinking about my hot butt, are you?'

'Yeah, I've checked you out, you'll do,' I say casually.

'You'll do too, I suppose,' he says back

Shit, it's getting hot in here. I open the window.

It's liberating. I'm not stuck in my head anymore, because my focus is on the road and keeping us both alive. And making sure I don't kill anyone or anything that appears in front of me. It's not long before I have to slam on the brakes for a person, then a cow, then a cow and a person.

Driving in India is not for the faint-hearted.

Haridwar is one of the seven holiest cities in India, believed to be a place for people tired of life. So, I'm in the right place. It's known as the 'Gateway to the Gods' and anyone who washes in the Ganges washes away their sins, or perhaps gets a bad case of dysentery– I forget the saying. I'll leave the dipping to the hardened locals and keep my sins with me on this trip, thank you. It's after dark when we arrive, but my guide has already called ahead and arranged a hotel. Apparently, this is how Sid rolls, with 'hook-ups' all over India. He explains that if he hasn't got a direct link, he'll know someone, who'll know someone, who'll know someone else, who can arrange whatever he needs in any city in India – and, in this case, what I need in Haridwar. It's the way India works; people will just help you out.

'If you're well-connected enough and rich enough?' I ask.

'You're right.'

I'm right!

Haridwar is spirituality on acid. After parking the car in a dodgy-looking car park (to be honest, I'm unsure if it'll still be in one piece when we return), we walk along narrow lanes lined with stalls selling every kind of Hindu memorabilia; some sell bangles, others jewellery or street food. I go slightly mad for the tacky religious trinkets and am instantly drawn to a glow-in-the-dark flying Hanuman, complete with his weapon of choice – the mace – and I buy eight. I decide they'll make the perfect gift for everyone I know. Who wouldn't want a plastic glow-in-the-dark monkey god?

Some of my favourite childhood memories are of Dadima telling me stories of the gods at bedtime. At the time, I thought they were simple fairy tales, like everyone else had heard, but Dadima was telling me stories about the ten Sikh gurus and my favourites always involved Guru Nanak, who turned his back on the family business to become a travelling sage with two disciples, one Hindu, one Sikh, preaching the idea of one god, no caste or class or religion for that matter. The dude was ahead of his time. I also loved hearing fables from Hindu mythology like The Ramayana, which tells the story of Prince Ram who is exiled into a forest for fourteen years with his wife, Sita, and his little brother, Lakhshmana. Sita is captured by the demon Ravana, so Ram, Lakhshmana along with Hanuman, his magic powers and his army of warrior monkeys went on a mission to rescue her. After their exile they return to their kingdom and people lit divas along the path so they would find their way back and that is why Diwali is celebrated and candles are lit. The magic was endless to my childhood ears, little boy gods with elephant heads, goddesses that slew demons and rode tigers, great

Mughal emperors who built palaces for their beloved wives. Stories about the universe and reincarnation and time. All of which were enchanting tales that I couldn't get enough of.

'More, Dadima, more!'

'There are plenty more, let's save some for tomorrow.'

Bedtime with Dadima was the best.

It's still warm after dark and the streets feel like a film set. Never have I been to a place more atmospheric than Haridwar. The place is alive and bustling with families out eating street food, most of whom will be here on a pilgrimage to visit the five main temples in the town, or one of the many others; or to float the ashes of a departed loved one down the Ganges, or have a puja with a priest by the river or be absolved of their sins; tourists who have come for a trip, people registering births and deaths and those, like me, who have come to find their family's history, if it exists.

It feels so good to be here with Sid. I notice he looks a little tired. His voice is a little deeper, his eyes and with those ridiculous eyelashes half-shut, he's even more attractive. It really feels like me and him against the world, in our own little bubble. I can't help but feel excited.

'Is this a good place to try some street food?'

'Are you in India?' he says, grinning and brushing back his hair. The action lifts his T-shirt and I notice a flash of his abs. I feel the urge to take his T-shirt off. Am I actually licking my lips?

'I'm famished,' I say, turning to look at the food stalls.

We stop at a small vendor selling chaat. Street snacks are designed to get your appetite going, so I plan on sampling a lot. I'm definitely Indian when it comes to my eating habits. I'm quite partial to the odd meal between meals. I order some bhel puri, avoiding my favourite pani puri because we can't be sure the 'pani', or water, which is used to make the tamarind sauce, is filtered – and that would be an utter disaster for my delicate Western digestive system. Water is something I have to be very careful of, so we are buying bottles and bottles of mineral water, which seems criminal in a country where so many still don't have access to any water at all, let alone clean water that won't make you sick.

I inhale the smells of the puffed rice, fresh-chopped onion and tomato, sev (which adds crunch and texture), tamarind chutney, chopped green chillis, coriander and a sprinkling of this particular vendor's chaat masala, and it's done, in seconds. Watching his hands prepare the plate was mesmerising and over in a flash.

'Is chaat lunch or dinner usually?' I ask Sid.

'Chaat fits in anywhere you like – it's in addition to.' The vendor passes the bhel puri to Sid, who hands it to me and winks. Who looks that sexy while winking? 'I personally think it's delicious all on its own.' He takes a bite, his eyes still on me, and I realise just how nice his lips are. I shake my head. I should not be thinking about Sid's mouth.

I eat some of my own chaat and I totally get it. In this moment, eating the bhel puri down a narrow alley, with a cow trying to manoeuvre past, and hordes of spirituality seekers, I can completely understand why Sid would have chosen to stay in India rather than anywhere else in the world. The street food alone is a great reason to stay, but it's more than that. There is something in the air, here. Maybe it's because I feel closer to Dadima and my family, my father through my grandma, but this place really does have a way of making you feel at home.

Sid has booked a hotel right on the banks of the river. It's not luxurious, but it's better than a luxury hotel ever could be – full of character, it's an old haveli mansion house converted into a heritage hotel, painted pink on the outside. Inside it's an oasis of calm with a beautiful courtyard in the middle and perfect clean, comfortable rooms with beautiful big teak wooden beds. It's perfectly magical.

We decide to stay in for dinner, too tired to venture back out. I'm quiet as we eat, overtired from the journey, overly stuffed from my two consecutive meals, and nervous about what tomorrow might bring.

We head up to our rooms, which are right next to each other. He walks me to my door. I open it then turn around to face him. He's leaning against the door frame, looking down at me through those goddam eyelashes. It might be the extra chilli or it might be the way he's looking at me, but blood rushes to my face. I feel as if I'm burning up.

'Where do we even start?' I ask.

'I made another call.' *Of course, he has, Annoying, Connected Sid.* 'To a hook-up, and we have to get up early to see a man.'

'About a dog?' I say, reflexively.

'No, why would we need a dog?' I decide I will never be able to explain this expression in a way that would make sense.

I scrunch my face up, about to say something, but notice the softness in his eyes and stop short. I feel drunk. For what feels like a lifetime, I do nothing but stare back. He bends down to kiss me, and the moment his lips touch mine, I'm done for. He strokes his thumb along my jaw then cups the back of my head, his hand gently gripping my hair, before deepening the kiss.

I have never been kissed like this . . .

We stumble backwards into my room, never breaking contact. There's nothing I can do to stop this from happening. There's nothing I want to do to stop this happening.

I close the door.

I wake up feeling weightless, content. And turn. But Sid is no longer in my bed. Did I dream us having sex last night? I notice it's only dawn, which is amazing considering how difficult I usually find getting my ass out of bed. Early mornings back in Manchester are my nemesis. There, the sun streaming through my windows makes me shrink away like a vampire but, here, now, in this alien place, in this new world, with no signs of my old life whatsoever, waking up at sunrise just happens. It happens because I'm excited by what this day will hold, and the answers I might discover. But also because being in one of the holiest and busiest cities on Earth, waking up first thing seems appropriate. My spiritual clock realises that dawn is the best time to arise here as I head down to the steps of the Ganges.

I'm not alone in waking early. I knew I wouldn't be – it is seen as a virtue, as Dadima and Mum have told me, and shown me, most of my life. It doesn't matter what time I ever got up, they had always been awake for hours and managed to achieve more in a morning than most people would in a day. They would have prayed, cleaned, cooked two or three curries (waking up to the smell of onions, garlic and ginger is the definition of growing up brown) before I'd even brushed my teeth. I never could understand why they cooked first thing in the morning, when most other people, the 'normal' white people, would cook dinner just before dinner. I realise now it's because we do things according to daylight hours, because there was no electricity in Punjab, or at least no guarantee the electricity would stick around. Morning cooking sessions remain. Plus, everyone knows any curry tastes better a few hours after it's cooked.

My stomach rumbles as I sit on the steps by the banks of the Holy River Ganges, just outside the hotel. It's the perfect spot to watch people go for a dip in the river, and to stop myself from thinking obsessively about Sid and what's going on between us. I look at them and imagine what sins they need clemency for. Did the two teen girls sneak out last night? They look like they share a secret. Is the man in a shirt and tie, trousers rolled up to his knees and his belt pulled a little too tight, asking forgiveness for wearing his wife's underwear, perhaps? The thought makes me chuckle. Is the pious-looking young man having dirty thoughts? I look at the priests conducting the various pujas and artis taking place and remember I'd heard that some of the priests love nothing more than to rip tourists off. I wonder if they see that as a sin, or whether they have a sin-free pass, a virtue ticket for the holy only.

A young woman is praying hard, tears rolling down her cheeks, and I wonder what her sin is. Hating her husband or her mother or her father or hating her life? I wonder what emotion she is feeling. She looks so utterly broken and in pain – or is it rage she's feeling. The rage that comes with being a woman, when you're powerless? Am I just projecting my own feelings onto this woman because, deep down somewhere inside me, I feel rage? Maybe her heart is simply broken.

Sitting underneath a pink and orange rising Indian sun, I can already feel the heat that will only intensify as it continues to rise. The morning light shines on the ripples in the water as I watch the spectacle in front of me, the volume only half as loud as it will get to in just a couple of hours, and I'm allowing myself to feel something. For the first time, I'm actively trying to clear my head, instead of letting the thoughts and questions buzzing around find a place to get comfy. I'm just letting myself be, not overthinking, and so my mind wanders to Naseeb, to this woman I have never met, never seen, will never touch, will never know.

I take her letters out of my bag, for what feels like the hundredth time. Sitting here, with Naseeb's letters in my hands, I feel as though this is the closest I will come to knowing her and her life. This woman resides in me somewhere. I feel her in me. Maybe today I will get some of my answers, but I know I shouldn't get my hopes up.

Naseeb was so smart, from her letters, and had so much to say, I wonder what she would be doing if she was my age? Naseeb, born eighties Britain! She'd be more successful than me, no doubt. A lot more fearless, maybe. A high-flying human rights barrister or a journalist, I should think. Would she have wanted children? What kind of mother would she have been in a different place, a different time? A brilliant, progressive one, I reckon. And maybe married or maybe not, it's irrelevant. The point is, she would have a say. Yes, she'd definitely have a say.

Or, maybe, just like me, she'd be crippled by fear, never really doing much, always worried on some level about doing the wrong thing.

No – no, not Naseeb. She would be incredible, my best friend too, my confidante. I feel her in every breath, like I was meant to find those letters. I'm meant to be right here. I'm meant to be on this quest. I'm meant to be sitting on the banks of the Ganges, at sunrise, watching a woman in a white saree with a shaved head descend the steps as though she's the only person in the world.

August, 1946

Jaan

I was so, so happy the day you came home to me. The entire village was lifted that day.

I wanted to be held in your arms for an eternity. I never ever wanted you to let me go.

The smell of you brings me such comfort as you talk into my ear in whispers at night in bed, so that your parents can't hear. I miss being held in your strong arms, the place where I feel safest.

Why did you have to go again? Did they need to post you somewhere else? I wish we could have come with you.

We got you so briefly. You were so tired, and I loved soothing you in my arms, stroking your hair in bed, cradling you, protecting you. In our world, in our love, we are equals.

Please make sure they don't push you too hard at work. Eat well and try and rest.

Our daughter Preet is well. She is our pride. She is so loved. She misses her papa.

We all do.

Come home to us soon.

You are in my prayers.

Your jaan,

Naseeb

Chapter Thirteen

Sid sits down next to me and makes me jump, nearly knocking the glass of hot spiced chai he has brought for me out of his hands. I smile and suddenly become aware of my body, which feels alive and sensual like never before; there's an effortlessness between us and I'm happy and relieved to see him and grateful for the tea, which is shockingly sweet – so much so I grind my teeth and my lips recede. *This really is a nation with a sweet tooth*, I think.

'She's a high-caste widow,' Sid says, sitting down next to me, noticing who my attention is on. 'She'll wear white sarees and have a shaved head for the rest of her life.' I look at him, markedly shocked. 'White is the colour of mourning, and she will no longer need to make herself beautiful, you see.'

'But that's so cruel! She's still human, still a woman. That's so dehumanising.'

'Mm hmm, some women live like pariahs after they lose their husbands. She could even be ostracised from her family and her community for the rest of her life, too. I'm not sure whether she, personally, is made to live away from people but, by the way she looks and how she has probably been made to dress, her family uphold these old traditions.' He turns to look at me, looking quite serious as he says, 'Widows are seen as cursed. Not all and things are changing, but we are a nation of 1.4 billion, so we have every variation amongst us.'

'Tradition?' I almost spit out my tea. 'It's barbarism!'

Then I notice another woman descending the steps.

'She is part of the hijra community,' he says.

The people-watching here is on another level.

'Trans?' I ask.

190

'Transvestites, transsexuals, transgenders, eunuchs. The oldest Trans community on Earth. There's mention of them in ancient texts but their community was outlawed under the British, along with homosexuality. And now a third gender is recognised in law, here in the East – far more progressive than your West!' he says with a smile and then continues. 'Modern and ancient, progressive and regressive, they sit side by side in this nation.'

We sit in silence after that, sipping our tea, watching the woman. Sometimes, I think the same about my own family, how progressive and utterly regressive sit next to each other. Young and old, parents trying to bridge the gap. Another door unlocks inside me. The weight of potential is heavy. If I can find out the secrets of our past, maybe I can join the disparate dots in my own life. I've always felt as if I've been fighting a battle at home, with Mum or the aunties, and I thought coming on this trip and finding out about where I come from might help me give them a break, but now I'm beginning to realise that I'm just another young woman in a long line of women in my ancestry who is fighting against a system of oppression. This trip is making me bolder.

'I could get my answers today, Sid. By tonight, I could know what happened to Naseeb . . .'

'Seriously? Has nobody thought to digitise the system?' I say in exasperation.

Haridwar is a city of records. Families have been coming here for centuries to record births and deaths, priests recording the information for them. Only, the system isn't computerised. That would be too easy, too efficient.

The priests are the gatekeepers, and the first task, the first mountain to climb, is to find the priest who holds the key to the cupboard which contains the book or scroll that has your family's details in it . . . *Simple, right*? It's a true North Indian Hindu genealogy-charting system. I'm impatient to find out more, anything more, and we ask a few people based on the little information I have. But the records are kept in cupboards in rooms all over the city. So first we have to find the right priest – and there are *thousands* in Haridwar.

Sid walks up to a group gathered on the banks and speaks to them in Hindi. I walk up and stand next to him.

'Yes, the name is Saul. S.A.U.L.' I'm chipping in, but they just look at me quizzically and go back to paying attention to Sid.

Then one pandit begins to shake his head more vigorously than the others. Apparently, this is an affirmative. He thinks he knows just the man – and it is always a man. And he can take us for a small fee.

'He's going to charge us?' I ask.

'Well, it's how they make their living. Oh, and he did try to rip us off.'

We're an 'us' now. My heart flutters.

'Heard your English accent and thought he could swindle the tourists. But it's sorted.'

'If these records had been digitised, it'd be so much easier,' I say.

'Yes, but this is India, madam. Ready for mission find the priest?'

'Ready as I'll ever be, captain.' And I stand to attention and salute. Feeling excited by the prospect.

We travel along narrow alleyways and backstreets, old homes and rooms practically stacked on top of each other. We turn up at a few rickety old houses, speak to a few priests who look after the scrolls of people with the same surname as my family. But none of the families are mine. It's dead end after dead end, frustrating and exhausting. We seem to be getting nowhere.

'We need a bit more information,' Sid says, hands open, no sign of frustration in his eyes. *Goddammit, why does he have to have such* nice *eyes?* His kindness and patience seem to grow in proportion with my agitation.

I wanted to do this journey by myself, but I've not been alone for the entire trip, so I think I need to shift my thinking. Why haven't I done that already? I speak to myself, standing hands on hips, as Sid looks at me, waiting for me to say something. *This is the moment you need to give in and do the thing you never do – the thing you hate doing – and ask for help. You already have Annoying, Helpful Sid helping you, and he's doing it for nothing, out of the literal goodness of his own heart. And you – you, Baby* (oh, very stern, but yes, this is working!) *need to get a grip. You are not above asking for help. Everyone needs help. And, right now, you need the only person who can possibly help.*

'Hi, Dadima.'

'Ooohh, Baby, so nice to hear your voice, beta. All OK? How is India? Not too hot? Are you enjoying? How is your tummy? No Delhi belly? Are you safe? No issues? The food is delicious, isn't it? I'm so happy you went to the Golden Temple and got blessings. I'm sending you my blessings now. Your mummy isn't here.'

Trying to actually get a word in to ask Dadima my questions is always the biggest challenge.

'That's fine, Dadima. It's you I need to speak to. I'm in Haridwar.'

'Haridwar?! Are you on a pilgrimage, Baby? I thought you wanted to rest in a five-star hotel and get expensive massage, to help with your relaxing.'

'I am here to relax, Dadima, but I thought I should know a bit more about the culture . . . and history.'

Silence.

'About who *we* are.'

'Who *I* am.'

'Why are you asking this, Baby? Why did you go to Haridwar?'

'I just, well, there's some things about our family that I'd like to know more about. I don't really know much about our history, so I'm here to find our family scroll.'

Silence.

'I just need a bit of information, Dadima, if you can help me.' I am beginning to think this was a very, very bad idea. 'Have you ever been here?'

After what feels like an age, Dadima speaks.

'I suppose it was only a matter of time before you would want to know everything; you modern girls always have so

193

many questions, always asking, asking, asking. Baby, I will not stop you, this is your history. But I cannot tell you everything, I only know what I know, the rest you can only find out yourself.'

Dadima is being cryptic, but then, so am I. I'm not revealing the truth about the letters and neither is she, but I know we are both thinking about them, and about Naseeb.

'I did go to Haridwar with your grandad, after we were married. I didn't go in to see the pandit, that was Grandad's job, but I do remember an old house with a blue door – oh, and an enormous banyan tree in the middle of the courtyard. And monkeys! Give them our surname, as well as the last place we lived before we moved, just outside Amritsar. Maybe this will be enough to help you.'

'Thank you, Dadima.' I pause, before ending with, 'Between you and me, yeah?'

'Yes, beta, between you and me.'

'What's between who?' I hear Mum shout in the background.

'Your mum is back,' she says to me and then shouts to Mum, 'It's BABY, SHE IS IN HARIDWAR.'

The phone then cuts off only for a FaceTime request to come through.

'Hey, Mum, hey, Dadima.' It's nice to see them both, even if the camera is far too close to their faces and constantly moving, so I'm catching glimpses of their chins.

'What are you doing in Haridwar? Your masi tells me you are now on a fact-finding mission about the past? As long as you are OK, looking after yourself, not eating anything to upset your tummy, staying out of the sun.'

I'm aware that Sid is right beside me, overhearing Mum. He gives me a knowing nod then begins to walk away, probably realising that I'm mortified at Mum talking to me like I'm seven years old.

'Yes, Mum, I'm having a great time. Being well looked after.'

I get a warm feeling, almost a tingle, at what feels like an in-joke between me and Sid.

194

'Where is he, then? This young man who is looking after my daughter?'

'Erm.' Oh, shit. They want to meet Sid. Why am I feeling nervous? There's nothing to be nervous about, it's not like there's anything going on. Or at least there wasn't, until last night.

Sid appears behind me on the screen and I see Mum's eyes widen and Dadima's eyes soften and relax.

'Hello, aunty.' He's smiling and confident.

'Ah, the gentleman looking after my daughter. Thank you, Siddharth. She's not too much trouble, is she? She's quite feisty, our Baby.'

Mum!

'No, she's lovely, aunty, and it's no trouble, honestly. Nice to meet you.'

'Oh, such a nice-looking man thinks my daughter is lovely. So, Siddharth, my sister tells me you run your own business?'

OK, that's quite enough chit-chat between Mum and Sid.

'Mum, Sid has to go.' I'm pushing him away from the phone.

He's barely a few steps away and both Mum and Dadima start talking about how handsome he is. Dadima can't stop smiling. I walk away from Sid as quickly as I can.

'You two! I'm here to find out about history, not find a husband.'

'You could do both,' says Mum and winks.

'It's been so nice to see your faces in extreme close-up, I love you both, got to go and find a pandit . . . and not for a wedding.'

Dadima's advice changes everything. It only takes another half an hour of asking for a house with a banyan tree in the courtyard to find it. A small, smiling pandit, dressed in a loin-cloth with beads around his neck and markings on his forehead, ushers me through a small door and into a tiny room filled with four metal lockers, a duvet on the floor being the only seating arrangement. He gestures only to Sid, asking him to sit, before Sid tells him it is me doing the searching.

The pandit shakes his head. 'It's usual for us to only deal with the men in the family.'

195

'Tell him there are no men in my family. I'm it. It's only me.'

Sid does so, and the priest, reluctantly, without saying anything to me, gestures for me to sit instead. He opens the door to one of the metal cabinets. It's stacked full of long, thin notebooks rolled up like scrolls, each with pages and pages filled with information of people's ancestry – records of births, deaths, marriages, dating back centuries. I can't believe what I'm seeing – how can the priest know where to look? How could he possibly remember? I'm not convinced this is any kind of organised system. How can it be? And yet, this has worked for hundreds of years, hasn't it? The priest obviously knows exactly which register to get out of the fifty or so in there.

The pandit sits next to me, cross-legged, unravels the paper and begins to flick through. It's many pages. This book goes back to the 1800s, he tells Sid, who translates for me. It's hard for me to imagine my grandfather here, with Dadima waiting outside. Up until a day ago, I had no idea that this method of recording data in India even existed. It blows my mind that my history has been sitting in this cupboard my entire life and I had no idea.

'Look here, Baby.'

The priest turns the book towards me, Sid translating in the background still, and there in front of me, on the page, written in English in my grandfather's handwriting, is his name.

Ranjit Singh married 1951
wife Madhu
son Jagtar born 1954

I'm shaking, I can't believe it. Seeing their names written down on this old piece of parchment has sparked something in me; I've never felt joy like it. Here's my dad. Here's Dadima. Here they are.

I found them.

When I was in school, we'd have talks from some of the other children's grandparents on their lives when they were younger.

Usually, they would tell us about the Second World War, rations, the good old days. After listening, I would go home and ask my parents about where we came from.

'Where was Grandad from and what did he do?' I'd try and ask Dad.

'He was from Punjab.' And then he'd swerve me onto another topic or Mum or Dadima would jump in with: 'So many questions all the time.'

The truth was that we didn't know our history, not really. Our ancestors didn't, and still don't, like to talk about that time, about the war, to Partition, to now. It made me realise that British people have history, they have records and documents and accounts, but so often, the people they colonised don't have that luxury. The luxury of history, of knowledge, or roots. Our history is too difficult to talk about, even amongst ourselves. So it's never discussed in homes as it's too painful and we are never taught it in schools as it's too dark, so we are left deprived of knowledge; the knowledge of who we are and what happened to us is stripping me of my context in the world. First they came and took our land and then they took our history, or whitewashed it.

Mum and Dad taught me that you live your life forward, ploughing on, looking only for success. What use is family history when we're here now? Fill the future as best you can, no need to ask your grandparents about the past.

And here I am, my fingers running over the page, over my grandfather's handwriting, over history. My history, written down, in a book. I try not to let the few tears that have formed in the corners of my eyes fall onto the page, as I look closer and further up.

Naseeb born 1923 married 1940
Deep born 1941
Preet born 1946
All died
August 1947

Naseeb. *Here she is . . .*

'I've found you,' I whisper, overcome by how connected I feel to this woman. A woman who now feels part of me, guiding me. This woman who nobody talks about, who didn't exist in my life, who I had no idea had a life.

Here is Naseeb recorded.

My fingers trace down the page to *All died August 1947*.

This hits me hard. My grandfather lost his entire family. His children's lives ended before they'd even begun.

'I see you, Naseeb,' I whisper again.

Thinking of all the forgotten women who died during Partition, whose names will never be said again, who will never be remembered. I'm thinking of them all. And I'm weighed down by it.

She's here, my grandad's first wife, and his two little children. *Oh, here they are.* I swallow loudly in the quiet chamber and look up to the ceiling to stem the pooling in my eyes. Seeing their names makes me feel something physical: a twinge in my heart, a punch in my gut. I can hear the blood whooshing in my ears.

I look further up the page and see the names of my great-grandfather and great-grandmother, but above her are only the names of men going back three more generations. It's unusual that the names of women in my family are even recorded at all. My grandfather must have insisted when he came here, with Dadima, in 1951. Just a few years after losing his entire family, and then marrying my grandmother, he would have come here to register his marriage, at the same time as honouring the lives of his first wife and two children, along with his parents.

The pain of that moment must have been devastating. I touch his handwriting, and wrestle with my pocket to take out my phone. I'm about to take a picture of the page when the pandit stops me, his arm outstretched. I look up: he's holding a pen.

Seven days ago, I was consumed by the petty goings-on of my job, allowing people to make me feel small, because I *was* small. On some level, I know that I agreed that I only deserved

198

what I got, that I wasn't worth more. And now I feel that something in me has changed. Something has tightened in my belly, a rod of steel inserted into my back. I was Simran who worked in marketing, trying to be like everyone else, and now I recognise I'm Baby Saul and I'm like no one else, I'm so much more. My family have survived great trauma, they uprooted from their land that was brutally torn in two, they started again to build a new life, once again building the land of the coloniser. Yes, they never spoke about what happened but it's in us, it can never leave us. The pain is inside us, it's what makes us. Understanding what I have learned so far has ignited the fuel in me; the fire inside me has been lit.

I take the pandit's pen and thank him. The magnitude and honour of the moment strikes me, and I write.

Baby

I've added my name to the history of my family, signing this record of us, so in years to come someone will see my name here, too. I can't stop smiling, looking at my name, and I actually whoop and cheer at this moment. Take that! A daughter, a woman, is writing her *own* name here today.

The pandit laughs at my reaction and it makes Sid smile, too. I take a deep breath and realise that that's it, though. There's no more information. I see their names, I know they existed, I know that Naseeb was Grandad's first wife and that he had two children, but they all died. Is this the end of my journey? It doesn't feel like it but maybe it is. I take my picture of the page on my phone and after Sid thanks the pandit for me, we leave.

'How are you feeling?' he asks.

'Strange. I'm happy to have found a record of Grandad's family, to see that Naseeb, Deep and Preet existed but happy my name is there too, along with Mum's, but . . . I guess the ending was never going to be happy. But knowing about Partition and really feeling it through real people are two completely different things. I feel so deeply connected to Naseeb, her story, Partition, all of it.'

'Well, it's your story.'

'I feel it, in my bones, you know.' I look up at him and into his eyes. Fast becoming one of my favourite things to do.

'This might be as far as I can go with this, which is upsetting, for more than one reason,' I say.

He looks deflated.

'It upsets me too. I'm having such a great time with you. About last night . . . Are you OK? We haven't spoken about it but . . .'

I interrupt with 'I'm OK.' Wishing I'd let him finish.

'Oh, OK, great.' He looks unsure.

'No, I'm sorry, I mean, I'm more than OK. It was fantastic, perfect. I'm not sure what to say that doesn't diminish it or make it seem naff.' I'm being refreshingly honest.

'It just felt so right,' he says.

'Right,' I agree.

There's a pause.

'It was so kind of out of the blue,' I add.

'Out of the blue? You wanted me from the minute you clocked eyes on me.' He widens his eyes.

'Oh yes. I'd almost forgotten that you also harbour an arrogant douche inside you.'

'Arrogant, yes, douche, no,' he adds.

It's so easy being with him.

The sun sets on Haridwar and we head, along with everyone else in India, it seems, back to the banks of the river. The evening pooja is taking place and the atmosphere is thick with incense, burning oil and body heat. Religious fervour is all around; I feel as though I'm at a music festival. The priests begin their Sanskrit chanting, with speakers amplifying their voices, bells are being rung, and I can hear the faint single note of a conch being blown in the distance. Once the prayers are over, those gathered all join in with the prayer for the river, 'Ma Ganga', the mother Ganges. It's so hypnotic and intense I can't speak – there are some moments in life that just need to be absorbed and this is one of those. I have never experienced anything like this, this mass of humanity and spirituality. Sid and I sit on the top of the steps leading down to the river, having managed to find a space so we're a part of the ceremony, but not quite in the thick of it because that would be overwhelming. We are squished close to each other, close enough for him to be able to hold my hand with no one seeing. I rest my head on his shoulder. We say nothing.

I need some time to think about what I've seen, to take it all in. I see a group of tourists watching the prayers, garlands around their necks and red tilaks on their foreheads, their eyes wide open at the incredible human spectacle in front of us. It really is something that can only be witnessed here. I'm a tourist, just like them. Or rather, I was. In this moment I don't feel like one anymore. I'm enjoying the anonymity of being Indian and blending in. My name is on a scroll along with my family – I do belong here too! My heart is heavy with the disappointment of all of this coming to an end. Ruchi was right: I already want to come back.

I feel so lucky to have found the scroll, that I got to see the names of my family written down, remembered. But the rush that came with the discovery of Naseeb and my grandfather is waning; what if this is all I will ever discover? I try to cheer myself up by imagining if it had all been digitised, as I had arrogantly suggested, I would never have had to come on this journey and I wouldn't have had the unique experience of Haridwar. What a privilege this crazy day has been. If this is indeed the end of my trip, then it's been a ride.

I take my phone out and look at the photo I snapped earlier, just to stare at the names. I zoom in as much as I can on every possible inch of the paper, as far into the actual page as my phone will take me. I feel like I'm traversing land, and if I could just zoom in closer, maybe I'll spot something else, something I've missed so far. I've zoomed in so much I've made myself slightly dizzy, but as I try and refocus my eyes, I find a small bit of writing next to the name of my great-great-grandfather.

'Hey, Sid, look at this.' I pass him my phone. He's been as deflated as I have since we came back from the pandit's house.

From here we set off back to the reality of Delhi and that will burst this perfect situation and I'm not ready for my time spent in a car with Sid to end.

He looks at the picture and then jumps up, grabbing my hand, and shouts unnecessarily close to my face, 'It's written in Urdu! We need to find someone to read it, to see what it says!'

Annoying but Helpful Sid is back on the case!

May 1947
Jaan

Preet is on her feet already. Our daughter has real spirit and determination. Deep is as cheeky as ever, he is your son through and through. I have him learning the alphabet, I want our son to get a good education, a degree even. He is missing you a great deal. We all are, my love. There isn't much more I can say about our children because the situation in Punjab is getting serious. There have been riots, looting and massacres in Lahore and Amritsar, and a few other major cities. Your parents try to hide it from me, to not startle the children, but there is even talk of leaving. A few months ago, there was little talk of the butchering entering Punjab, but now it seems our worst fears may be coming true.

A few people from the village are talking about heading to their ancestral village, from before they moved here. A few of the elders have been to see Pitaji to discuss us all leaving together. Your father has flatly refused. He says he has worked too hard since he moved the family here to leave now, and he does not think the trouble will come here. We live together in harmony with our Muslim neighbours. We have eaten each other's salt and there is great honour in this. We have our values, our codes. These politicians are stirring up trouble and there are gangs creating mayhem, but here I know that people are good and that we will be fine.

Pitaji and Mataji tried to keep me at home with them and the children but they are both sick and I needed to take a trip

202

to visit the doctor to get them some herbal treatment. On my way, I saw one of those modern British cars drive past me. I saw a driver, a well-dressed Indian man, a British officer and a beautiful smiling memsahib. I looked at the newspaper a few days later and apparently it was Nehru, this man Mountbatten and his wife, Edwina. I had seen them with my own eyes. I noticed her beautiful red lipstick.

There seems to be very little smiling in Punjab now.

Please write soon and tell me where you are, how you are, how soon you'll be returning home. And, my love, please tell me what to do.

You are in my prayers.

Yours always,

Naseeb

Chapter Fourteen

'Do we have an ancestral village, Dadima?'

'Of course, Baby, everyone does.' She says it like I'm an idiot. Which I guess, to her, is true.

'Could you tell me a bit more about it, please?' I ask, hoping she'll be a bit more forthcoming this time.

'It is the village where families will have lived for generations, before moving for work. This moving thing is only very recent, you know. The first time most people will have been made to move, forced to leave their homes, would have been during Partition.'

'But not Dadaji?'

'No, your great-grandfather moved to make a better life for himself and his family much earlier, and he did do well for himself, which is why he was able to educate your grandfather.'

We are still in Haridwar. Calling Dadima seemed like the only thing to do and, really, when is calling your grandma ever anything other than the *right* thing to do?

'I know about Naseeb, Dadima. I have the letters. Why did no one ever talk to me, to anyone, about her, about the letters? Why all the secrecy, Dadima?'

'Not secret, Baby. Just not know how to speak about it. Nobody talks about what happened. Nobody.' She is right, I cannot blame her for that. 'I never even spoke to your grandfather about his previous life. I once tried to bring it up and he became so angry, he threw the wooden chair he was sitting on against the wall.' She pauses, before continuing, 'He was angry, all the time, when I married him. He was sad, so very sad, and deeply wounded, but he could only express it through anger. I married an angry man, Baby. Do not make the same mistake.'

Dadima explained to Sid when I put her on loudspeaker that Grandad had fought in Burma during the Second World War. It was a terrible theatre of war for the British, and many Indian soldiers lost their lives.

'Your husband would no doubt have seen appalling things while he was there,' Sid says gently to her.

'Once, when he was drunk, he told me about his Naseeb, his first wife, and how much he loved her and his two children. He told me as though he was talking to himself, looking through me. He looked up and saw my face and slapped me hard before completely shutting down again. So, I never asked, and only know very little still.'

'He hit you?'

'When we were young it was not strange for a husband to hit his wife.'

'Grandma, it's abuse!'

'He was angry, where else was he going to take it out?'

'Don't excuse it. He was wrong. How about he didn't take it out anywhere? Or he takes it out not on a human being, not a woman? Or even better, learns to communicate his feelings?'

'Your generation is much better at all of this understanding feelings. We just put up with everything, it's how we were brought up, beta.'

I understand but I don't have to like it.

'I found the letters after he died and kept them in my peti. He had kept them all these years, brought them from India with him as his treasure. I knew nothing about them until then, and I'm sure he had planned on destroying them before he died, but he didn't get the chance. Your grandfather, he was a secret man. It is only when I read the letters that I understood. Most of women married in our time never knew love, but your grandfather made Naseeb feel love. His poor children . . . I do not know what kind of man your grandfather was for Naseeb, but from the letters, I know he was less angry.'

My heart breaks for Dadima, and I feel a flicker of rage in my gut thinking of Dadaji hitting her. I can't compute my angry grandfather and this loving husband. Life can really break you; our experiences fully shape and change who we are. He obviously never ever got over what happened. *No wonder my belly is so often full of rage*, I think. *Did I inherit the family trait?*

I've always felt unsettled and never been able to put my finger on why. Is it work, is it home, is it a system that doesn't see me, where I'm constantly having to push and persuade people to allow me to be me? But now I see it's also my history, my surroundings at home. It permeates into you. I'm surprised I function as well as I do, all things considered.

'I'm sorry I didn't tell you the real reason I came to India, Grandma. I'm sorry I took the letters, *your* letters, and didn't ask you first. That was very wrong. It just didn't seem right to talk to you, but . . .'

'It's OK, beta. It's OK. I had a suspicion you may have found them when you started asking questions about India and, of course, once I checked the peti, I saw they were gone.'

'You've known this whole time?'

'Of course. Dadima knows everything.' She chuckles.

'So, what else can you tell me, oh all-knowing Dadi of mine?'

Silence.

'Nothing.' *Oh, no, I've lost her. Please, Dadima, please don't put the lid back on the past now.*

'Please, I've come all this way. Please don't shut me out now. I want to be able to talk about these things with you, not bottle them up. Are you sure there is nothing else I should know?'

Silence.

'Please, Dadima. I need to know,' I whisper into the phone.

'What things should I tell you, Baby? How and where do we even begin? When you have seen so much, heard so many tales of terror during that time.'

'But no one has ever said anything about Partition to me.' I pause. 'What was it like for you, Dadima? What do you remember? I know it must be hard to think back to that time, but maybe it will help to tell your granddaughter?'

'Some memories are too painful to recall. But when you come home, Baby. When I see you. Then maybe let's talk.'

I know that Dadima's family had always lived in what became India; they didn't have to become refugees in their own land. When the land split in two, Dadima was only twelve, old enough to remember the terror. And she saw horror, they all did. This much Mum has told me. Her generation of women knew acutely the value of their lives and how precarious their existence was.

Now is not the time to have this conversation, to retraumatise Grandma. At home, face to face, is when I will talk to her, if she will talk with me about what she as a girl, and now as a woman, felt. I would like to get from Dadi her lived experience, from her own mouth, and I feel the urgency of time. Dadi is eighty-eight and I'm lucky to still have her, but I can't take time for granted anymore. Dadima needs her story told, too. I get a huge pang of homesickness; I want to be back with my head in Dadima's lap, I want her to stroke my hair. I'm even missing Mum.

'Will you tell Mum what I'm really doing in India?'

'She already knows.' *What? And she hasn't been messaging me non-stop?*

'Are you sure?'

'We decided not to bother you too much on this trip, let you see it for yourself.'

The only other information I get from Dadima is that she knew about Grandad's ancestral village because it's how her marriage was arranged. Through some convoluted extended family connection, all via the caste network, it was worked out. Grandad was totally alone and he didn't want a dowry, which was almost unheard of. Dadima's family wanted to get her married and the no-dowry offer was too good to give up for something as trivial as a thirteen-year age gap. Older men frequently married younger women, especially if it was their second marriage. I wonder if any older women married younger men for their second marriage, and my mind goes back to the widow on the banks of the Ganges. The double standards are everywhere.

It seems obvious now why Grandad couldn't wait to get out of India for a fresh start.

'He always told me he had great admiration for the British.'

'Even though they colonised the country and they were cruel?' I ask.

'He wanted them out of his country, yes, but he admired their rules, regulations and their order. Being in the army taught him a great deal and he respected his British commanding officers. So, Britain was always going to be where we ended up.'

It turns out there is a place not far from Amritsar where my family have lived for generations – another piece of family history I have no knowledge about. No one ever told me. But I also never asked. And that was what was written on the scroll in Urdu script: the name of the village.

It's on the drive from Haridwar back towards Amritsar, with Sid happily singing along to the radio beside me, that I fill him in on what Dadima told me.

He strokes my hair and leans over to kiss me – and nearly goes straight into the back of a motorbike with a giant bale of hay on the back.

'Keep your eyes on the road,' I say.

'It's getting harder to do, with you sitting next to me.'

I think I'm actually blushing.

I've connected my phone to the car system and we are listening to Jai Paul, perfect for road trips as you can't help but disappear into songs that connect with your soul. You have to stop what you're doing and be taken wherever it takes you.

The song playing is 'Jasmine'. It takes me back to the first time I heard it; late at night in a club, my ears tuned into it and I just had to close my eyes and let my body move with the groove. I was so consumed by it, I might as well have been the only person in the room. It was a spiritual experience and I remember wanting to share this magical experience, this all-consuming, magnificent feeling, with someone special . . .

And so we let the song play loud, in the car, and say nothing. We are just in it.

The fear of the unknown has haunted me throughout my life, yet I've never wanted to know more about my past. I've always I been so resistant to wanting to fully understand who I am, because it would mark me out as even more different to my peers.

I shake my head and look out of the window, see myself reflected back. I'm in the earth, in the trees, in the people. Not that long ago, I had very little connection to this place, because it never seemed relevant. My life was Bradford, and my immediate family were responsible for my world. That was all that was important, that was all I saw as defining me. But really, my story began when Dadaji left India for a new life in the UK. *I'm* the new life, I'm the product of that scary journey, of being brave enough to try something different somewhere else.

Have I really spent that life hating myself? Hating my name, my life, my family?

My family had to find a way of making sure the culture wouldn't vanish without a trace, and that was by bringing up children with a strict understanding of their heritage. I was the British experiment. Can you make someone fully British, without them losing their Indian values? Who decided which bits of the culture were worth saving and instilling in me? Was there a committee to create me?

I look across to Sid and my stomach does a little somersault. *God, I want to be held by him again!* I fancy him something chronic. There are so many thoughts jumping through my mind at once, I can't think straight and yet somehow, I've never been clearer-minded. I don't want to go back to the old Simran. Baby is becoming who she was destined to be.

July 1947
Jaan

Things are frantic and terrifying in Punjab. Why have the army taken you away? You should be here with us, with your family. The war is over, where are you?

I am having to take charge in the house, your father is sick and refusing to leave but people are going now in such a hurry and with only what they can carry. They are walking across the border.

The border, that seems like such a strange thing to say. How can this place no longer be India, they just drew a line? That's it. A line and we believe them.

I am now in a foreign country, where I am not welcome because of my faith. This is my home, my land. The milk from the buffalo that ate this grass from this soil nourished us. Punjab is a land of many and all faiths. We have lived together side by side always. And now the chaos has come.

The violence is everywhere and getting closer. Gangs of hoodlums, once sweet sons, now barbaric animals, are rioting. But much worse is happening to us women. Girls are being kidnapped, they are raping us, shaming us, parading us naked, in front of our fathers and brothers; they are branding us, killing us. This battle or whatever is happening is now being fought through us. I have heard that women are taking their own lives, jumping into wells. We are living in Hell and the shaitans are all around.

It is the end of the world, and you are not here with me.

I am so scared. I must choose to do what is best for all of us. I will do what a mother must do and protect her children.

May God protect us all. And if, my love, this does not end well, know that I have loved you with all my heart. I know we will be together again in our next life . . .

I hope you come home soon.

Yours always,

Naseeb

Chapter Fifteen

The village is about an hour's drive from Amritsar and only 30km from Lahore. We are so close to the border of Pakistan, to the line of divide.

The end of this story is not a happy one. It's a tragedy, the worst kind of unhappy story. The ending was written in ink on the scroll back in Haridwar, wasn't it? The words written in Dadaji's handwriting, the same handwriting that Naseeb would have read when his letters arrived, were clear. I wish I could have seen those letters, known what my grandfather felt when he was happy and in love, read his use of language and love expressions, seen his handwriting even, just known something about my grandad.

Naseeb and her children all died in August 1947. So why have we kept going? What more do I need to hear? I know why: it's because I have come such a long way both physically and within myself and I no longer want to hide from my past, from anything – I don't want to fear the unknown anymore. I want to embrace it, the bad and the good.

'What if this trip is futile? I should have been satisfied with the letters. The letters contain so much more than any history book could tell me. What could anyone in this village know?' I'm voicing my doubts out loud. 'What if there's nothing there, Sid? Another roundabout?'

'Because we are in it now and even if it is just another roundabout, it's OK. Right? We have discovered so much. Each other.'

He's right but I'm tired and homesick. It feels like forever since I was curled up on the sofa with my mum and Dadima. But I have a Sid, and Sids have an effortless way of instilling enthusiasm in those around them. He alone is managing to keep a small flicker of energy alive in me. I'm here now and might as well see this through. Wherever this story ends.

The village must be home to around a hundred families, and it's pretty basic, frozen in time. The buildings are old, single-storey brick houses and some have outer walls covered in some kind of mud. There are none of the big, white, modern homes here that I've seen dotted all over Punjab. This place has a sleepiness about it, a timelessness. It's dusty and bathed in sunlight. There is one main street, designed for a bullock cart, barely wide enough for a car, and off the one road there are small, cobbled alleys with houses dotted along. There's the odd square patch of grass where cattle are grazing, and we park up on the edge, by the well.

Sid has decided we will walk and knock on doors. Apparently, this is the best way to do our research, he tells me – 'groundwork'. Getting out and meeting people, collecting their oral histories. We walk past a small Hindu temple and then a shrine to a Muslim saint. This is Punjab.

Sid knocks on the first wooden door and a young woman opens it, wearing a bright yellow shalwar kameez, her head covered. She's the daughter-in-law of the house and no one else is in to help, but she sends us a few doors down, to a family who have been here for a long time. We pass a few children playing street cricket, with a wooden plank as a bat, and narrowly miss being hit by the ball. They look tiny and have the bodies and faces of toddlers but the sass and confidence of children twice their age. I guess you grow up fast in the pind. Sid throws the ball back to the little bowler, who catches it like a pro.

Sid knocks on the door and an old gentleman, dressed in jeans, an Indian khaki shirt and a box-fresh pair of Nike Air Maxes, answers. After a brief conversation with Sid, he invites us both in, but my eyes have caught something and I'm distracted.

'You do the pleasantries and find out what you can, I just need to explore,' I say to Sid, smiling at the man.

He looks confused but agrees. 'I'll be fine,' I add, giving his arm a squeeze.

I saw something sparkle from the corner of my eyes, just for a moment. Something is calling me and I start walking along the narrow path, down the alley to our left. I don't seem to have a choice; my feet are taking me there. I can see a small house at the very end, separate from all the others, at the edge of the village.

An old lady is sitting outside the door, on a charpoy. Some kids run past me shouting, 'Pagal buddhi, pagal buddhi.' Crazy old lady, a crazy old lady.

I aim for her, not able to take my eyes off her, and it looks as though she's staring right back at me. As if she can see inside me. The sun is beating down, bright and harsh, but she doesn't seem to mind at all. Dressed in a white shalwar kameez, her pure silver hair is scraped back into a plait. There's an air of mystery about her that I'm drawn to, a thread leading to her that I need to follow. She is magnetic. My instinct is to sit down next to her without even asking. And that's when I see her magnificent face. This old woman is beautiful, weathered, with wrinkles all over her face; she's utterly radiant.

A child runs past, shouting, 'She's dirty!'

Dirty? She looks incredibly well-kept and put together. There is nothing dirty about her. I turn my head to scowl after them and she looks directly at me, smirking, a knowing smile on her face. I see then what must have sparkled, what caught my attention from the distance. It's her eyes – they are the most incredible shade of green. It's as though there is a light shining out from within them; it's almost difficult to look at her, like staring into the sun.

I reach out slowly and touch her hand. I open my mouth to speak and find myself trying to converse in Punjabi for the first time in my adult life.

I put my hands together and greet her.

'Sat sri akaal, Bibiji.' *God is Truth, Grandmother.*

She simply nods.

'I'm looking for my grandfather's first wife; his name was Ranjit and his wife was called Naseeb. I'm trying to find out what happened to her. Naseeb?' I repeat her name, just in case the woman is slightly deaf, or can't understand me.

Her eyes widen and a look of pain shoots across her face. 'Naseeb Bhabhi,' she says.

'You're Billi!' I gasp, and with that glint in her eye, she nods.

Billi speaks slowly so I can understand her Punjabi. She doesn't stop looking me in the eye for our entire conversation.

I can't believe it's her. The little shadow, the little watcher, from the letters! The child who never speaks but sees everything. The outsider.

I hold her hand and ask her to tell me everything.

'What happened to Naseeb?'

I'm searching her face for any response. She turns her eyes away from me for the first time since meeting her, focusing beyond me instead, before closing them. As if to stop herself crying.

'You were there, you knew here. Please tell me what she was like. Tell me all about Naseeb and about her children.' I'm firing questions at her, not getting anywhere, but I can't stop. 'What happened to Deep and Preet?'

She squeezes my hand tight and says something I don't quite understand. I hear the word Naseeb and ask her to say it again.

'Preet, the baby, Kush Naseeb.'

Kush Naseeb means happy fate, so what does she mean? Preet had a happy fate? I can barely breathe.

'But they all died, I saw it, it's recorded. My grandfather lost Naseeb and the children.'

'No, not the baby, not Preet. Naseeb gave Anjuman her wish, her prayers were answered. Naseeb gave her a baby, a daughter.'

And then, as if in some kind of trance, Billi takes me back to August 1947.

'The first time I watched her I could not believe what I saw. Naseeb is beautiful, she is much too beautiful to be a besharama

215

who casts spells. I was told she was a witch who cast a spell on Ranjit Jijaji. I was told only shameless women don't have arranged marriages. I watch her by hiding. I was a little scared the first time but could not stop watching her. I think maybe she put a spell on me. I am not allowed in people's homes, but I had to see Naseeb Bhabhi. Not only is Naseeb Bhabhi the most beautiful woman I have ever seen, she is kind. Naseeb Bhabhi has the most beautiful heart in the village, so now I like witches.'

'Other children can go to school. I cannot. Untouchables are not allowed to sit next to other children, and they say we don't need an education. I wish I could look at the books the other children do. Sometimes I get a stick and pretend I am writing in the dirt. I write my name, only I don't know how to. Ma asks what education do I need when I will be cleaning other people's filth for the rest of my life? Ma says I should not wish for anything or have any hope in my heart, because my prayers will never be answered. Ma didn't need to tell me that, because I don't pray, not to God, anyway.

'I had two Bhabhis because of her, because I had Naseeb and Anjuman. I had the best days of my life with them. I was part of their gang. In the house, I would sit on the floor. I would try and not be there if Tej Masi was at home. But when it was just me with Naseeb Bhabhi and Anjuman Bhabhi, I felt free and happy. They let me listen to their conversations and let me play with Deep and Preet. I was allowed to hold the babies, too, when no one else was around. Babies are so pure that it is a curse for me to even look at them, but the shameless witch lady, she let me hold them and smell their soft heads and stroke their squidgy round bellies. I know what to do with babies, I have been helping Ma with my younger brother and sisters since I was little. I help Ma a lot.

'They would pray a lot for Anjuman Bhabhi because she had no baby. It's sad because Ma says a woman's job is to have sons for their husband. So, Anjuman Bhabhi is not working, she is not fulfilling her job as a wife. She cries, but we make her smile, and they pray to every god. I don't pray, but I like to follow them as they walk and see new places, new shrines and holy places. When I'm with them, no one bothers me as much. Even if others try and shoo me away, my two Bhabhis stop them and say, "She's with us, leave her be." Can you imagine the freedom? Is this how other people feel all the time?

'Then everything changed. People started talking about something called Partition, about the land being divided, about our home, Punjab, splitting in two. How will they split the land? Where will our house go? What will happen to all the water that flows through Punjab, will it pour into the crack? Our house is going to stay, Ma says, and we are going to leave. I've never been anywhere else, none of us have. Ma has never left the village, Ma is afraid.

'Every day I hear more shouting. Baba is shouting at Ma, telling her she needs to keep me under control, that I can't keep wandering around, that Ma gave birth to too many daughters. I don't want Ma to cry, and I want to help her and be a good daughter, but I also want to be with my Bhabhis.

'On the morning we are due to leave, I sneak out of the house to see Naseeb Bhabhi. I wanted to say goodbye. She is staying in her house and Baba says they are foolish people, Baba who refuses to leave. Said they are a crazy old family who don't know what's good for them. But I know it's because Naseeb Bhabhi has magic powers, and she will protect them. She is a besharama witch, she is my goddess.

'I waited in a corner outside her house and then I saw Anjuman Bhabhi arriving, constantly looking over her shoulder, looking scared. I ran up to her as Naseeb Bhabhi opened the door, and she jumped back before she can see it is only me. Naseeb Bhabhi also has fear in her eyes. She hugged Anjuman and then held me tight and kissed my head. Bhabhi has always been kind to me, but this was the first time she has held me or kissed me in this way. At first I felt my body stiffen, reflexively, because nobody touches me and I don't know how to react. But I remind myself I am with my goddesses, I am safe, and I take a deep breath of Naseeb Bhabhi's scent. Naseeb Bhabhi always smells clean. She tried to bathe me once, but I would not let her, and she told me why it was important to keep myself clean, especially when it is my time every month. I was embarrassed – nobody should talk about such things, Ma says it is dirty. But Naseeb Bhabhi is shameless, and she is my goddess, so I listen to her. It is our secret that she tells me such things.

'Naseeb Bhabhi took Anjuman and me into the house, and the door is relocked. I have never been inside before. Her house has two rooms and a vehra and they have their own buffalo! I live in one room with everyone. Two manjas are put together with a soft, clean home-made mattress. The blankets are folded and stacked at the bottom. There is a small rocking cradle for the baby too.

'Anjuman and Naseeb are talking frantically, fast fast, crying crying. I cannot understand much of what they are saying. They are talking of the way women are being treated, killed and touched and taken and thrown away. It's everything Ma told me men would do. But they seem shocked, less prepared for it than me. This place is rotten now, the earth is bad, and I want to tell Naseeb Bhabhi to leave with me, that I will look after her, but I hear her saying she will not go from her home. She is not listening to Anjuman either, shaking her head, and Anjuman Bhabhi is crying crying crying.

'Anjuman tells her about her family coming from another town on a train. I have never been on a train before, I wonder what it's like. There is danger all around, Anjuman says. I have been told this since I was a little girl. But this time it is different. This time the danger is everywhere, for everyone and I have never seen these two brave, beautiful women talk to each other like this, their heads so close together, holding each other.'

'I'm alone, Naseebo. I have no one.'

Naseeb Bhabhi tells Anjuman she's not, hugs her and looks her in the eyes for such a long time. I hold my breath as she turns, crouching down to reach the cradle, and picking up a sleeping baby. *Preet*. With silent tears rolling down her cheeks, she hands Anjuman her baby.

'What are you doing? No, no, she is your daughter.'

'Please. Please take her. Do this for me. Please help my daughter survive. If I come out of this, if it is God's will that I live, I will come and find you and all will be fine, but should the worst happen—'

'No, Naseeb, I can't—'

'Should the worst happen, please, Anjuman, raise my daughter as your own. Is she not already your daughter too? Please, show her a life full of love, please teach her to read and write. Please, love her as your daughter. I'm begging you, Anjuman. Take her. Take Preet. Save my daughter.'

'Anjuman Bhabhi got her wish. My goddess granted her a baby.'

I feel this story in the pit of my gut. My tears flow from deep inside me and I have no control of them rolling down my cheeks. Naseeb gave away her baby to Anjuman. I can't imagine the pain and desperation a mother must be in to do this, or the capacity of love. She wanted to protect her daughter at any cost and also gave Anjuman her longed-for baby.

My instinct is to reach out to Billi, to give her a hug. She flinches at first, but I can't let her go. I almost collapse onto her, and her skinny, frail arms hug me back. There is more strength in them than I know, and she holds me tight while I sob into her arms.

I look up at her and ask desperately, 'And what about Naseeb? What happened to Naseeb? To your goddess?'

But she just shakes her head.

'I don't know. We left with all the other Hindus and Sikhs and her family refused to leave.'

I'm still hugging Billi, weeping for Naseeb and for Billi.

'Making friends, I see,' Sid says. I extract myself from Billi's arms and turn to him. He notices my tears and frowns, concern etched in his features.

I stand up and fall into his arms, still weeping, repeating: 'Preet is kush naseeb, Sid. It's Preet, she was given to Anjuman. She didn't die.'

He holds me and, for the first time in my life, I really let another person do it. See me in this state, with my emotions undone, because I need it.

Chapter Sixteen

'Your morning chai, Madam.'

Sid hands me a steaming cuppa and gives me a kiss before heading back into his apartment.

I breathe deeply.

It's a foggy Delhi morning and I'm on the balcony listening to the birds, mainly crows and parakeets, sipping my first cup of piping hot chai of the day. Which Sid brings me every morning. It's bliss.

We got back to Delhi two weeks ago and I am a different person to the one who left here. And Sid, who has been through it all with me, has seen me in a way no one else has. He has been with me for this entire transformation, if that is what is happening. Now, when I look at him, my heart wants to burst out of my chest. It's overwhelming.

I'm staying with Sid in his beautiful two-bedroom apartment round the corner from my masi's place.

For a man living on his own, Sid's home is immaculate. He has incredible taste and an eye for design and detail. Indian craftsmanship is celebrated throughout his small but swanky pad. There are two bedrooms, two bathrooms, a kitchen, a large living room and a stunning balcony which overlooks a private park. He has beautiful hand-made shelves, very cool framed works of art, both old and new graphic design works by young artists, the odd antique sculpture and a well looked-after record collection, which includes Prince. Bonus points for the Prince, because he really knows his stuff.

'It's the 1994 release of *The Black Album*,' he says casually.

Music nerd and history bore. He really is a renaissance man.

I've explored Delhi with Sid. He couldn't wait to show me the layers of history in this crazy city, from the artefacts of the Indus valley civilisation, to the incredible architecture and creativity of the Mughals, the Red Fort, the Jama Masjid, the hustle and bustle and intense energy of ramshackle Old Delhi, to the leafy surrounds of the diplomatic district with its expensive shopping malls and green spaces. We have been for sunset walks around Humayun's tomb, and sundowner drinks on rooftops overlooking the thirteenth-century tower, Qutub Minar. And now I'm not just looking at it all as a tourist. I'm seeing history and stories and destruction and creation, lives torn apart, new ones built. I'm connecting to it all. I'm falling in love with India. I'm falling in love.

He joins me on the balcony.

'You know I now have to find out what happened to Preet and Anjuman? I can't come this far and not. She's Grandad's daughter and she might have survived, had a life, children, even? Imagine. And they'd be related to me.'

'There are people who try and track down what happened to families torn apart by Partition, people finders, but it's not going to be easy,' he says.

'I want to at least try.'

Life is glorious. It's laid-back, full of art and laughter and conversation, the most delicious food I've ever eaten, with an undercurrent of risk and pure naughtiness. My clothes have even become more laid-back. I wake up in the morning and put on an Indian cotton kurta over jeans, or one of the bohemian dresses I've found in the market that make sense here, but I'd never dream of wearing back in concrete Manchester. We go out for dinner, we watch movies, we read to each other, just like Ranjit and Naseeb did, but the conversation that preoccupies most of our time and is constantly on my mind is finding Preet. It's my obsession. I've come much further than I ever thought I would when I unearthed my family treasure in a drunken stupor. I had no idea what those letters would reveal, I just knew I had to follow their lead.

222

I've had so many of my questions answered since meeting Billi, but I also feel like I've a whole bunch of new ones, mainly about the baby, Preet. Is she alive and where might she be? I also can't wait to get back and tell Dadima everything.

Things are even in a good place with Mum. We spoke about the letters and Sid, and I think instinctively she knows I'm in a much happier place in my life than I have been for a long time and this makes her happy and, wonderfully, our relationship feels easier.

I love spending time at Sid's place; we listen to so much music and talk about everything, as though we just want to soak up every drop of thought and opinion. I want to know what he thinks about everything and, more importantly, he wants to know my thoughts too. Sid often plays records. Sometimes it's a classical raga by Pandit Ravi Shankar, or his daughter, Anoushka Shankar, sometimes a great new electronic album – he's introduced me to a whole world of Indian DJs and even Western classical which I've never spent much time listening to, even a British punk band called The Sex Patels, who I love. He can translate the words of Jagjit Singh ghazals for me, that I've loved listening to my entire life but never fully grasped the meaning, until now. And sometimes Sid reaches for my cup, places it on his gorgeous wooden coffee table, and lifts me to my feet to spin me around. And sometimes, when I drop my Friday night bangers' club mix we just dance like idiots, making each other laugh. I can dance with abandon in front of him, as though I'm back in my flat in Manchester. It's a powerful feeling of pure romance that runs through my veins, and I can't get enough.

Staying with Sid has caused not a small amount of outrage amongst my family, however – Masi in particular.

'What will people say? My neighbours?'

'Ah, those *people* again. They can't get enough of my life, can they?'

Masi seemed so cool when I first met her, but my relationship with Sid has revealed the extent of her open-mindedness, or lack of. Moving in with a boyfriend is like most other things in

223

India – not straightforward. It's allowed, legally, but the moral code you are meant to abide by is still somewhat different. And I'm from Britain, so my moral code is questionable.

'It's not right, Baby. I need to discuss this with your mother. I'm not comfortable with all of this shady-boy business. Too much responsibility for me.'

I want to cry with laughter at whatever *shady-boy business* is but I'm too annoyed with her. Why am I her responsibility, why is this all about her?

'You want to hold a conference to discuss my life?'

Talk about creating a drama.

A family summit is called with Mum to discuss a decision I have made, at the age of thirty-six. Once a baby, always a baby. We all jump on a FaceTime, and Dadima makes a last-minute surprise appearance, holding the phone so close to her face and at completely the wrong angle, so all we can see is a close-up of her nostril hairs.

'You have given her too much freedom, Didi.' Masi's opening gambit.

No, you can't have a woman with too much freedom, she might do something shocking like make her own choices.

'She should be staying with me while she is in Delhi.'

'Mum, please. It's no big deal. I'm staying with Sid. We are seeing each other. It's only round the corner from Masi's,' I say, pleading with Mum, already prepared for her to support Masi.

Mum tries to speak but Masi jumps in.

'She has lost her traditional values, Didi. We are still a conservative community here, people talk. What if something happens to her, she gets pregnant?'

Oh Jesus! I'm exasperated.

Again I see Mum attempt to jump in but Masi's on one.

'I still have impressionable children at home. Ruchi looks up to Baby and Ruchi is a good girl, I don't want her being corrupted and led astray, Baby giving her ideas about living with boys.'

It's not boys you have to worry about, I think to myself.

Mum is frowning.

'We were never allowed to do any of this, Didi,' Masi says to Mum.

'Oh, Honey, I've heard enough. Bas kar,' Mum says firmly.

Well, I wasn't expecting that from Mum.

'We are from a different time! Things have moved on. My daughter is no corrupter and I'm so cross that you could even suggest this. She's your niece, you should love her like your own.'

Mum's incensed and I can see Honey Masi shrinking.

'She's a brilliant daughter. The best. I trust my daughter. It's her life now, to live as she pleases.'

Good Lord, is this really my mother? Go, Mum!

'You bring up your children the way you want. If my own daughter, your niece, is so shameful, you don't have to see her.'

'Didi, it doesn't have to come to that.'

'I thought you said this boy was wonderful? It was you who insisted they travel together in the first place!'

Exactly, Mum. Answer that charge, Mas! She had not only actively encouraged it, but Masi had orchestrated the entire thing.

Something had changed with Mum, and I liked it. I know she is probably over the moon that I have met someone, especially an Indian, and wants me to do everything to nurture the relationship, even if that means living in sin in India. I'm not sure how any of my family would have stopped me from doing it anyway. Falling out means more drama, and no one wants that. It's the choice that Asian parents have when it comes to their daughters' lives, either oppose their decision and risk losing them, or trust them, go along with their choice and continue to have a daughter. Not a hard choice, really, is it?

After THE phone call and being admonished right royally by Mum, Masi takes a few words from Ruchi – wonderful Ruchi.

'Mumma, Baby Didi is not a baby, plus she's always lived her life. She's not from here and being cross and forcing her to stay with us will destroy your relationship. And Sid is great! He's the best.'

Masi is nodding, feeling contrite.

'Plus, my plan worked. Why do you think I invited him round for dinner in the first place?'

So it *was* a set-up!

Chapter Seventeen

'There needs to be a commemoration, some kind of public acknowledgement that this happened,' Sid says one afternoon, in the orange glow of the sun, as we sit outside reading together.

He's reading a book I've recommended him, borrowed from the library, which tries to explain what happened. The main narrative that has filtered down is that women went bravely to their own deaths, as though it was their choice, that they *had* a choice. How do we begin to heal if we don't know the truth? What do we do with these stories now we know them? What do I do with all this knowledge, this pain? Are all Indian women walking around with this burning rage that has been passed down through generations?

We began this journey together, and Sid wasn't about to let me down on the next part of it. My quest goes on. My main focus as I sip my chai every morning, as I unconsciously sway to the music that beats in the house, the thing that preoccupies my mind, my one burning question: is Preet alive? And if she is, can I find her? Since my magical encounter with Billi, I can't stop thinking about any of them, the whole host of people buried in my family's memories. I think of Billi's story over and over: Naseeb giving Anjuman her baby, but then what? It's so hard to imagine Naseeb doing that, from what I know about her in her personal letters, but learning about the horror of Partition puts it all into perspective. It makes sense that Naseeb would have thought giving up her child the best way of saving her. Naseeb's sacrifice was the biggest act of love I've ever heard of.

Sid explains there's a Punjabi word, 'sahnjhi', which means shared, or common. Daughters of a village are seen as sahnjhi – they are everyone's daughter. A beautifully communal sentiment when we all know, still in this day and age, that it takes a village to raise a child. That is, until all hell breaks loose, and then it's every woman and child for themselves. I'm consumed by reading the stories of what was done to women during that time. It's pure horror. But the story of these women doesn't end with Partition.

'Did you know, Sid, that so many women were abducted – approximately seventy thousand – that both nations thought it best to "recover and restore" women back to their families?'

He puts down his own book to listen.

'Some of these women had had children or were now married, most would have been raped. But they were forced back to their original families by the state, actually forced, and guess what? Most of the families rejected the women because they were tainted.'

I sigh deeply. 'I wish there were some stories of resilience and hope.'

'Your family story has some hope. There must be others, but not recorded.'

I take some heart in what he says, but when I think about what was done to the women, my body burns with rage. I feel the pain of these women, of Naseeb. It sits deep inside me. It has always been there, I think, but now I'm allowing myself to feel it, and the feeling that comes is fury. So many women had no agency or say over their own lives, and it was less than eighty years ago. Even my encyclopaedia, Sid, who seems to have read a book or an article about everything, had no idea about the extent of what happened to women during and after Partition.

Maybe it's alive and knows what it needs – to work its way down the family tree to get to the generation who know what to do with it, how to deal with it, talk about it. *I need to talk about it.* To Dadima.

What does this mean for Naseeb? Did she die or did she survive? But like so many women, her true fate will never be known, and I just have to reconcile with that. Preet, though, Preet is different. Sid mentioned, after reading an article during our first week together, when all the excitement of new love and old leads had collided, that there is a people-finding service. It was set up to reunite lost ones and loved ones separated during Partition. Even now, people use them, reach out like I did, to find the ending or beginning to their family story. I feel overwhelmed with sadness, and yet this is also the happiest I've been in ages.

My phone is ringing. We try to ignore it and carry on sitting together, thinking, talking over everything, weighing our options. It stops and then starts ringing again. And again. Who needs to speak to me that urgently?

'It's Mum!' My mum is FaceTiming – I'm not really in the right frame of mind for this and Sid knows.

'Call her back later,' he says.

But Mum calls back again immediately; it's as if she can sense my finger hovering over the phone screen.

'Hi, Mum! Sorry I missed your call, I only just got back on the Wi-Fi.'

There is only silence on the other end of the line. That's not like my mum – she is usually halfway through a sentence before I've even finished saying hello.

'Mum?'

I hear a choking sob at the end of the line, a hiccup and gasp as she tries to speak through her tears. Mum is sobbing. I don't know if I've ever heard her cry like this. Fear grips me. Something has happened.

'Mum? What's happened? Are you OK? Mum?' My voice is rising.

She finally manages to get out a single word and my heart drops into my stomach. Everything around me goes cold.

'Dadima . . .'

'No!' I shout, my knees buckling.

229

'Dadima sanu shad ke chalegayee. Baby, your dadima has left us.'

Time stops.

I can feel every part of my body so acutely, but I don't feel as though I have any control over it. It is as though my muscles have just atrophied, and I can hear the blood whooshing in my ears. My knees do not seem able to do their job anymore. They have just packed up, abandoned me. I collapse onto a chair. I am undone.

Sid is by my feet, holding my legs, looking at me with deep concern in his eyes.

I know this feeling well, this unbearable ache. I know what a shattered heart feels like. Mine had smashed to pieces once before, when Dad died, and I realised that it was only just beginning to mend itself, only to be destroyed once again.

'What happened, Ma?'

'Her heart just stopped, Baby.'

I cling onto the phone as tears roll down my face, swallowing hard, not wanting to let go of my connection with Mum, even though neither of us is speaking, only crying.

I take a deep breath, I need to get the words out.

'Mumma . . . I didn't even get to say goodbye.'

'Come home, Baby. You will get to say goodbye.'

And all of a sudden, the only thing that matters is getting out of India and getting home.

Why had I even come here in the first place? How could I ever have left the people I love most for such a thing? Why didn't I spend as much time as possible with Dadima while I could? Why did I think there would be more time? Time to talk things over, to ask her questions? How could I have been so stupid, even after losing Dad?

Nothing made any sense.

All I feel is pain and guilt and remorse. Guilt for being so far away from Mum and Dadima, guilt for going off and leaving them behind.

I look at Sid.

How do I treat his feelings with care, when I don't even know how to deal with my own?

'I need to get home.'

'I'll book you on the first flight.'

I can't get out of the chair just yet but he's already at his laptop.

'I can see there's a flight to Amsterdam; you can change there and get straight to Leeds Bradford Airport.'

He's thinking of everything.

'I need to pack but I can't even think.'

My legs are both lead and jelly.

'Don't worry, I'll pack your suitcase. Just, Baby, please don't worry.'

'What about us?' I say.

He sits in front of me.

'We will figure it out. Just don't think about anything other than getting home and being with your mum, where you need to be.'

Inside I am destroyed, but somehow, I am still functioning. My survival instincts kick in as I realise I don't have time to crumble or think about my pain. I need to be home for Mum, for Dadima. To say goodbye.

Why was I so far away? What was I doing here? These thoughts keep looping through my head as I go through the motions of existing in this strange in-between space, no longer on an adventure, no longer doing a runner, only wanting to get back to where I came from. To be back with everyone who knew me, who knew my dadima.

I couldn't believe I wasn't going to see her again. I need to tell her about everything: my life, my feelings, what I'd discovered. I need to ask her so many questions. I need to know everything about her life, who she was, what she was like as a little girl, a young woman, a wife, a mother, an immigrant. I want to know about all her feelings, her innermost thoughts, how she did it, how she got through it all.

I want to put my head in her lap and have her stroke my hair. I just want to look at her face, study the lines and ask her about who she is. I didn't get her lemon pickle recipe from her.

I needed more time.

'My destiny is cruel, Sid.'

'Don't say that. We found each other, didn't we?'

'Yes, but now both you and Dadima have been taken from me in one day. The two people who have my whole heart.'

I'm holding him tight at the airport, my tears staining his T-shirt. I want to leave a mark.

He looks down, holds my chin in his and kisses me gently. People turn to look at us but we are lost in each other.

'You, Yorkshire lass, have got me. Go and be where you need to be. I'm here for you.'

Usually, I'd be trying to figure out what to do about his feelings, how to ease his pain; usually I'd be thinking about him, but today I can only think about me and Dadima.

He makes it as easy as possible for me to leave him.

He stands and watches me as I disappear into Departures.

The flight home feels endless. I put on film after film, but nothing holds my attention. I weep silently, discreetly, staring out the window. On that flight home, I feel truly lost, floating in the clouds and utterly disconnected.

It is raining as I get out of the taxi and look up at the familiar house, shivering with a mixture of shock at this cold, damp climate and trepidation as to what awaits me. I feel sick to my stomach with nerves about setting foot in the house and, at the same time, I'm convincing myself that maybe it was all a mistake. Maybe I will open the kitchen door to find Dadima standing over the cooker, making a pan of chai, her turning to look at me. I'd never known this house without Dadima, this life without her. She was constant.

I walk into the kitchen and there is Pinky, making tea. She comes straight over and hugs me as I hold back my tears, still feeling numb.

'I'm so sorry, Baby,' she says, giving me a squeeze that comforts me even as I weep. 'I'm so sorry.' I nuzzle my face into her neck and I squeeze her back.

In the living room, the furniture has all been moved back and white sheets laid down to cover the carpet. Mum is dressed in a white shalwar kameez, head covered in a white dupatta, flanked by a few aunties, all dressed in white. They have come to pay their condolences.

Our death rituals are like weddings, a communal affair not requiring a formal invite. But right now, I wish I had my home and my mum to myself. I try to hold back but it is impossible. I collapse into her lap and start to sob.

'Mum, I spent too long thinking about me! And I don't even know about Dadima's life,' I say as I cling to her.

'Your grandma had very good life, Baby,' says Mum, in a gentle voice I almost don't recognise. She puts a hand up to my hair and strokes it very gently.

One of the elderly aunties speaks up suddenly.

'What your grandmother lived through couldn't have been easy.'

The others suck the saliva through their teeth, parting their lips to make that distinctly Punjabi noise of agreement.

'Adapting to a new country, this cold weather, the terrible food.'

Again, the same noise and a shake of the head.

'And after living through Partition.'

I look up quickly, and the old lady looks at me, all the ladies in the room look at me.

I swallow back my sobs and say in a high, plaintive voice that barely sounds like me, 'She never spoke about it, *nobody* speaks about it! What happened was so awful, horrifying, and then you all came here, and no one said a word.' I throw this accusation at them all. I know I am really asking Dadima how she could have kept it all from me.

'There are some things you don't know how to speak about, beta. Things that have been seen and done that should never have been witnessed, things that change a person. We came here to get away from the past. And for girls like you to have a better life,' she pleads with me and Mum nods.

It is comforting talking to Dadima's friend. I sit next to her for a while and give her a hug. It makes me feel closer to my grandmother, being with someone from her generation. This woman, who I only ever thought of as being the one with the tough skin on her heels, the one with hairs on her chin. She was just one of Dadima's many friends, another old lady with iron grey hair in a pastel-coloured shalwar kameez who sat with her in the Gurdwara and used to tell me off for running around or being too loud. But in this moment, she is a haven and I see her as a woman who has lived a life, maybe many different lives. As a pioneer who travelled to a foreign land and survived this country's hostile environment. I see her and I'm overwhelmed by what they did, this generation of women, who just got on with whatever life threw at them, the generation who didn't have the privilege of thinking about themselves or their own needs, who did everything for everyone else, but mainly their children. For better and for worse. Yes, they spoiled their sons, they uphold the patriarchy, they have not listened to or under-stood the wishes and desires of their daughters – but maybe they were conditioned by their environments. Maybe they felt they had no choice.

My wonderful grandma who only ever gave me love and never judged me or my choices (all right, maybe a few of my sartorial choices when I went through that emo phase), she was kind and patient and full of love. But what about all the pain she must have had deep within her, the pain that I feel so intensely now? The pain that's inside me. When I think about Dadima, I think about Naseeb. I think about Anjuman, Billi . . . I think about them all, the generation who know something about humanity, something dark, they've seen it. Knowing it and seeing it are not the same.

234

They *know* pain. The pain of having the earth taken away from under your feet. Your home. The only place you feel safe, where you nurture and nourish your children. With the flick of a white man's pencil, the slicing of a map by men, it's gone, cruelly taken from you and you are too insignificant to have a say and your men, the ones who are supposed to protect you, they are the ones to fear. They do the only thing they know to do and destroy you, the women. When have women ever felt safe around men, even their own?

Talk about trust issues.

Once most of the visitors have left, I leave the living room to find some solace.

I switch on the little Golden Temple lamp by Dadima's bed and press play on the CD. Still in her old CD player, she's had for years, this particular album is not available anywhere.

Mum and Pinky come in to join me. All three of us sit on her bed.

'Why did she have to die?' I say to no one in particular. I know there is no answer that can comfort me.

'It was her time, darling,' Mum says, kissing my forehead.

'I just want to smell her rubbing Astral cream onto her hands.' I pause and then wail, 'I can't believe I'll never eat Dadima's roti ever again.'

This thought tips all three of us back into tears and the room is very quiet.

I keep repeating the same question, torturing myself with it. 'Why did I go to India?'

'You had to go, Baby,' Mum says.

'I'll never forgive myself for not being here for her, though.'

'Baby, your dadima was so happy you were there, that you went to India. She was so, so happy for you. We both were.'

I look at Mum curiously. She hasn't mentioned much about India, her family there. Or even Sid.

'You gave her so much pleasure and joy in life. Your trip of discovery to India lifted something for her. You opened the door to a secret she could never unlock. She carried it somewhere inside her, always there, like a little knot, but you untied it. It's your generation that can do this, it's the greatest gift you gave your dadima.'

I'm listening intently to Mum, for once not wanting to interrupt her.

'But I kept it a secret, the real reason why I left.'

'You have no secrets from us,' Mum smiles. 'Well, maybe I didn't know all the ins and outs but your dadima knew everything, she always knew everything, she knew the letters were gone.'

Now all three of us are smiling.

'We carry so much inside us, don't we?' says Pinks.

'And so much we don't even know we have inside us, Pinks, that came before us, so much was done to women, those who survived to have future generations did just that: survive. No, not only survive, but they also thrived like warrior goddesses. We know we feel something deep in our bellies – you know it, don't you, Pinky, you feel it too? It's a power.'

She's looking at me a little confused, but I carry on. My mind fizzing, I start to talk about pain passed down through generations of women. About the pain I have been carrying my entire life. Well, that ball has well and truly burst now, and it's in every part of me.

'It's like I've connected to every single woman in my ancestry, to every single woman in Punjab. I've connected to my history, I know who I am more than I did before I left. There's something in me that's changed but I can't tell you how, I'm just different, more grounded, more determined—'

'More in love?' says Pinks, with a wink.

I think of Sid and smile, the jig is up.

'Show us some pics, then!'

'Oh Pinky, he is very good-looking, even Dadima thought he was, what do you say, pengy?'

We crack up.

236

'It's peng, Mum.'

While I'm fumbling around in my bag looking for my phone, I pull out the little freezer bag that Dadima gave me when I left for India with her humbugs in it. Only three left.

Chapter Eighteen

'You coming for a drink, Baby?'

'Nah, you're all right, Sups, not tonight.'

'Ah, come on, mate, I'll buy you your first whisky soda!'

I smile and shake my head. She knows I'm not coming out. I used to be the first one to get a round in, to make the claim that a packet of peanuts counted as dinner. That was before.

It's back to work as usual. Nothing has changed (except now people call me by my real name) and yet everything is different. I'm more serious at work. Same me, maybe more confident, and not to be messed with – the new (old) name might sound gentle to some people, but I've never been fiercer. And definitely not the first out to the pub and the first at the bar.

I still love it, still have a laugh with the team, still love a gossip over chilli sauce with Jojo and Sups, but the noise of the place has turned down in my mind. I've turned down the work frequency and realised I have other priorities, other things that matter to me.

Work has stopped feeling like my whole world and that's a good thing. Is this what they call perspective?

And I made a big decision about work.

'What do you mean, you're resigning, what will we do?' Sups was fake-shocked when I told her.

Jojo on the other hand simply said 'Finally!' And shook my hand.

Zero regrets. Liberation.

I feel lighter in one way. I've let go of the things that felt so important before India and now seem petty, but I'm also weighed down and leaden in another way. I'm sad. Sups can see it, Pinks gets it. I've been through so much and it's altered me. I went on an adventure, learned my history, lost my beloved grandma but in the process discovered who I am. I'm awake. I'm changed. I've fallen in love. I'm heartbroken.

I want to do more with my life. Maybe write about my experience. Naseeb's letters have inspired me to do something more with my passion for words and writing. Knowing about her life – and her death – has somehow given my life meaning, given it a purpose. My existence is far more miraculous and precious than I ever understood. I was so ungrateful before, took so much for granted, let things happen to me instead of making the most of every moment. For the first time, I feel connected to where I come from, to my past, and it is helping to guide me into my future. I have a duty to Naseeb to live a full life of meaning and passion, to live.

I wrote to Sid. Sent him an actual letter in the post. A love letter. It made sense, felt romantic. Although not as romantic as Naseeb's achingly beautiful letters, but still poignant – doing justice to what we went through together, what we had. Having to write full sentences without the use of an emoji was something of a learning curve. Being earnest, sincere, was an even steeper one.

No response yet. I've never anticipated my mail before. Mail used to be something to put in a pile, statements never to be looked at, but now I run home from work to see if there's an envelope with my name on it in his handwriting on my doormat. And nothing. I am crushed every single time. But then, what did I expect? A Bollywood ending?

I stayed in Bradford for a week after Dadima's funeral. I didn't want to leave Dadima's space or Mum. Poor Mum. She looked so frail and lonely. She just lost her husband, and now Dadima. I spent the week just wanting to look after her and make sure she knew I was there for her, that I love her. I wanted to be kind, and suddenly it was easier to be patient, because I know

now that time is so precious. All the people I love seem to slip through my fingers, so I need to cling onto Mum, make every second count. And when she says something ridiculous, I just take a breath and smile, because we only have each other now.

I reluctantly left the cocoon of my family home to go back to my life. Back to my flat. The home that I had loved so much, been so proud of, but I felt nervous about it, going back to a place that I was last in when I was someone else.

It was so obvious that something was missing in my life. Someone was missing. I missed him. But there was nothing I could do about it. Neither of us was prepared for a long-distance romance, we'd not even really discussed it as an option.

I was getting into my head and questioning everything. Was it even a relationship? Did we even know each other? Was he even real? Was it just romance out of circumstance? Yes, we'd had an incredible adventure but it was three weeks. What are three weeks compared to a lifetime?

Or like Naseeb said in her letters to Ranjit, was our meeting destined in the stars? Had I known Sid for many lifetimes? It felt like that when I was with him.

Much of the time I kept my mind occupied with the discovery of Preet. The baby who was passed from one woman to another, friend to friend, sister to sister, Sikh to Muslim, Indian to Pakistani. She was the gift of motherhood that Anjuman longed for. Naseeb had granted her wish and in doing so, kept her daughter alive. Gave her the chance of a life of love.

Grandad's daughter.

My aunt. My *aunt*. A connection to both Dad and Dadima.

If indeed she is alive. If I can find her.

This is what I plan to do tonight rather than go to the pub: continue my research into Preet, where she and Anjuman could have gone.

My desperate need to get to Pakistan was a welcome distraction from the longing to be back with Sid. To be back in our little bubble, our adventure, where I had someone I could trust, someone to support me. My flat felt empty without him and he'd never even been there. How could I even begin to figure out how to find Preet, how to get to her, without him being helpful?

'I don't know what you're doing here, back in grim Manc. Just get yourself on the next flight out to India. Have the Bollywood romance – you've got the name for it now.'

This was Johnny's advice. I am back in their flat eating chocolate. Expensive chocolate. Oh well, it's got to be better for me than the house red at least.

'My life is here. I love Manchester and Mum and you two. I couldn't leave this.'

Henry looks up at me from under his eyebrows and frowns.

'This is not it, Baby. It used to be, before you realised there's an entire world out there, a world with a Sid in it.'

'But he's there, I'm here. East and West. We have lives. It was a beautiful holiday fling, that's all,' I say mournfully and shove another truffle in my mouth. They're delicious. 'Anyway, I need to look after Mum.'

'No, you need to live your life.'

'I am. I'm going to write. I know there's more to life than marketing.'

'Hallelujah!' Johnny shouts and throws his hands in the air for added drama.

'But I can't pine for him when being together isn't a possibility. His life is there, my life is here. It's just better I shut down my feelings rather than suffer every single day,' I say, convincing no one.

'I'm not sure feelings are that easy to tune in and out of.'

'They are for me. My Indian woman skills are kicking in – it's called self-preservation. I can't mope around, and the relationship is at an impasse. I just need to get on with my life.' I brighten and almost manage an enthusiastic grin as I add, 'Plus, I've got my trip to Pakistan on the horizon! It's OK. *I'm* OK. I got a lead.'

I head back to my flat to save myself from diabetes, grabbing one last chocolate for the long walk across the corridor. Back in my own space I light a scented candle rather than saving it for when guests come round. I'm treating myself tonight, I'm worth a Diptyque Feu de Bois. I put on my dreamiest Spotify playlist, which is a bit painful as there are songs from my time in Delhi with Sid on there, but it's perfect for my mood. Melancholic. Next, I go in the fridge to create one of Dadima's old Indian face pack recipes: a spoonful of yogurt, a tiny bit of turmeric and a teaspoon of honey.

The mask gets applied, with a bit too much turmeric, making me look jaundiced. I sit back on my sofa, my cosy slipper socks keeping my toes toasty, to scroll through Deliveroo, while knowing full well I'll end up ordering a Nando's.

Here in the sanctuary I've created for myself, I feel utterly hollow. Dadima and Dad are gone forever but I have to live with it and adapt. Death happens. They're gone. But Sid is still alive and breathing. He still exists on Earth, miles away from me. And I can't bear it. Alone, trying to relax, pretending that I'm OK. The minute I stop and allow myself to feel my feelings, I realise life is intolerable without him. What am I doing?

I'm weeping and causing my yogurt face mask to melt into my mouth, and it tastes sour and sweet, but mainly sour.

Who am I kidding with the 'I'm getting on with my life' bullshit? He's all I ever think about. I see him everywhere. I imagine him picking me up from work, us going to the movies, going for a meal, on the night bus home – no, we'd get Ubers. I imagine him in my bed, watching TV. Maybe I'd come home from work and he'd surprise me with a romantic week away. Another road trip together, this time to Europe. He'd take me to Paris. Maybe we move to London together and walk along the South Bank, go and see exhibitions, go to clubs, see plays. Live life. Autumn walks with his arms around me. Living in a love bubble. Or just staying in and ordering a Nando's. The fantasy in my mind is so real and so cruel. It's torture but I can't help myself.

So this is heartache.

Pinks calls, probably to check in on me. She's such a bloody good friend, so attentive.

'Hey, you! Everything OK?'

'All good, over here. Peri peri chips on the way. Living my best life. How about you, how's work?'

I move away from talking about me. Pinky has started work at a law firm in Leeds.

'Oh, I love it.'

'And what about Anoop? Has he sorted himself out?'

'Yeah, I think not having me around has made him appreciate me. We are going on a trip to Scotland, just the two of us.'

'That's great.'

I think of Sid in Scotland in an Argyle sweater and wellies. The image makes me smile but also pierces my heart.

I get off the phone quick as I want a night to wallow in my self-pity. I want to feel my heartache, I want to sit here and think of nothing but him.

I turn up the music.

There's a knock at the door and I wonder what Johnny or Henry might have forgotten to tell me. Or one of my other neighbours telling me to turn down Joy Crookes. I consider ignoring them, but they knock again. I stomp to the door.

I fling it open.

Sid is standing at my front door, a suitcase by his feet. He's here! I willed him into existence.

'I have brought a letter for you from Delhi.'

I say nothing, just stare. Frozen in time.

It's only when he slowly leans forward to kiss me that I finally wake up and know it's real. I reach up for him, cannot wait to feel his lips on mine.

'You know you taste like yogurt?' he says.

Epilogue

My nerves kick in as soon as I'm off the plane. I'm on Pakistani soil, the soil where Naseeb lived and died. Punjab, but from the other side. My story resides here too.

Sid was his usual wonderful self before I left. He was the only one who didn't put the fear of Pakistan into me, he wonderfully did the opposite. He made sure I was ready to soak up a privileged and life-changing experience. What a fantastic opportunity to have in my life, to hopefully find my aunt, my dad's stepsister. I also get to see the great city of Lahore.

'Once the capital of Punjab, it's so steeped in history and culture and so magnificent they called it the Paris of the East!' He excitedly tells me. *Of course, my wonderful history nerd.*

'Visit all the sights . . . The Badshahi Mosque, which is right next to the Gurdwara and the tomb of Maharaja Ranjit Singh – oh and go to what used to be the red-light district, Heera Mandi; there's meant to be a fantastic rooftop restaurant perfect for sunset and to hear the evening call to prayer. You lucky thing!'

How does he know all this stuff?

'And try all the food.'

'I will.'

'And . . . '

Getting out of the front door was hard.

'And look after yourself.'

'Yes.'

'And come back to me soon.'

I'm at the Allama Iqbal International Airport in Lahore, feeling dazed, dressed modestly, with a bright-red cotton scarf I bought in India around my neck. I'm breathing in the new air but slightly stressed at being alone and stepping into the unknown. Heck, this is turning into a habit.

I'm convinced I'll be pulled out at Customs to explain why I'm in Pakistan. I always worry that I'm going to be pulled out in every queue in every airport, even when I have nothing to panic about. I literally teeter on the edge of hysteria every time. I've never taken drugs in my life, and yet I worry someone may have put a kilo of heroin in my luggage! Since Sid is used to travelling to meet potential clients for his business, he told me he gets pulled out for 'random' checks most places he visits. I guess he's got one of those random-looking faces, huh? My Customs experience is smooth, though, and when asked why I'm visiting, my palms perspiring like never before, I tell the truth.

And this time I speak in Punjabi.

'I'm here to find out what happened to my family during Partition.'

The customs officer shakes his head. 'Terrible things happened. My own family had to leave Ambala in India to come to Pakistan. We are the same people. I hope you find your answers, Baby.'

I like that he looked at my name and chose to say it, as though I was a part of his family. It moves me the way he welcomes me here, even to find answers of that time. It's such a wonderful moment, so warm and welcoming, and the first moment in a long while I feel the magic of having a name as disarming as Baby. Well done, Mum! Finally, I'm owning my identity, in more ways than one.

I step out into the heat of the great city of Lahore and acknowledge that Naseeb is with me. She's in me, even though I know I will never know what happened to her, where she ended up. I feel her presence now more than ever. Naseeb, the holder of secrets, who left all her secrets to me, it feels. Have I followed all the clues, have I arrived at the final secret? Come on, then, Naseeb, where have you led me?

I've hired a car with a driver to take me to an address in a leafy suburb, not too far from the old centre of Lahore.

We pull up on a road lined with two-storey houses, each one with a large metal gate and beautiful bougainvillea plants flowing over the top.

I'm nervous as hell. What am I doing here? I don't think I've ever experienced a feeling quite like this. My stomach is doing butterflies and, sitting in that poor driver's car, the air conditioning on full blast as I have a full-on meltdown, it hits me that, four months since quitting my job, I find myself in Pakistan. Not just that, but I'm about to knock on the door of someone who may be my dad's older sister. My grandfather's child. Naseeb's baby. And I am all alone. I'm winded by the pain of missing Dad and Dadima. But then it's their voices I hear, giving me the strength to get myself out of the car.

I wonder if my grandfather ever visited Lahore. He must have done; being in the army, he must have seen so many places. I make a mental note to make sure I visit the main sites in the old walled city before I leave, all the places Sid mentioned, to make sure I walk in my grandfather's footsteps, just in case. I have to be prepared that this really could be the biggest waste of time, that whoever this woman is that I'm about to meet, she may know nothing about Preet or Naseeb or Anjuman. I've been told that the lady who lives at this address may know *something*, and nothing more. *Why have I come here on a maybe? What was I thinking?* A maybe is better than nothing, that's why. Because I need to see for myself what it was like. I need to see what happens when an arbitrary line is drawn down the middle of a country, and how quickly a place can become distinct. What happens over seven decades? Do people change? I need to walk the streets my grandfather would have walked, to see the great city of Lahore, because it's a city that people shed tears over when they heard it would no longer be in India.

So, here I am, on a maybe. *No going back now.*

I knock on the gate with shaking hands, and it's opened by a man in his late forties. I'm taken aback, because he looks a bit like Dad. My heart jumps and I can't help but grin at him, not saying anything to him until he has to repeat himself.

'Yes? Who are you? How can I help?'

I finally fall out of my reverie. 'Erm, yes, salaam alaikum. I'm Baby, from Bradford, and I've been in India for a while . . .'

Baby from Bradford, what kind of an opening line is that? I engage my brain to get to the point, because this guy is looking at me as if I've escaped from an asylum. I can see he's closing the gate a little and looking over my head, to see if there is anyone else with me. I decide to just be upfront. *Come on, Baby from Bradford, you can do it.*

'Sorry. I'm here trying to find . . . Preet? Do you know if there is someone, or was someone, called Preet living here?'

'Kaun hai Hassan?' I hear a voice. A woman's. *Who is that*, she is asking.

'Someone called Baby? From Bradford?' he calls out. 'Your name is Baby?' he asks me.

I nod.

'Let her in,' the voice calls.

I step inside the gate and look to my right, where in the middle of a beautifully manicured garden, with exotic flowers in full bloom, sits a lady. She is surprisingly youthful, dressed in an elegant dusky-pink shalwar kameez, with a diaphanous dupatta draped over her shoulders. Her long grey hair flows around her like a mane, with eyeliner framing her perfect almond eyes. She looks like Dad, too. I shake as I approach her.

She gets up, moving faster than I'd expect for a woman her age, and hugs me, holding me tight. She then holds my face in both her hands and looks at me, really looks at me, as if she's searching for something, as if she's always known me, as if she *sees* me. I recognise a fire in her eyes that I have seen in my own, and then she smiles.

'There you are,' she says. As if she's been waiting her whole life for me.

I follow her inside her home, through some wide-open glass doors. The room we enter is magnificent, filled floor-to-ceiling with books. I've entered a lifetime's worth of reading. I glance at all the authors she has here. Amrita Pritam, Khushwant Singh, Saadat Hasan Manto, Rabindranath Tagore, Hilary Mantel, Emily Dickinson. I spot *Wuthering Heights*, a couple of Hanif Kureishi, the Bruce Springsteen autobiography. I'm awestruck, taking in the rich and decadent décor, beautiful lamps, two stunning rugs, a vase of fresh roses and a colourful taxidermy butterfly in a bell jar.

I like this woman.

'Now, tell me, Baby, what brings you to Lahore? To me? Are you my past, my future, or both?' Her English is immaculate, with a beautiful Pakistani lilt. She's effortlessly elegant, has obviously been well-educated and has a youthfulness that makes her seem younger than her seventy-seven years.

I make a few false starts, stumbling over my words, unable to look her in her fiery eyes.

'Here, take your time.' She hands me a glass of water for which I'm very grateful, suddenly realising I haven't had any water all morning and I'm massively dehydrated, and massively flustered.

You can do this, Baby. You can do this. I breathe, and then I begin.

'My grandfather's name was Ranjit Singh Saul, he married my grandmother in 1951. But, until 1947, he was married to a woman named Naseeb. They had two children together, named Deep and Preet. Ranjit was away working in the army when the violence broke out; he was never able to go back to his village and believed his family had all died during Partition. They had all gone. He truly believed he was all alone. So, he remarried and had my father. A few years later, he and his small family left India and Punjab forever, and moved to England, where I was born.'

Oh, wow, all of that really did come out. But I can't stop now. 'Do you recognise the name Ranjeet? He was married to Naseeb, and she had a best friend . . .'

Silent tears roll down her cheeks as she finishes my sentence for me.

'Anjuman. Her best friend was Anjuman.'

She is nodding towards the end of my story, and I look in her eyes as she says, 'I am Preet.'

I fall out of my chair to her feet, put my head in her lap, and weep.

Naseeb has led me to her. I found her for you, Naseeb.

So, this is home, I think. *It's not about the place, or even who you are with. It's how you get to feel inside.*

I am home now.

Acknowledgements

I have a few heartfelt thanks yous to dish out because this book would not have happened without the dedication and support of a collection of excellent people.

Firstly, to you. Thank you for taking the time to read this book.

I am blessed to be surrounded by epic women, you'll notice how many as you read this page.

Thank you to the tag team of editors who helped bring Baby to life:

Beth Eynon, who knew this was the story I had to tell, who fell in love with Baby and made me believe in myself. Melissa Cox, for the vision, support and the podcast-length voicenotes that kept me sane – and her sublime eyeliner and kickass boots. Salma Begum, for totally getting it. Katie Brown, for her magic sprinkles, clarity and ability to have a small baby and edit a book about Baby!

My brilliant team at Bonnier: Perminder, Margaret, Jess, Elinor, Emily, Laura and Chelsea.

My badass bitches at Curtis Brown:
The best in the business, Cath Summerhayes. Thanks for telling me I have a book in me. Turns out I have at least two. What a ride this is turning into.

Annabel White, Jess Molloy, thank you.

My extraordinary agent, friend and confidante, Meryl Hoffman. Thank you for everything you do. Above and beyond.

The consigliere, Elli and Josh for keeping my life in order.

TEAM GLAAAAAAM. Big up my hype crew. Krishan Parmar, Oskar Pera, Sarah Jane Wai, Narad Kutowaroo, Heidi North.

Thank you for building my confidence, making me look sparkly, genuinely caring, being the best at what you do, being a right laugh and helping me SERVE!

The best PR team in the business. Team Dundas Max, Ros, baby Martha (welcome to the world) Abi Etchells and Tori Jones.

So many amazing friends who have supported me. I'm blooming lucky to have a crew, a forcefield of ace mates around me. Sangna, Nerm, Adrian, Amy, Ben, Yen, Elaine, Casper, Laura, Hannah, Reva, Anoushka, Rajiv.

Nikita Gill you are a very special soul. Thank you, little sister.

Special mention to the cosmic fairy, Krupa – your vibrations are powerful! And talking of vibrations, thank you to Claudia Tomaz for your healing hands. I also have to mention Nikesh Shukla and Salena Godden because their energy and good vibes reach far and wide. They boost and connect so many and should be recognised and thanked for what they do.

All of the above are mighty human beings.

There's an even bigger army who make up my treasured community. I'm so grateful to have you in my life, know who you are. I see you.

And to my family:
Mum, Dad, Kul, Shivani and our light, Vaneesha. My day ones. The core of my world. Thank you for your unconditional love and trust in me. We've been through a lot, but it feels like the best time right now. I know I'm not perfect but thank you for always being there without judgment. I love you.

Thank you to Hackney Marshes for providing me with nature and adventure.

Thank you Universe, you magnificent, unfathomable wonder.

And most importantly I want to acknowledge all the people who lived through Partition. And those who didn't survive. The unknown names of all the women whose lives were taken. I honour you all. You are not forgotten. To those ancestors who sacrificed so much. You are deep inside us, you walk with us. You give me the courage and strength to continue to live my life with purpose and passion. You are the fire that rages in inside me. I am here because of you.

My gratitude is eternal.